WHISPERING

WHISPERING

Jane Aiken Hodge

Thorndike Press
Thorndike, Maine USA

This Large Print edition is published by Thorndike Press, USA.

Published in 1995 in the U.S. by arrangement with St. Martin's Press, Inc.

U.S. Softcover   ISBN 0–7862–0457–5 (General Series Edition)

The text of this Large Print edition is unabridged.
Other aspects of the book may vary from the original edition.

Set in 16 pt. New Times Roman.

Printed in Great Britain on acid-free paper.

British Library Cataloguing in Publication Data available

Library of Congress Cataloging-in-Publication Data

Hodge, Jane Aiken.
   Whispering / Jane Aiken Hodge.
      p.   cm.
   ISBN 0–7862–0457–5 (lg. print : 1sc)
   1. Large type books.   I. Title.
[PS3558.O342W48   1995]
813′.54—dc20   95–7910

CHAPTER ONE

The rain came down in torrents. The hired post-chaise leaked. Jeremy Craddock congratulated himself that it was only a child he was fetching. A young lady would grumble. He just hoped the nuns had her ready for him, the timing was tight enough as it was. A quick anxious glance at the watch on his fob confirmed this, but it was no use telling the coachman to hurry. Heavily bribed, he was doing the best he could with the tired horses that were all the Bath livery stable had had to offer. But at least the man knew the way to the convent, which was more than Jeremy did himself. Why should he? He had never been in the town before, did not much like what he saw of it now.

The sound of the wheels changed as they left paved and terraced streets behind and crossed the river to climb a hill. He pulled out his letter of instructions and peered at it in the bad light of the wet August morning. No need, he knew them pretty well by heart, but no time must be lost in misdirection. Here at last were the gates Senhor Gomez had described in his letter. A child ran out through drenching rain to open them and the carriage moved forward up a tree-lined drive. He had never visited a convent in his life and visions of hands extended through iron gratings ran through his head. It was a relief to have the carriage stop on a gravel sweep outside a perfectly normal pillared Palladian entrance.

A swift dash through the rain. The big door had already swung open. An ordinary maidservant stood there, bobbing an ordinary curtsey.

'The Reverend Mother,' he told her. 'She will be expecting me. Mr Craddock.' Time seemed to drip away down his fingers with the rain from his coat-sleeves. The girl had taken the hat he handed her, but looked puzzled. 'There's been no orders, sir,' she said. 'They allays sends to let us know when someone's coming. Specially a gentleman.'

'No orders? But there must have been. Senhor Gomez wrote at the same time as he wrote to me. I've come for Miss Gomez,' he went on. 'I hope she's packed and ready.'

'Miss Gomez?' Something more than surprise in the girl's face? He was trained to read faces, and thought so. 'But she's—' She stopped. 'I'll pass the word to Reverend Mother,' she said. 'If you'll wait in here, sir?' She took his heavy greatcoat and opened a door upon a dank, dark parlour.

'Don't lose any time about it, there's a good girl.' He slipped a coin into the ready hand. 'I've none to spare.'

'I'll do my best for you, sir.' His smile, and the coin, had charmed her.

2

Left alone, he ran fingers through his fair, short crop, glanced in the glass over the chimneypiece to make sure of the set of his cravat, and got out his letter of instructions again. He knew what it said. Gomez had written to the convent by the same post as he had to him, and told them to have the child ready. 'She will be no trouble, I promise you.'

Reverend Mother was not behind gratings at all. She was standing by a welcoming fire, a formidable woman in black habit and white wimple. 'Mr Craddock.' She did not offer to shake hands, keeping her own folded. 'In what way can I serve you?' She did not suggest that he sit down.

It irked him. 'You have surely heard from Senhor Gomez?' he said.

'No. Should I have?' Heavy black eyebrows were drawn into a frown. Of puzzlement, or of anger?

Why should she be angry? 'Yes,' he said. 'Senhor Gomez wrote and asked me to fetch his daughter, take her to Portugal with me.'

'You are going to Oporto?'

'Yes. If I catch the ship. I trust you have the child ready, ma'am.'

'I have had no letter. This needs thinking about. You had best sit down, Mr Craddock.'

'Thank you.' He waited until she had done so. 'I can only think that Gomez' letter has gone astray,' he said. 'You would perhaps like to see mine.' Lucky he knew its contents so

3

well, there was nothing in it she should not see. 'Thank you.' She read it quickly, efficiently, coldly, as, he thought, she probably did everything. He found himself wondering what it would be like to be a child in her care.

'I know the hand, of course.' She gave him back the letter. 'There is no question but it is from the child's father. And the instructions are clear enough. As it happens, her things are packed and ready. It seems to me that I have no alternative but to let her go with you.'

'Packed and ready?' Now she had surprised him. 'But you said you had not heard—'

'Nor had I. I think it only right to tell you, Mr Craddock, that the young person was about to be expelled from our establishment.'

'Expelled? Why?' And then another equally relevant question. 'And where to?' A glance at his watch reminded them both of what he had said about haste.

'Appalling misconduct.' Now he knew why she was angry. 'She is in isolation, Mr Craddock, and was to stay there until she went to her mother's family.'

'The old mad woman down in Wales? But, ma'am—'

'You address me as "Reverend Mother," Mr Craddock. Yes, I wrote to Lady Trellgarten to tell her I was sending the young person to Trellgarten Hall. She was to have left tomorrow. You come most timely, Mr Craddock. Senhor Gomez appears to think it

4

safe enough for the child to return to Oporto. It had not, frankly, struck me as at all a possibility. I am responsible for the girl, after all. I could hardly send her off to be snapped up by a French privateer, or, worse still, be subjected to the kind of savagery that the French soldiers inflicted on the city two years ago.' She was on the defensive now, and he was glad. She had not wanted, he thought, to wait until she could get a reply from Oporto. What in the world could the child have done?

'Oh, it's safe enough now, ma'am.' He was not going to call her Reverend Mother. There was not much that was reverend about her, he thought, nor much that was motherly either. 'With Lord Wellington in control,' he went on. 'He has Masséna well and truly on the run, and not in the direction of Oporto, thank God. The English merchants are all taking heart and making their arrangements to go back, those who did not go when the Lines of Torres Vedras held so splendidly last year.'

'That jumped-up Indian general,' said the nun, and made him angry.

But there was no time for that. Another glance at his watch. 'If you would be so good as to have the girl fetched? It's a blessing she is packed and ready to go. And I am sure I can count on you to make your explanations to Lady Trellgarten. I suppose I should know what terrible sin the child has committed.'

'Insubordinate, unruly ...' She rang the

5

silver handbell on her table and gave instructions for Miss Gomez to be fetched. 'She's been a disruptive influence ever since she came, three years ago. If I had known—' She stopped. 'If it had not been for the family connection ... A bold, rebellious girl, Mr Craddock, wicked herself and a cause of wickedness in others. And then, this!' She had risen to move over to the writing desk under the window and came back with a piece of paper in her hand. 'Did you ever see anything so scurrilous, Mr Craddock?'

His training stood him in good stead. He did not laugh. But it was a wickedly funny caricature; the bold, black strokes summing up everything he had himself found to dislike in the Reverend Mother. 'Scandalous,' he said. 'But,' diffidently, 'you do not think it suggests a certain artistic talent?'

'Talent!' she snorted. 'Talent should be put to the service of God, Mr Craddock, not the devil. I found a group of my young ladies laughing over it. Laughing!' She was about to tear the paper across but he reached out and took it from her.

'Do you not think her father should see it? To make him understand—'

'You're right, of course. There are probably others; I would just as soon not see them. But, Mr Craddock, am I not to meet your chaperone? As responsible for the child, I feel I should do so.'

'Chaperone?'

'You have surely brought an abigail, a respectable young female, a companion for Miss Gomez?'

'For a child? I thought her too old for a nursemaid.' Had he thought about it at all? 'I am her cousin, ma'am, her aunt's son, with three sisters of my own. She will play no tricks on me, I can promise you.'

'You wilfully misunderstand me, Mr Craddock. A chaperone! The proprieties! You keep calling her a child.' She turned at a knock on the door. 'Come in.'

Not a child. The dark-haired girl who stood summing him up with bold black eyes was very nearly as tall as he was. Now she sketched elegant little curtseys for them both. 'You sent for me, Reverend Mother?' Her hands were folded in front of her; everything about her seemed demure and was absolutely not.

'Yes.' The old nun's tone was uncompromising. 'This is your cousin, Caterina, Mr Craddock, come to fetch you on your father's orders. I hope you will behave better to him than you have to us.'

'Father has sent for me? To Oporto?' She turned eagerly, held out her hand to Jeremy. 'Oh, I am so glad to meet you, cousin. When do we go?'

'This instant,' he told her. 'But first I think you should apologise for all the trouble you seem to have caused here.'

7

'Oh?' A slight gesture on his part had drawn her attention to the picture he was holding. They exchanged one quick, understanding glance. 'Yes.' She turned to the old nun. 'Reverend Mother, I apologise. You will be glad to see me go, I know, and I am glad to go. But I thank you from my heart for all you have done for me.'

She meant it, Jeremy thought, and thought that the old nun believed so too. 'Bless you, my child,' she said, surprisingly. And then, to Jeremy, 'But this question of a chaperone.'

'Yes,' he said. 'I understand now.' He turned, smiling, to Caterina. 'I thought you a child still,' he told her. 'I did not see why Reverend Mother spoke of the need for a chaperone. I do now.' Back to the nun. 'It is but to apply to my sister in Bath,' he told her. 'I know you will trust me with Miss Gomez for those few miles. And we must be going or we will lose our ship. Are you ready, Cousin Caterina?'

'Yes, cousin,' she said with deceptive meekness.

*　　*　　*

The post chaise stood ready; her small trunk had been strapped up behind; the rain had stopped; Jeremy handed Caterina ceremoniously into the coach, and got a mischievous look of thanks. 'Such a perfect

8

gentle knight, cousin.' And then, as he joined her in the carriage. 'Are you my cousin?'

'Of course I am.' Now she had shocked him. 'You mean you were not sure, and yet you came with me?'

'I'd have come with the devil to get out of that place,' she told him. 'And not to the depths of Wales to rusticate with poor mad granny either. You do come very timely, cousin. Thank you.' He was arranging the shabby travelling rug around her knees. 'And now for your sister in Bath.' She was teasing him. 'What are you going to do about her?'

'You saw through that.' With a rueful look.

'I most certainly did. It was a miracle the old beldame did not. She is usually quicker than that, to give the devil her due, but I suppose she was so glad to get rid of me ... And without the expense of sending me into Wales, either, which was bound to be a consideration for the old skinflint. So—no sister in Bath?'

'No. Just one much older brother.'

'Whom you don't much like.'

She was dangerously quick, this unusual girl. 'No. We don't see much of each other. I invented the three sisters for your old dragon's benefit. I thought they would make me seem more reliable. Just as well I did. Your father called you a child. How was I to know?'

'How was he? We've neither met nor written for over three years and didn't see all that much of each other before that. I was a bitter

9

disappointment, don't you see, a mere girl. Girls don't run vineyards. And then my mother was so disobliging as to die. No son. No heir. Very inconsiderate, he thought that. They were her vineyards, you see. What he married her for.'

'His now, surely.'

'Oh, that's of course. Do you know my father?'

'We have not met, no. Only corresponded. I look forward to meeting him.'

'No law against that,' she said. 'So you don't know what has made him relent and have me back.'

'Relent? But he sent you home for your safety, surely?'

'It made a most convenient pretext. With the French holding Lisbon, the Spanish holding Porto, and the English ordered to leave. But this is not home. I am not English, cousin, I am Portuguese like my father.' She had switched into fluent Portuguese to say this.

If it had been meant to baffle him, it failed. 'Of course,' he spoke in Portuguese as idiomatic if less fluent than hers. 'I had quite forgotten, finding you in such very English surroundings.' That was careless of him, he thought. He must not let this surprisingly grown-up child throw him off balance.

'Where are we going?' she asked now in English, surprising him again, not at the question but at the fact that she had not asked,

10

nor he answered it sooner.

'Into Bath for a change of horses. Then to Falmouth. There's a ship loading there. When she is ready, and the wind serves, she will sail. And I mean to be on her.'

'So masterful! And what about my abigail, cousin? You have not been to Porto, I take it, so you do not know what a scandal broth they brew in that tight, smug little British community. I don't suppose you much wish to have to marry me on arrival. Though really,' judiciously, 'there might be something to be said for it.'

She had silenced him, and knew it. 'Here we are, almost into Bath,' she went on in the same reasonable tone. 'If you will have your coachman follow my directions, I think I can find us a chaperone. She's an old friend. I promised her long ago that she should share my fortunes, if any. I had been wondering how in the world to get her to Trellgarten if I had to go there. This works out most admirably. We need to turn right here, cousin.'

'Who is this? And will she agree to come?' But he gave the order.

'Oh, she'll come all right. She's a friend, I told you. We met—No, I don't think I will tell you how we met. You might be shocked.'

'I think I am beyond being shocked.'

'Good,' she said. 'Left here, tell him, then right at the corner and stop at the end of the mews. I just hope Harriet is in.'

11

'Harriet?'

'Harriet Brown. A dear friend. And I promise you will make a most convincing chaperone. We may have to outfit her a little. Are you game for that, cousin?'

'Your father undertook to pay your expenses.'

'Handsome of him. For once. I do long to know why he decided to have me back. Tell me, if Harriet is there, how long can she have to get ready?'

'Half an hour at the very longest. I want to be well on the road before we stop for the night.'

'I should just about think so,' she agreed. 'Bath is another fine spot for scandal. I'm glad you do not intend to rack up at York House with me. Even with Harriet in attendance.'

'York House is well above my touch.' He meant to quell her.

'Not above my father's,' she reminded him. 'Here we are.' The carriage had pulled up at the end of an extremely unsavoury mews. 'With luck, if Harriet is home, we will be no more than fifteen minutes. If it's to be longer, I'll let you know.'

'But I am coming with you.'

'Oh no you are not. I go alone or not at all.' She was ready for this. 'Be reasonable, cousin. Look at me. Look at yourself. You're a swell. I'm—just a girl. I can go down there without being noticed; you cannot.'

It was true. He had been momentarily appalled at her plain, even dowdy appearance when she joined him in bonnet and pelisse. 'We will buy you some clothes in Falmouth if there is time,' he told her and realised that he had let her win her point.

'Splendid.' She turned back to smile at him from the carriage step. 'And Harriet can have mine.' She looked up at the coachman. 'If you want to walk the horses, there's some open ground over there.' She turned and walked swiftly away down the crowded, insalubrious alley, only her erect carriage and purposeful stride differentiating her from the shabby crowd around her. He should not have let her go. Could he have stopped her? 'Yes,' he said irritably in answer to the coachman's question. 'Walk them as the young lady said.'

Young lady. He had thought a young lady would grumble at the leaking carriage, and that was one thing his surprising young cousin had absolutely not done. He looked at his watch. She had been gone five minutes. He had known her now for not much more than an hour, and, amazingly, he was regretting that from now on they would have a companion, this mysterious Harriet Brown who lived in such a poor way, and whom Caterina had met in circumstances that, she said, would shock him. He rather looked forward to the process of getting to know this cousin of his, and perhaps letting her learn how very little there

13

was in the world that shocked him. The younger son of a younger son, he had been fighting his own battles for ten years since his father died bankrupt when he was fifteen. And fighting them, he reckoned now, with some success. After all, here he was, on a secret and fascinating mission to a strange country, and he could congratulate himself on having acquired an equally fascinating companion.

What would she be saying to her friend Harriet Brown? He wished he could be a fly on the shabby walls that enclosed their confidences.

* * *

'So that's our story,' Caterina summed up for her friend. 'We met when the carriage nearly ran you down. I was on my way to —what did I go to alone?—my drawing lesson. The other girl was ill. I made the carriage stop; you weren't badly hurt but I insisted on taking you home.'

'You're a great insister,' said Harriet Brown lovingly. 'I take it this gentry cousin of yours has found that out by now.'

'He's learning. And less of the cant talk, if you please. It was the penniless gentlewoman I recognised in you, don't forget. There should be a word for gentle girl, should there not?'

'What we are not,' said Harriet. 'There,' she closed the shabby little portmanteau. 'That'll

14

do me till we get to Falmouth and the gentry cousin fits you out like the lady you always were. I can't wait to get into that gown of yours. It's short on you, and a bit tight; skinflints, those nuns; it'll do me a treat, but I reckon the cove's in for the fright of his life when he sees you rigged up proper. Good,' she wrapped herself in a shabby shawl. 'That's the last bit of cockney you'll hear out of me, Cat my love, and what a strain it is going to be.' She had modulated into the genteel accents of an abigail.

'No, no,' protested Caterina. 'You are coming as friend and chaperone, not abigail. Not so genteel if you love me!'

'Which I do. And so we should, shouldn't we, you and I. What we've been through together.' Quickly, lovingly, they embraced.

*   *   *

Jeremy Craddock thought Miss Brown a sad, pale little shrimp of a thing, all bones and angles, in her darned shawl and shabby bonnet, and it surprised him when it was she who asked the question he had been expecting from Caterina.

'I'm ashamed to have to confess it,' he told her, 'and to two such intrepid young ladies, too, but I have been ordered to Oporto for my health. The doctors advise some winter sunshine for a problem of mine.'

15

'I just hope you get it then,' said Caterina. 'I thought everyone knew about the winter rains in Spain and Portugal since Sir John Moore's terrible retreat on Corunna. And Soult's flight from Porto, come to that. It was the weather saved him, if you ask me. And what a pity that was. But what's your complaint, cousin? You don't look like an invalid to me. Is there anything Harriet and I should know? In case you were to take ill during the voyage.'

'Oh, it's nothing.' He had not expected to dislike this so much. 'A slight tendency to the falling sickness, that's all. It has unfitted me for the army, much to my regret. There's an American lady has lived in Oporto for a year or so, a student of Dr Mesmer's. They say great things of the cures she has worked. I expect you will think me a hypochondriacal fool, but I have allowed myself to entertain hopes of her treatment. It's a deuced inconvenient complaint to suffer from, as I am sure you two young ladies will understand.'

'I should just about think so,' said Caterina. 'We had a girl at the convent for a while. She used to foam at the mouth and fall down, and we had to force her teeth open so she didn't bite her tongue. I'll be able to do that for you, cousin, if need be. No need to fret.'

'What happened to her?' This was very tiresome indeed.

'Oh, Reverend Mother sent her home in the end. She said we were a convent, not a hospital.

16

She wasn't a great one for loving kindness.'

'I've not had a seizure for years,' he hastened to tell her. 'But something happened last winter that made the doctors a little anxious. Rest and sunshine, they said. In happier times I'd have gone to the south of France, or Italy.'

'Combining health with pleasure,' agreed Caterina. 'Never mind, I don't suppose it will rain all the time in Porto, cousin, and you will have plenty of distractions if you like cards, and dancing, and gossip. But tell me about the American lady. What in the world is she doing in Porto?'

'She and her brother were expelled from France, where she went after studying with Dr Mesmer in Switzerland. She's an outspoken young lady, as I believe Americans tend to be. She was a friend of the former Empress Josephine and said something a little too frank when Napoleon divorced her to marry Marie Louise of Austria. The tale is that she and her brother had to leave on the first ship—and it was taking supplies to Soult when he held Oporto.'

'Why do you say Oporto when Caterina says Porto?' asked Harriet.

'She is right and I am wrong,' Jeremy told her. 'Porto is the Portuguese name for the city. It means port, of course. It's only we English who have tagged on the "O" from the Portuguese for "the". Should I try to change my habits, do you think, cousin?'

17

'It depends which society you mean to join,' Caterina told him. 'The English or the Portuguese. They don't mix much, I should warn you. I wonder where the American lady and her brother have managed to fit themselves in. What is her name, by the way?'

'You've not heard about her?'

'How should I have? I have heard about as much from Porto these three long years as I have from the moon. I don't even know if my friends survived the French massacre two years ago. I don't know if I have any friends.' She reached out to clasp Harriet's hand. 'I can't tell you how glad I am that you are coming with me, Harriet dear.' And then, to Jeremy. 'Is the nameless American lady young?'

'I believe so. Miss Rachel Emerson. Her brother is a good deal older, I understand, and has acted as her manager in this strange career of hers.'

'You mean she is in the way of being a professional healer?' Caterina had recognised the note of disapproval in his voice.

'She does it for money, if that is what you mean.'

'As a doctor would, surely? Tell me, cousin, is it because she takes money for her healing that you disapprove of her, or because she is a woman setting up as a healer?'

'A bit of both, I suppose.' Ruefully. 'I hope you never draw my caricature, Cousin Caterina. You see too far into a man's
18

thoughts for comfort.' And that was all too true.

'Ah, but I like you, Cousin Jeremy,' said Caterina.

*　　　*　　　*

'There you are!' Ralph Emerson came angrily out on to the tiny balcony with its high view down the Douro River to the sea. 'I've been hunting everywhere for you. What is this about Mrs Ware cancelling?' A big, burly, fair-haired man, he had the remains of what had been striking good looks, marred now by broken veins, too high a colour, and a look of habitual bad temper.

'Not very far to hunt.' Rachel Emerson put down the shabby sheet she had been darning and looked up at him with large, thoughtful grey eyes. Much younger than he was, she did not look in the least like him. She was small and neat-featured, he was large and flamboyant; where he was ruddy, she was pale. 'You know I like to work out here in the evenings. The light is better, for one thing, and I love to see the colours changing on the river. You were right to insist on a place with a river view, even if it is such a tiny one.'

If she had hoped to placate him with this remark, she failed dismally. 'And whose fault is it, pray, that we cannot afford a better place? What have you done now, to offend Mrs

Ware?'

'Nothing that I know of. She just sent a note to say she was sorry, she was too busy to come. One of the children is ill, I expect.'

'More likely she is not satisfied with the treatment she is getting! I've told you over and over again that they want a show, these stupid Englishwomen. It's not enough just to lay your hands on them. They want dark curtains and soft music, all the trimmings old Mesmer supplied. And the group thing, the holding of hands, the magic circles—'

'That was Dr Mesmer's way.' She had said all this many times before. 'Mine is different, Ralph. Different, but just as effective. He told me so himself. He said my hands were quick to feel trouble, and quick to soothe it. He told me to concentrate on that. And you know I have had results—'

'Those suggestible French! Of course you have. Rub them with sweet oil, smile your charming smile, and hey presto, they are cured. The English are quite other; and so I warned you when we came here. They need the hocus pocus.'

'And that is just why I did not want to come.' This was an argument, if you could call it that since he always won, that they had had many times since they left France. She had longed to go home to New England and safety, had found herself reluctantly in Oporto instead. And now, of course, it was all her fault that the patients who had flocked to her at first were beginning to fall away.

'Closed shutters and dramatic lighting.' He had said this to her many times before. 'And the group holding hands, so the electrical magnetism runs through them. That's what you need. I'll look after the lights and the music. All you have to do is manage the sufferers, as you so well know how to do.'

'But that's not the way I can cure them.' She had said this to him many times before. 'It's feeling them, and listening to them, by ourselves, together. That's how I can help them. You know it really, Ralph. Why do you pretend not to?'

'Because I like to eat, I suppose. Look at that pile of bills! I hope you have some idea of how we are to pay them, because it is more than I have.'

She was silent for a long minute, gazing across to the south bank of the Douro and its busy fringe of shipping. Then she looked up at him: 'You do not think there might be something you could do? With the town so busy as it is, and the troops and supplies coming in for Wellington, and business beginning to look up just a little at last?'

'And what, pray, do you think I should do? Hire myself out as a copy clerk, perhaps, to one of those stiff-necked British merchants? You know what would happen then! We'd be done for socially, you and I, and you could whistle for any more customers. God knows we are on sufferance enough as it is. A little better than the sawbones, and not quite so good as the Chaplain. God, how I hate the British.' And then, gripping her wrist with a hand that hurt. 'And if you are fool enough to tell anyone I said that you'll be lucky to live to regret it.'

'You're hurting me,' she said. 'Who would I tell? I've no friends, only customers, as you choose to call them. Yes, Tilly, what is it?'

'A note for you mum. No answer needed, the man said.' Tilly was a handsome black girl who spoke the lilting English of the southern American states. In hiring her in preference to a Portuguese servant Ralph Emerson had imitated the British merchants he disliked so much. Like them, he had not troubled himself to try and learn the difficult language of the country and preferred to be waited on by servants who could understand his shouted commands. 'Well, what is it?' he asked impatiently.

'It may be work.' Rachel handed him the letter, preferring to do so than to have him demand to see it. 'It's from Senhor Gomez—'

'Rich as Croesus. Lives beyond the Franciscans—' He was reading the letter. 'Of course! He's the one married an English vineyard, and the girl died. Some whispering about it, by what I've heard. The baby was a girl. They don't reckon much to girls, here in Portugal.'

'Who does? This must be a relative of his wife. Coming out from England for his health.'

'The falling sickness. You are going to cure him, my girl. And I am going to make the financial arrangements with rich Senhor Gomez.'

'I did cure someone of it once, do you remember? Dr Mesmer had given up, gave me a free hand, said I could hardly make matters worse for the poor girl.'

'Pity it was a girl,' he said. 'Let's just hope you can bring it off with this Jeremy Craddock.'

'I must do it my own way.' She had been steeling herself to say this. 'If I am to have any chance of success I have to work on Mr Craddock as I did on poor Lucy.'

'And how did you work on poor Lucy?' His tone was faintly mocking.

'I saw her alone. Many times. We talked. I—it's hard to describe—' She hated talking to him about her cures, but knew she had to make this clear. 'I touched her, felt what was wrong, we worked together on it.'

'A lot of female mumbo jumbo. It will be interesting to see how you go on with this Mr Craddock. Do you think he will be consumptive too? An interesting invalid with long golden hair and deep sunk eyes.' While they were talking his eyes had gone on looking past her to scan the animated scene on the river below, even busier than usual at this evening

23

hour when merchants were being ferried home from their wine lodges at Villa Nova de Gaia on the south bank. They had one floor of a tall, thin house, tucked in among the steep alleys that led down from the Cathedral to the river, and the windows looked across the bridge of boats that spanned the river and downstream to the far view of São João da Foz and the sea. 'There's a ship coming in now,' he said. 'She must just have made it across the bar with the tide. Heavy loaded by the look of her.' He had picked up the glass he kept handy. 'English, of course. Maybe your patient is on her. Had you paused to consider, my dear, what the Oporto tabbies will say if you insist on seeing this interesting young invalid alone?'

CHAPTER TWO

Jeremy Craddock was amazed at how much money the two girls contrived to spend in Falmouth, and taken aback at the results. 'I see now just how right your dragon of a nun was to insist on a chaperone,' he told Caterina, when she and Harriet joined him in their inn parlour, transformed into young lady of fashion and respectable friend.

'Thank you, kind sir,' she dropped him one of her demure curtseys. 'We will do, you think, Harriet and I?'

24

'You will most certainly do. Aside from the fact that Miss Brown is much too young! May I pour you a glass of wine, Miss Gomez?'

'Ha! It's "Miss Gomez" now! And glasses of wine! I am grown up at last.' It was the first time on the journey that he had offered it. She sipped. 'And very nasty it is too. You wait till you taste our Colares wine, Mr Craddock.' She emphasised the surname, teasing. 'You will find it quite a different thing. Oh, I can't wait to get home. Will we sail in the morning, do you think?'

'If the wind holds. Captain Barker expects a swift and easy voyage, I am happy to tell you. Are you young ladies good sailors?'

'I am,' said Caterina, and, 'Lord knows,' said Harriet.

'I don't know either.' Smiling at Harriet. 'This long war has made travel impossible. I was too young to take advantage of the peace in 1802—or at least that is what my tutors said. I was wild to go.'

'And the grown ups wouldn't let you?' said Caterina. 'Poor Cousin Jeremy, I know just how you felt. Just the same, you must have been grateful to them when war broke out again and Boney clapped all the English tourists into gaol. Just think, you might be there still.'

'A monster of a man,' he told her. 'A danger to the world. We have to beat him. Do you think your father will quite like your calling me

Cousin Jeremy, Miss Gomez?' More and more he felt things going too fast for him.

'I've no idea. I'm not sure I care very much either. To have a father's rights, you need to act like a father.' She flashed him one of her wicked smiles. 'I'm sorry. I am shocking you again, am I not, cousin?'

'I am beginning to think it was a very odd nunnery of yours,' he told her.

'That they did not teach me better manners? Oh, to do them justice, they did try, those poor nuns. With prayers and fasting, mainly. The fasting on my part, you understand, and the prayers on theirs.' And then, suddenly sober. 'But I should not laugh at them, they were wonderfully good to me, really. And I repaid them with mockery. I sometimes think I am not a very civilised person, Cousin Jeremy.'

'Of course you're not,' put in Harriet lovingly. 'You're a savage, Cat, but sometimes in this world one needs to be.'

'You're certainly a chameleon,' Jeremy said. 'A man does not know where he is with you.' It was true. He found her profoundly disturbing. He wanted no truck with women, never had, not since the childhood night when his adored mother came to his bedside, cried over him, kissed him passionately, and was gone in the morning. She had eloped with his father's best friend, and he had promised himself, as he grew painfully up, that he would never let a woman get under his guard again. Now he shepherded

26

his little party briskly off to an early bed and retired himself hoping strongly that they would be able to sail next morning.

But they woke to the still, clear light of what felt almost like an autumn day, and a message from the *Anthea* confirmed that there was no hope of sailing until that evening at the earliest.

'Wonderful.' Caterina smiled across the breakfast table at him. 'Harryo and I had to waste all yesterday shopping, today we can explore this nice town. Do you know it used to be called Pennycomequick, Cousin Jeremy? The girl who brought our water told us.'

'And how you understood her is a mystery to me,' said Harriet. 'So broad as she speaks.'

'I love languages, they interest me. I even contrived to persuade one of the nuns to teach me a little Latin until Reverend Mother found out and put a stop to it. A waste of everyone's time, she called it. But, come, cousin, where shall we start? Out on the cliff walk or over to the castle?'

'The cliffs, perhaps, if your shoes are stout enough for such walking.' He had been very much aware of curious glances at their little party and had even wondered whether he should not hire a local girl to go along as abigail, but something Caterina had said about her father had made him baulk at this extra expense.

It was a happy day. The girls proved good walkers with none of the squealing and

27

demands for help he expected from young ladies. They found a broad turf path along the cliff overlooking Falmouth Bay where they could walk three abreast and listen to larks singing high above them. 'This is better than the castle.' Caterina turned to look back at Pendennis Castle on its headland. 'I needed this air. And so did you, Harryo love, though you were never one to grumble as I do. But you begin to look yourself again today, I am glad to say. Oh—' She turned impulsively to Jeremy. 'I cannot begin to tell you how grateful I am, Cousin Jeremy.' And then: 'But what a wretch I am. I never thought to ask whether you felt well enough to climb up here. You don't talk about yourself much, do you?'

'It's a dull subject.' Half of him wished Harriet away and the other half was deeply grateful that she was there.

'Then we will talk about something else,' said Caterina cheerfully. 'What shall it be?'

Inevitably, this meant a little silence, which was just becoming awkward when they came on a cliff-top tavern and stopped to drink mugs of strong local cider and eat cold beef and pickles. 'Oh, what a happy day,' said Caterina as they turned back towards their inn.

But Jeremy had resolved that he would suffer from seasickness on the crossing. To his relief, they were summoned on board that evening and sailed with the dawn wind. He had been glad to find that there were a few other women on board, soldiers' wives on their way to join their husbands in Oporto or up river. Consigning his charges to the women's quarters, he made a painful apology. 'I am so very sorry; I don't feel quite the thing.' The ship was listing sluggishly this way and that on a rising tide. 'If you will excuse me. I know you by now as amply able to take care of yourselves.'

'Of course we can, Cousin Jeremy. You take care of yourself.' Caterina smiled the smile that was beginning to touch his heart.

*   *   *

'Thank goodness for a moment alone.' Caterina had steered her friend to a quiet corner on the upper deck of the ship. 'Now, tell me about your trouble with your mother, Harryo. How could she send you to that dreadful place?'

'To teach me a lesson,' said Harriet. 'Mind you, money has been tight lately. Everyone has been feeling the pinch, what with the war going on for ever and the harvests so bad and all. And mother's is the kind of business feels hard times first. People can be very ruthless, Cat, when their own comfort is threatened. I was one less mouth to feed, see.'

'Yes, but you've been worth your weight in gold to her, and you know it. There must have been more.'

29

'Of course there was. She had found me a good match, hadn't she?'

'Oh,' said Caterina. 'Now I begin to see. Tell me about him.'

Harriet made an expressive face. 'A tanner in a very good way of business and smelled of it. Twice widowed, eight small children. He'd worn them out, Cat, those two poor wives of his. He needed a new drudge and picked on me. I wouldn't have minded the children, poor little things, but he was gross, Cat, aside from the smell. If she wanted me to make that kind of match, mother shouldn't have sent me to Miss Shepard's school to get ideas above my station.'

'Amongst other things,' said Caterina dryly. 'I wonder what inducement he was offering your mother.'

'Just money. Mother would do anything for money as we both know. So when I refused the tanner she sent me away to her friends the Joneses. Ten children, they have. Governess! Maid of all work, more like. Skivvy. And I didn't much like the way he was beginning to get me in corners. I was never gladder to see anyone than you, love.'

'Thank goodness you let me know where you were. But your mother, Harryo. Is money really so tight with her?'

'Well, she's missing what the tanner promised her for me. And she's certainly glad of what she gets from you. No need to worry,

30

so long as you can keep it up.'

'That's why I am going to Portugal,' said Caterina.

* * *

'There you are at last.' Five days later, Caterina made room for Jeremy between her and Harriet at the rail as the *Anthea* drew in towards land. 'We were afraid you might be dying down there in your cabin, but thought you would not be best pleased if we came to enquire. I do hope you have not had one of your seizures.'

'Not precisely.' He loathed to have to say it. 'But I have to confess that the mere possibility of one makes life on shipboard somewhat risky.'

'I should just about think so. Suppose you lost consciousness on the top deck and fell overboard? But we would have looked after you, would we not, Harryo?'

'I don't suppose Mr Craddock would have liked it much,' Harriet smiled at him.

Something had changed about her, he thought. What was it? Pink in her cheeks, something about her hair ... 'You are quite right, Miss Brown,' he told her. 'I just hope you ladies have enjoyed your voyage.'

'We've loved it.' Caterina answered him. 'Haven't we, Harryo? I have taught Harriet some Portuguese, the ship's officers are our

31

slaves, and the captain has the most improper ideas concerning Harriet. No need to look so alarmed, cousin, he has a wife and six children at home and we have behaved like the patterns of propriety we are.'

'I shall be very glad to see you safe into your father's hands,' he told her.

'I just hope he will be as glad to receive me. Oh, look!' She pointed ahead. 'I can see the castle at Foz—good God, they have repaired it—and the Clerigos tower beyond. Oh, Harriet, we are almost home!' She turned to embrace her friend and Jeremy suspected that it was to hide the sheen of tears in her eyes, and could not help being moved by it. Just as well they were nearly there.

'You can see the bar now,' Caterina told him. 'Captain Barker knows his business, I can tell; the tide is full and the wind behind us; there will be no difficulty getting past it. When the weather is bad, you have to land here at Foz,' she explained, 'and get carried ashore by the fishwives. I have never thought it would be very comfortable.'

'I am glad to hear there is something that daunts you,' he told her.

'Many things, cousin. I am terrified of mice, and I don't like thunder much either.'

'What are you afraid of, Miss Brown?' He turned to include Harriet in the conversation.

'Hunger,' she told him.

'Oh, Harryo!' Caterina caught her friend's

hand. 'I'm ashamed—'

'Nonsense.' And then, changing the subject. 'Lord, what a lot of boats. I do hope we don't run one down.'

'We won't,' said Caterina. 'The Portuguese are nimble as fish in the water. It's the way to travel of course; the roads are so frightful. All those little boats you see ahead are taking businessmen home from their work at Villa Nova—much quicker than going round by the bridge of boats. Father had his own man—old Felipe. I wonder if he survived the massacre?'

'Massacre?' asked Harriet.

'Two years ago, when Soult took the town. Horrible. The Portonians were the first to revolt against the French after they invaded the year before. They freed themselves, under that great man, their Bishop, while that lazy crew down in Lisbon waited for the British to come and free them.' She turned on Jeremy. 'And then you defended Lisbon, and let Porto go hang.'

'You know that's not fair, Miss Gomez.' He must go very carefully here.

'Do I? What about Sir Robert Wilson and his loyal Lusitanian legion? Where were they when Porto needed them? Enrolled there, trained there, and then marched away into the mountains—'

'And very gallantly they served there,' he told her. 'Robert Wilson and his tiny band of Portuguese kept the French guessing all that

33

winter. Things might have gone very differently if it had not been for them.'

'They would have been different in Porto if they had been there in the spring.' She turned to Harriet. 'The Bishop built fortifications, tried to defend the town, but there was so little time, and too few trained men ... The French broke through—they were savage, out of control, people fled across the bridge of boats and it gave way under their numbers. Imagine! A cold April day, and the river in flood ... Nobody knows how many died, how many were killed by the French in the town—'

'The French did help to rescue people from the river,' Jeremy reminded her.

'Some of them did! The ones who weren't looting and killing—'

'A sack is always a horrible affair,' he told her. 'And I did hear that the Bishop had withdrawn across the bridge of boats the night before, even perhaps given orders for its destruction.'

'That's a wicked slander.' Furiously.

'Probably. He would hardly have been made a member of the Council of Regents down in Lisbon if anyone had believed it.'

'Yes. I shall be sad he's not here,' she said. 'He's my godfather; he was always good to me.'

'But what happened afterwards?' asked Harriet. 'In Porto, I mean. I'm very ignorant, I'm afraid.'

'Like everyone else in England,' said Caterina. 'And why not? A small, unimportant far-off ally.' And then, with a sudden smile for Jeremy. 'You're going to tell me I am being unfair again, and I suppose you are right, really. What happened, Harriet, was that Lord Wellington turned up, like St George in the pantomime, and got his troops across the Douro when Soult wasn't looking, and retook Porto in a day. I just hope you British are valuing the place a bit more highly now, Cousin Jeremy, but I doubt it. No lines of Torres Vedras for Porto; we must make shift to defend ourselves.'

'I really don't think the question is going to arise,' he told her. 'Oporto's moment of danger surely passed when Masséna turned east instead of north after giving up hope at Torres Vedras. And if there were any cause for anxiety, I should have thought you would have found this ship's cargo reassuring.' He was furious with himself the moment the words were spoken. The less he saw of this dangerous girl, the better.

'Oh, what are we carrying?'

'Just war material.' He made it vague. 'Look, that must be the bridge of boats.' The river had narrowed and deepened while they rounded a series of bluffs on the north side. Now he could see the unmistakable bulk of Oporto's cathedral ahead of them, above the pontoon bridge with its busy morning traffic.

35

'And is that the Clerigos tower they say is the highest in Portugal?'

'Yes. And we just passed our house. Look, Harryo, on the hill there, with the white terraces.'

'It looks huge,' said Harriet nervously. 'And what's the church we are coming up to now?'

'That's the Franciscans', with the monastery behind. Yes, I thought so—' There had been a quick series of shouted orders and the ship was turning across the river in a wide curve. 'We are to moor at Villa Nova de Gaia on the south bank. That's where your war materials will be unloaded, Cousin Jeremy. And very welcome too, if any of them get left here in Porto. That's the English Factory, by the way.' She pointed to a solid grey building on the north bank. 'Where the British wine and dine each other and keep us junior allies at arm's length.'

She had tried him too far. 'Miss Gomez, I beg you to think about what you are saying. You know how small a society it is we are about to join; your father is one of the few people with a foot in both camps. I have been wondering if he has not perhaps sent for you in the hope that you will help him improve relations between the British and the Portuguese, vitally important in these dangerous times. It is true,' he admitted, 'I had heard that the British tend to keep themselves rather to themselves in Oporto. But neither of our countries has so many allies against

36

Napoleon that we can afford to affront each other. I do beg that you will try to think of yourself as British as well as Portuguese.'

'After the way I was treated at that school? You ask a good deal, Mr Craddock.'

'That school was not all England. It was Roman Catholic to begin with.'

'And so am I.' Dangerously.

'I beg your pardon. I had quite forgotten. Well, Miss Gomez, if you cannot think of yourself as British, by all means think of yourself as Portuguese, and remember we and the Spanish are all the allies you have got. Dislike us British if you must, but for all our sakes, do, I beg of you, try to keep a civil tongue in your head.' He stopped, appalled at his own frankness, and saw with deep relief that she was laughing.

'Lord, what a scold,' she said. 'I never had an elder brother, but I am sure that is just what he would sound like. Are you proposing to be a brother to me, Mr Craddock?'

'I should like it above all things.' He saw with relief that they were nudging their way in to the quay. It was high time this conversation ended. 'Can you see your father in the crowd there?' He was glad to be able to change the subject so suitably.

'My father? You surely don't think he would waste valuable time coming to meet me? One of the servants will be there to see to the baggage, of course, but I imagine that we will be left to find our way home unaided. You are coming to stay with us, I hope, cousin?'

'Your father was so good as to invite me.' He was less and less sure that this was a good idea. 'I shall most certainly take advantage of the invitation for a few days,' he went on. 'Then I think I must look out for bachelor quarters convenient for the lady who I hope is going to treat me.'

'You make me ashamed.' Her smile was friendly. 'I keep forgetting you are a sick man. You conceal it so well. Will it be too tiring for you to cross by ferry and walk home? I promise you, it is much the quickest way.'

'Of course not.' More and more he hated to play the invalid, but it must be done. 'I have done nothing but rest on board ship,' he told her. 'The exercise will do me good.'

The quay rocked under Jeremy's feet. His carefully learned Portuguese seemed useless against this barrage of noise as men in red caps and women in flat black hats swarmed on and off the ship, carrying luggage, shouting greetings, stinking of garlic and something else he could not place.

'There's Felipe.' Caterina put a hand on his arm. 'This way, Cousin Jeremy. Keep close, Harriet.'

'I certainly will,' said Harriet. 'This is worse than Bath market any day.'

'Certainly different,' said Caterina. 'Here we are, Felipe. It's good to see you.' She shocked

38

and amazed Jeremy by kissing the grizzled servant on both cheeks. It was cool comfort to see that it surprised him too. 'How are you all, Felipe? How is Maria?'

'Dead.' The old man turned to spit on the quay. 'The French killed her.'

'Maria? Dead?' She reached out a groping hand, and Jeremy caught it. 'She can't be! How?'

'Not now,' the man said gruffly. 'Later, *minha senhora*. This way. The boat is waiting for you. I will see to the luggage.' And they obeyed him in taut silence.

* * *

'I think I have spotted your patient.' Ralph Emerson made room for Rachel beside him on the little balcony and passed her the glass. 'Standing with two ladies on the quay just upstream from the ship.'

'Yes, I am sure you are right, that must be Mr Craddock. I wonder which of the young ladies is the romantic Miss Gomez.'

'What makes you think her romantic?'

'Have you not heard the story? Mrs Ware told me the last time she came for treatment. Of course it was given out that Senhor Gomez sent her home for safety during the first French invasion in 1808, but the facts of the case were that he had found her in a compromising position with a young neighbour of theirs. You

39

know how those houses beyond the Franciscans' all have gardens running down the slope of the bluff. Well, there was a path through at the bottom, a convenient summerhouse, a charming young Romeo of a neighbour. Boy and girl stuff, of course, nothing to signify, but you can see why Gomez thought he should pack her off—a motherless girl—to some reliable English nuns.'

'So,' Ralph Emerson said thoughtfully, 'damaged goods!'

'Nothing of the kind! She was a child, remember, can't have been more than twelve or thirteen.'

'"Younger than she are happy mothers made,"' he quoted at her.

'*Romeo and Juliet!* And look what came of that. Do, please forget I told you, Ralph.'

'I like you to tell me things. Who was the Romeo?'

'Mrs Ware didn't say, but she did mention that he had left town. Joined the Loyal Lusitanian Legion, I think she said.'

'He is probably dead in that case. Their casualties have been frightful, I believe. End of a sad little story.' He took the glass back from her.

'They are preparing to unload the cargo already. Wasting no time I see. You have to give it to the British, they are hard workers. What does it look like to you?' He passed her the glass.

'Heavy stuff. Hard to see. The hatches are open; they are swaying it up, but look, Ralph, it's not going ashore.'

'No more it is. They are loading it straight into river boats. Someone must have worked hard to have them organised and ready. You're right, it is heavy stuff, by the look of it. Now, I wonder: downriver to defend the harbour mouth, or upriver for some mad plan of Lord Wellington's. Either way, the Portonians won't be best pleased when they see it being dispatched elsewhere. Look, there's Craddock helping his young ladies into a boat to cross the river. The one in colours is most probably Miss Gomez, don't you think?'

'Yes. The other will be her companion. Mr Craddock is much younger than I expected. From what Senhor Gomez said, I had thought him middle aged.'

'He don't look precisely crippled with illness either. Quite the young gallant. I think I shall have to chaperone you when you start on him with your miracle hands, my dear.' His tone was faintly mocking as it so often was when he talked of her healing powers.

'No!' She turned on him angrily. 'You know I would be able to do nothing with you there, laughing at me.'

'Then perhaps you should invite Miss Gomez's companion. She don't look much of a dragon to me. You might find her presence less formidable than mine. Lord, look at that for a

41

heavy load!' He turned back to watch the activity on the dockside.

'It's dinner time, Ralph.'

'To hell with dinner. Let it wait.'

*   *   *

Other eyes, behind other spyglasses, were also watching the unloading of the *Anthea*. On the second floor balcony of a prosperous house in the Rua Nova dos Inglesas, Mrs Ware handed the glass to her son. 'There's Caterina Gomez! I'd know her father's boat anywhere, so shabby, and that dour old Felipe of his. At least she looks quite the lady.'

'And why should she not, mother?'

'Well, you know the stories. We are going to forget them, of course. After all, poor child, motherless, no proper female companionship, and that ramshackle household full of hangers-on and priests. How was the poor child to know how to go on? I just hope she proves educable. Lord knows, she's young enough still.'

'Going a little too fast, aren't you, mother? I've not said I'll do it, even if old Gomez don't change his mind, which ten to one he will.'

'But, dear boy, just think how wretchedly we are placed! With your father's death at such an awkward moment, and this cruel war, ruining everything for everybody, and those Portuguese merchants the only ones who have contrived to come out of it with their businesses intact. Frank, do please remember that it seems to be Miss Gomez or starvation.'

'Suppose I decide I would rather starve, mother? Or do a job of work, perhaps? I was talking to Major Dickson at the dinner for the Prince of Wales's birthday the other night. He seemed to think he could find work for me if I were so minded.'

'Work for you? What kind of work, for goodness sake?'

'You don't think me capable of working, do you, mother? And whose fault was that but yours and my father's? Having me educated at Eton and Cambridge like a gentleman, when I should have been learning my trade. Well, it may surprise you, but when I told Dickson I was a senior wrangler in mathematics he seemed quite interested. Said he wanted to talk to me again, but would be too busy while the *Anthea* was unloading. I think he is having a hard time of it with some of the English officers here; they rank above him in the English army—his rank is Portuguese you see—and you can imagine how they feel about that.'

'Lord, yes! I was talking to Mrs Bland the other day, and she said most of the Portuguese levies—what do they call them? *ordinanzas*— were no more use than girls from the seminary. No clothes or shoes, and half-starved most of the time, and the officers not much better. She had thought of going with her husband when he moves up country next week, but he advises against it. He came through the mountains with Dickson and says the conditions are little short of barbarous. And as for the roads! Dickson has written Lord Wellington urging a change of route, because the one from Peso da Regua to Trancoso was so dreadful. The gun-carriages would be shattered to pieces, she says. But he doesn't seem to think conditions at Pinhel would be any better from her point of view and urges her to stay here where she is comfortable.'

'Which I am sure she is glad enough to do,' said Frank. 'But, mother, should she be telling you the things her husband says to her? I know we are all friends here in Oporto, but you must remember what Dom Antonio the Governor said just the other day about careless talk and the possibility of French spies among the servants.'

'What a slanderous thing to say! I trust my American blacks just as I would English servants. Just think of the way they looked after things for me here during the French occupation! When I got back there was not so much as a spoon missing. And as for that Antonio, he may be acting Governor in Colonel Trant's absence, but there is no need for him to give himself such airs. Look,' she handed him the glass, 'they are disembarking now; you can get a better view of Miss Gomez. She looks well enough to me; dowdy provincial

44

clothes, of course, but what else would you expect of a girl straight from the convent. I'll soon put that to rights. Who is that man gallanting her?' Sharply.

'Oh, that must be her cousin. Gomez asked him to bring her out; he's coming for his health—hopes for a cure from Miss Emerson, I believe.'

'Oh—an invalid.' She dismissed him, relieved. 'Much good may that Rachel Emerson do him. Calls herself a healer! All she did was put her hands on my head and ask me a lot of impertinent questions! I'm not going back to her in a hurry. A pair of charlatans! I cannot imagine how they came to be admitted into society.'

'They had introductions to Joseph Camo, I believe. And you know what a debt we all owe him for the way he looked after our affairs while we were in exile in England.'

'Exile.' She sniffed. 'What an odd word. And I have always been convinced that that man Camo had his share of the goods from those merchantmen that were snapped up by the French.'

'Very likely,' said her son. 'But he did us yeoman service, just the same. He mixed up the figures so successfully that the French did not dare distrain the half of our British property for fear of offending their American friends. You know how badly they want the Yankees to join them against us.'

'Much use they would be. And how do you know he didn't blind you with his figures too? That's probably why we find ourselves so poor now. What he saved from the French, he quietly took for himself.'

'Mother, will you listen to me for once? I understand figures too, and I know what a good job Joseph Camo did for us. I do beg you to watch what you say about him. He's been a good friend to us all, but I tell you, he could make a formidable enemy.'

'He's like all the rest of those Americans,' she said. 'He smells of the shop. No wonder he was prepared to sponsor those dubious Emersons. And besides, you have only to look at him to see that he has Portuguese ancestry; no wonder he goes on so well here. Dark-haired, large-nosed and oily like the rest of them.'

'Mother!' He was exasperated. 'Do you want me to marry Miss Gomez and her fortune, or do you not?'

'Well, of course I do. Whose idea was it anyway? And, really, she could be a lot worse by the looks of her.' She put down the glass as the little party landed and vanished into the network of alleys behind the quay.

'Well then.' Quietly now, but with emphasis. 'She is half Portuguese remember. Her father entirely so.'

'But she has been to school in England for— what would it be? Three years? Surely that must have civilised her. She needs to learn to dress, of course, but let me alone for that. I would never have suggested the match, my dear, if I had thought she would come to us with a lot of sluttish Portuguese habits ... I have your interests too much at heart for that, my dear boy.'

'If you truly have my interests at heart, mother, I do beg you to be immensely careful what you say. I know it is hard to remember, here in Oporto, with things so nearly back to normal, but there is still a war being fought up in the mountains, hardly two days' ride away.'

'As if I would forget! Do you realise that it is only a few weeks till vintage—such as there will be this year, after all the fighting upriver—and Major Dickson who you are such friends with has taken over every available boat on the river for his mighty secret operations. *And* all the oxcarts upriver, Helen Bland says. It is going to be a black year for the wine trade, dear boy, and how we are to get through next winter is more than I can imagine.'

'We'll manage, mother.' He said it more cheerfully than he felt. 'And I promise you, next year will be better.'

'I cannot imagine what makes you think so. So far as I can see, this horrible war is going to go on for ever. And all they send out from England is powder and shot!' With a despairing gesture at the busy scene around the *Anthea*. 'I wrote your Aunt Betty to send me all

47

kinds of things I needed, and I bet you a pound to a dollar that there is nothing on that ship but arms and ammunition.'

'I hope you are right, mother.'

*   *   *

A Londoner, Jeremy Craddock thought he was used to city streets, but nothing had prepared him for the noise and filth of Oporto's narrow, steeply climbing lanes. He began by trying to give an arm to each of the young ladies in his charge, but soon recognised that this was impossible, and agreed tacitly to follow Caterina's lead, with Harriet between them, looking terrified he thought, and no wonder. Caterina, on the other hand, was quite obviously in her element, ploughing her way through the crowds, with what sounded like an exchange of insults from time to time when someone got in her way. It was a far cry from the apparently demure young lady he had rescued from disgrace at the convent. But then, for how long had he been deceived by that modest front of hers? Not for long after he had seen her drawing. He thought, with something between regret and relief, that his fears of becoming attached to her had been quite groundless. There was no place in his life for this young amazon. He might as well have stayed on deck and enjoyed the voyage.

It irked him a little in retrospect, and he

spoke more sharply than he intended when she paused to wait for them at the top of one of the steep flights of steps that punctuated the alley. 'How much further, Miss Gomez? We are getting quite breathless, Miss Brown and I. And attracting a great deal of attention. I begin to think we should have hired sedan chairs after all.'

'I'm sorry. You are probably quite right, but it is a last taste of freedom for Harryo and me. Once we are behind the great doors of my father's house we are going to have to behave like the young ladies we are supposed to be.' She shouted something firece in Portuguese at a group of ragged children. 'Don't give them anything, Harryo, you'll have the whole quarter on our heels.'

'But they look so wretched,' said Harriet. 'I thought I knew what hunger looked like, but this is worse than anything ... Even the pigs look starving.' The noisome alley that they were climbing seemed to be shared equally by pigs, hens and ragged children.

'At least the pigs don't beg,' said Jeremy Craddock.

'You would beg if you were as hungry as these babies are.' Harriet turned on him fiercely, her whole face suddenly hard and sharp.

'Don't, Harryo,' Caterina's voice was gentle. 'Don't think about it. Please.'

'I'm sorry,' said Harriet. 'I don't know

49

what's the matter with me. It's the heat, I think, and these poor children...'

'I know,' said Caterina. 'But, remember, love, the kind climate makes their lives easier. And, look, the worst is over now; we're getting into the better part of town. No more pigs, Mr Craddock, and we will be smelling the flowers in my father's garden soon.' She had turned left at the top of a flight of steps into a slightly wider alley running between high walls, and Jeremy saw evergreen trees rising above them.

'It's good to be out of the crowd,' he said. 'Keep in the shade, Miss Brown, and you won't mind it so much.' He took Harriet's arm as a group of priests dressed all in black surged past.

'So many priests,' she said. 'They fair give me the creeps.'

'Nonsense,' said Caterina. 'They are just a lot of harmless old men.' But Jeremy noticed that she got out of their way like everybody else, as they marched along the centre of the narrow street, black robes flowing behind them.

'Here we are.' Caterina stopped at a door in the wall to their left, and tugged hard on the bell pull beside it. 'Home,' she said and Jeremy wondered if there was a question in her voice.

The big door swung open on to a green courtyard, and instant pandemonium. Three black-garbed old women plunged forward to seize and hug Caterina, passing her between them like a child's toy. A group of other servants stood around shrieking welcomes.

'Enough.' An upright, white-haired old man in rusty black had been standing a little back from the animated scene. Now he stepped forward and bent to kiss Caterina's hand. 'You are dearly welcome home, *minha senhora.*'

'Oh, Tonio.' Her eyes were full of tears. 'I am so very sorry about Maria.'

'I try to think of it as the will of God, but it is hard. Father Pedro says thoughts of vengeance are wicked, but I tell you, *senhora*, if a Frenchman were to come in at that door, now, I would kill him with my bare hands.' He looked down at them, surprised at what he had said. 'It is good to have you back, *minha senhora.* Your father expects you in his study. You and the *senhor.*'

'Miss Brown had best come too,' said Jeremy. 'Unless any of your servants speak English, that is.'

'Gracious no.' Caterina found the idea absurd. 'Yes. Come along Harriet, he can't bite you.' Jeremy wondered how sure she was of this.

The house door faced them across the courtyard, standing open in welcome. Jeremy had a vague impression of an old, asymmetrical building, set about with flowers and covered in vines, before he followed the two girls into a dark, cool corridor.

It was suddenly quiet as the door swung to

51

behind them leaving the chattering servants outside in the courtyard. 'This way.' Caterina led the way down what seemed an endless passage, dimly lit from the occasional open door to left or right, then paused before knocking once, firmly, on the door at the end.

CHAPTER THREE

The dark room smelled of dust and damp. Senhor Gomez was busy behind a huge desk piled high with papers. He rose, tall and gaunt, to survey his three visitors with a cold eye.

'Father.' Caterina offered her cheek for his reluctant kiss.

'Caterina. Welcome home.' He spoke with no trace of feeling, turned to Jeremy. 'Mr Craddock, thank you for bringing her.' He held out a limp hand to Jeremy's warm clasp. 'And this is?'

'Miss Brown. Harriet Brown.' Caterina spoke into the little silence that followed the question. If she had hoped Jeremy would answer it, he had failed her. 'My friend—and chaperone.'

'Chaperone?' With a look that made Harriet quail. 'She don't look fit to chaperone a mouse. Your idea I take it, Mr Craddock. My daughter was never one to think of such fal-lals. Pity, perhaps.' With a darkling look

52

for Caterina.

'No, sir.' Jeremy spoke at last. 'Reverend Mother's idea. From your letter, I had taken Miss Gomez to be a child, never thought of the need; Mother Agnes pointed it out to me, and I was grateful to her.'

'And she produced this amazon from her kitchens?'

'No, father,' said Caterina. 'Harriet is a friend of mine. I asked her to come and she did so as a favour to me. She is my guest.'

'Is she so?' The two dark glances met and held. 'Then, welcome, Miss Brown. I am sure you and my daughter will prove admirable company for each other. And for Mr Craddock. And now, if you will excuse me, I have work to do.' With a gesture to the huge ledgers on his table. 'I will look forward to seeing you at supper time, Mr Craddock.' He did not try to make it convincing.

'Thank you, sir.' Jeremy held open the door for the two girls, resolving to start looking for lodgings at once.

Back in the long corridor, Caterina watched him close the study door behind them. 'I won't apologise for my father,' she said. 'What's the use? But I do welcome you both.'

'Is he always like that?' asked Harriet.

'When he speaks at all.' Caterina moved back down the long hall to open a door and lead the way into a room that contrasted in every respect with the gloomy study they had just left. This was a woman's room, full of light and colour, opening on to a shady terrace. 'My mother's sitting room,' she told them. 'I used to think father stopped speaking after she died. It was Maria told me how wrong I was. Tonio's wife.' She was fighting tears, and Harriet looked at her in astonishment. Through all the trouble they had shared, she had never seen her friend cry. 'Maria brought me up,' she told them. 'In so far as anyone did. She loved me. Now she is dead, and I never thanked her.'

'There is no need for thanks,' Harriet told her. 'Not when you were as close as that. She will know.'

'But I didn't even say goodbye. Father wouldn't let me; said there was no time, hustled me on board ship as if the devil was after me.'

'Well, the French were,' said Jeremy.

'Yes, and Father wanted no reminders of his English connection. I don't know—and I don't want to know—what expectations you have from my father, Mr Craddock, but as a friend, let me tell you one thing about him. There is just one love in his life, and that is his vineyards. He married my mother for them— and for an heir to inherit them. And what he got was me. Maria told me that after he learned from the doctors that mother could not have another child he never spoke to her again.'

'But, surely, you can inherit?' This was Harriet, surprising the other two.

'Oh, yes, I can inherit, but if I marry the

54

name goes, don't you see? They won't be Gomez wines any more.'

'And that is so important to him?' Jeremy Craddock could not believe his ears.

'Oh, yes,' she told him. 'More important than anything in the world, Mr Craddock. Never forget that in your dealings with him.'

'Thank you,' he said. 'I won't.' He felt himself in deep water again. 'Lord, how bright the sun is.' They had moved out, by common consent, on to the vine-hung terrace, and he had been gazing down to where the river sparkled far below them. He put a hand to his brow. 'Will you forgive me, Miss Gomez, if I play the invalid and rest for a while?'

'Of course. How thoughtless of me. Poor Cousin Jeremy, do you feel one of your seizures coming on?'

'I confess I have felt better.' He made it rueful. 'Stupid of me; the doctors warned me about dazzling light ... I am ashamed to confess it, but I do long for a darkened room.'

'And you shall have one. We will all be the better for some rest and quiet before the delights of a family evening. I should warn you, cousin, that we keep Portuguese hours here; breakfast and dine early, with a siesta after and a light supper at night. The British, of course, stick to their own ways. It makes social intercourse a little difficult.'

'I wonder what the Americans do,' he said. 'I do feel the sooner I get in touch with Miss

Emerson the better.'

'I'll find out her where she lives while you are resting,' she promised him. 'And I will have something to eat sent to your room, cousin. It's a long time since breakfast.'

'It certainly is,' said Harriet. 'I am starving.'

The rambling house was immensely confusing. It had been built on various levels along the ridge, with steps up and down into its different wings, which must have been added haphazardly, as they were needed. Jeremy was pleased to find himself alone in a remote guest wing with a view across the gardens to the stable block. 'But don't try to go out that way,' Caterina warned. 'It's quite the wrong direction, and you will get lost in the alleys for sure, and very likely robbed too, or mobbed by beggars which would be almost as bad.'

'You mean the front door is the only way out?'

'Yes. My ancestors were thinking of Spanish invasion when they built the house. You probably noticed how solid the door is, and the gate of the stable yard is almost a fortification. It stood in good stead when the French invaded; they didn't get in here, which is why we still have our valuables, and the gold plate in the chapel.'

'They'd surely not have taken that?'

'Oh yes they would! They took everything, cousin. The silver altar in the cathedral was only spared because someone had the wits to

56

paint it over to look like wood. What they saw, they took, and anyone who protested got killed. Tonio told me about Maria. She was visiting her sick sister when the French stormed the defences and poured into the town. Unlucky for her; it was a house on the main road; a group of soldiers burst in, demanding food. Maria's niece Francesca was there—she was my age, and very lovely, skin like a lily. Maria and her mother tried to protect her—no use, they killed all three women in the end. With the children watching.'

'You ought not to know these things,' Jeremy protested.

'Why not? They happened. Better say they ought not to happen, Cousin Jeremy.' She swept the room with a swift, hostess's glance. 'Ring the bell if you need anything. Someone will come in the end. We'll leave you to your rest.'

'I hope you are not putting me in a guest wing miles from anywhere,' Harriet said nervously as they retraced their steps.

'No, no, love.' Caterina squeezed her hand. 'You are to be next to me in the women's wing. You will find the sexes kept very strictly separate, here in Portugal. I hope you won't find it too odd.'

'I think I'll like it.' Harriet sounded surprised.

Having settled Harriet in her room, Caterina put on a wide-brimmed hat and went out by a side door into the gardens. Drifting, apparently aimlessly, from terrace to terrace, she worked her way gradually down towards the lowest level where, in winter, a roaring stream plunged down the narrow gorge to the river. The terraces got rockier and less well cultivated as she descended, degenerating at last into a tangle of vine and jasmine and myrtle bushes. The garden had evidently been allowed to go back to jungle while she was in England. At first she thought the way down from the lowest of the cultivated terraces had been blocked off, but when she reached the seaward end she found the beginnings of the narrow path that led on down. Glad that she was still wearing her serviceable travelling dress, she gathered its skirts in a firm hand and started carefully down. It got easier as it went on; the servants who had made the path as a short cut to their friends working on the estate across the gorge had had the wits to keep its start as unobtrusive as possible. If she had not expected it to be there, she would not have found it.

Parts of the bottom terrace had been eroded by the winter torrent that was now nothing but a dry bed. She made her difficult way back inland along it and found, as she had feared, that the rustic summerhouse that used to command a view of a small waterfall had been systematically destroyed. She stood looking at it for a long minute, remembering, wondering

… then moved on, past its ruins, to where the gorge narrowed enough for a tall man to cross it. Here, too, everything was very much as she had expected. A barricade had been built of the timbers from the summerhouse, but had been subsequently broken down so that the way was open to anyone brave enough to cross.

She turned to retrace her steps. If she had hoped for a miracle, it had not happened. She had learned nothing that she had not expected, and, furthermore, she must not let herself be found down here. It was hot work climbing back up the path, and she was at the top, sitting on a stone bench, brushing burrs from her skirts, when something told her she was no longer alone.

The monk had come so silently along the terrace that it was only the smell of incense clinging to his brown habit that alerted her. She stood at once and made him a civil curtsey. 'Forgive me, father, I did not hear you.'

'I did not mean to startle you, my child.' He was automatically blessing her as he spoke. 'You look hot, daughter. Should you be out here in the sunshine after your exhausting journey?'

'The air is doing me good,' she told him. 'And I wanted to revisit my childhood haunts, but,' looking ruefully down at her skirts, 'the lower terraces seem to have gone to rack and ruin; I could find no way down to the stream.'

'I should hope not!' He gestured her to seat

herself and now sat down beside her, the smell of incense stronger than ever. 'The scandalous path across the gorge has been blocked for years. That is the past, to be forgotten. I am charged to say that to you by your father. As his spiritual guide, and I hope, his close friend, I am delighted to greet his beloved daughter. We are to be good friends, you and I.' It sounded as much threat as promise.

'Thank you. But—' She hesitated. 'I had thought Father Tomas—' He had been her father's resident confessor when she left, an amiable old man who thought of nothing much beyond his food and his drink.

'Father Tomas died two years ago. Of what looked very much like a surfeit, I am sorry to say. I trust things have gone on more regularly in this household since I was so fortunate as to be asked to take his place. I am Father Pedro, child. Forgive me for not introducing myself sooner. I had hoped that your father would have told you of the rock on which he now, I am happy to say, builds his security.'

'If you know my father,' she told him bluntly, 'you surely know that he does not waste much time—or talk—on me.'

'Something that I may be able to rectify, dear child. I am happy to tell you that I have managed, God helping me, to bring Senhor Gomez to a state of grace in which I devoutly hope his daughter will soon join him. The past is to be forgotten; a hopeful future lies before you. I trust you have come back from your exile the obedient daughter so good a father deserves.' He laid a soft, dry hand on hers and she was suddenly afraid. 'It was natural to wish to revisit your childhood haunts,' he told her. 'But I trust you were saying goodbye to them, Caterina. You are a woman now, and a handsome one, and your father and I feel it is high time you were married.'

'Married? Oh, no!' It was startled out of her.

'Indeed yes. The friends of your childhood are mothers long since. Your father and I have thought long and earnestly about your future. It has not been easy. I have told you that the past is to be forgotten, but of course it is not quite so simple as that. There were, I am afraid, whispers at the time of your sending away; the best of servants will talk; that Maria seems to have been a chatterbox if ever there was one. But we won't speak ill of the dead.' He had recognised her angry reaction. 'It means, I am afraid, that marriage with a son of your father's fidalgo friends is out of the question. It would never have been easy, what with your foreign blood, and, now, your foreign education. I am sorry to have to tell you, dear child, that your looks are a little bold for a girl of your age and breeding. You should not meet a man's eyes when you speak to him. Not even those of a holy father like me.'

'Forgive me, father.' She made it meek, and sat looking down at her folded hands, fuming,

61

wondering what he would say next.

'As for Luiz de Fonsa y Sanchez.' He spoke the name that had been in her thoughts all day. 'You are to forget him, child, as his family have. Or remember him only in your prayers, as a lost soul. When Soult's French troops fled from Porto two years ago Luiz de Fonsa y Sanchez went with them, as their friend and ally.'

'I don't believe it!' But it would explain so much. All that dreadful silence. She thought about it. 'What had they done to him?'

'Who?'

'His family.'

'They were angry with him, of course. Rightly so. His fault, the whole sordid business. I think the discovery killed his mother; she had such hopes of him, her only son. And then, when he went off with Soult, his father struck him out of the family records. Cherish no hopes of him, my daughter. So far as Porto goes, he no longer exists.'

'And the old lady?' Caterina made herself ask it. 'His grandmother? She loved him so.'

'A sad story. A great lady, I believe. I never saw her. She is shut up there, in her own rooms, quite out of her wits. Your doing, and her grandson's. The house is a fortress these days, shut up. Sanchez sees no one, does not even come to church. A scandalous, shameful business ... I beg your pardon?'

'Nothing, father. Only, if you hold me to

blame for all this, I am surprised you and my father are even thinking of arranging a marriage for me.'

'That is what I am trying to explain to you, child. It has to be to an Englishman, and soon, before the whispers reach the British community. What of your cousin, Mr Craddock?'

'What?' Caterina could not believe her ears. 'But he's not Catholic.' It was the first of the objections that crowded her mind.

'Dear child, you have not been thinking about your position, your predicament. If a son of the church were to sue for your hand, it would be our duty, your father's and mine, to tell him the sad truth about you.'

'Whereas you feel free to pull the wool over the eyes of a mere Protestant!' She saw she had made him angry, and knew it for a mistake. She needed to know about their plans for her. 'Forgive me. It was the shock. I have thought of Mr Craddock only as a cousin. And he is not a well man, father.'

'I know. The falling sickness. Here on some wild goose chase for a cure from that American charlatan, Miss Emerson. That is why your father and I thought it best to offer you an alternative. I hope you see what a great deal of thought we have put into your unfortunate position.'

'I do indeed, father. I promise you, I am doing my very best to be grateful. And who is the alternative you have to offer?'

'Frank Ware. You must have met him, I should think, as a child. He was finishing at Eton when the French invaded the first time. His parents got out on the last boat, and I am afraid their affairs were not luckily handled for them in their absence. Some say that old Mr Ware died of the shock when he got back and found just how bad things were. His wife sent for young Frank from Cambridge. He's no fool, that young man. He saw how bad things were and set his mind to practical ways of improving them. There would be no difficulty about your continuing to practise your faith, and bringing up the children in it. And Ware would be happy to join his name with yours.'

'You mean you have talked to him about it?' Now she could not help letting her fury show.

'Of course. What did you imagine? So long as the young man likes you well enough, and I can see no problem about that. Mind you, if you had arrived on the best of terms with your cousin, Mr Craddock, we might have been prepared to think again. But it does not seem as if that is the case.'

'No. I do not propose to marry, father. Or rather, I look upon myself as already married.'

'Absurd.' And then. 'You can't mean—no, impossible.'

'In the eyes of God,' she said bleakly, and knew she had made him angry again.

'Childish nonsense. Put it out of your mind,

Caterina, and listen to the last alternative I am authorised to put before you. If indeed you do not feel yourself fit to marry, and I would respect you for such feelings, there is, naturally, another path open to you: the veil. Your father is prepared to dower your entry into the convent of the Little Sisters of St Seraphina, here in Porto.'

'The silent order! Never.'

'These are your choices, daughter. If you have been deluding yourself with the idea that your father considers leaving his fortune to you as a single woman, to play ducks and drakes with as you please, I beg you to put it out of your mind once and for all.'

'Thank you, father,' she said. 'You have made things very clear to me. The past may be forgotten, as you say, but it is not forgiven. I will think hard about what you have said to me. And now, if you will excuse me, I find myself a little fatigued by my journey.'

CHAPTER FOUR

One evening with Father Pedro and Senhor Gomez was quite enough for Jeremy Craddock. The two girls stayed almost totally silent throughout the frugal meal. Jeremy did not blame Harriet for seeming overwhelmed by the company, but he was surprised by

Caterina's unaccustomed silence. She did not come to his help when her father and the priest joined in baiting him about the inadequate support they felt the British government was giving to Portugal. Too little, they called it, and too late. He was quietly fuming when they turned to Wellington and dismissed him as a do-nothing Indian general who had retired, they said, to sulk behind the lines of Torres Vedras, leaving the town of Coimbra to its fate. But he held his tongue, and promised himself to find lodgings and move out next day.

To his relief, Gomez did not appear at breakfast and Caterina seemed to have emerged from the cloud that had surrounded her the night before. She enquired kindly about his health, and told him she had found out where the Emersons lived. 'You'll never find it by yourself, cousin. They live in one of the alleys below the cathedral, not the town's most elegant district. I'll send a servant to show you the way; he speaks a little English.'

When he thanked her and went on to say that he hoped to find himself somewhere to lodge, she smiled at last. 'I don't blame you, cousin,' she told him. 'I only wish I could do likewise. I am afraid it won't be easy, though, here in Porto. Now I know how things go on in England I can see why the British are so rude about our *estalagems*—our inns. Porto holds nothing to compare with that splendid inn at Falmouth! Oh, what a happy, hopeful time that was.'

'Indeed it was.' Jeremy suddenly felt immensely sorry for Caterina, condemned to the company of her dour father and his attendant priest, with only Harriet for support. Just the same; 'I am glad you have Miss Brown with you,' he told her.

'And so am I! I owe a great debt to you and Mother Agnes and your concern with the proprieties.'

Something in her tone made him anxious for her. 'Cousin Caterina, if things do not go right for you here, if you ever felt the need of my help, you would ask for it, would not you? I'm your mother's kin, after all. I have been thinking about her since I saw her sitting room yesterday. It must have been so strange for her, coming to live here.'

'Do you know,' she told him, 'I have been thinking of her too. And, thank you, cousin, I'll remember your kindness.'

*　　*　　*

Jeremy enjoyed the morning walk through the teeming city. They crossed a large, noisy, open marketplace where black-clad country women shouted their diverse wares. The piles of eggs, scrawny, cackling hens and lavish heaps of fruit and vegetables made him wonder about the difficulty the English troops were said to be having in feeding themselves off the

67

countryside. He must come back here on his own. But first he must get to work. They had left the market now and were climbing a narrow, ill-paved street of what looked like a better class of shop.

'Rua são Antonio,' said his guide, confirming this. 'And that is Santa Caterina, where the *fidalgo* ladies order their clothes. But we go this way. The cathedral is up there—' Pointing to another tangle of alleyways thronged with people and overhung with grimy-looking washing.

'I can't see it.' Jeremy stood aside as two sedan chairs confronted each other in the narrow road, followed by a torrent of oaths from the porters.

'Of course not. There are no long views in Porto. It is built too close. That is why you need a guide, *senhor*.' He turned into a narrow alley slanting downhill, and Jeremy, who had always prided himself on his sense of direction, knew he was totally lost.

'This is the house.' The man rapped at a door set in a tiled wall. 'I will wait, of course, and see the *senhor* back.'

'Thank you.' Jeremy had given up hope of being independent for a while.

The door swung open on to a dark stairway, lit from somewhere far above. A handsome young black woman greeted Jeremy in lilting, fluent English and led the way upstairs.

Two steep and noisome flights up, she flung

68

open a door and ushered him into a blaze of light. Dazzled for a moment, he remembered to put his hand to his brow, as if in pain, then advanced into the surprising room. Brilliantly whitewashed, it was hung with coloured shawls of green and blue and azure to give the impression of some fantastic under-sea cave. The light came from a balconied window, where a woman was standing, looking out.

'Mr Craddock.' She came to him out of the light, like a revelation. 'I am so very glad to see you.' She held out a slim hand and he held it for a long moment, gazing at her.

'But you are young!' She was not only much younger than he was expecting, she was beautiful, with the frail, pale elegance of a wood nymph, a water sprite. Pale golden hair hung unfashionably to frame the ivory face with its huge grey eyes.

She was smiling at him with pale coral lips. 'Is that so terrible, Mr Craddock?'

'It is a great surprise. I had imagined—' He paused. What had he imagined?

'A crone? A sybil with three teeth and tangled grey hair? I am sorry to disappoint you, Mr Craddock, and in fact I have to return the compliment. We had thought you an older man, my brother and I, from what Senhor Gomez said. So what's to do? You see, I much prefer to work entirely alone with my patients; it is a very personal business, as I am sure you will understand. But I am afraid we may start tongues wagging here in gossipy Porto if we do so. My brother suggests he sits with us and pretends to be made of stone, but the trouble is he is something of a cynic where my gift is concerned. I am afraid I could not hope to succeed with him present, however quiet he kept.'

'No, I can quite understand that. But, Miss Emerson, how can I let you ... It is you the talk would harm ...' Should he suggest that Caterina or Harriet might act as chaperone? But to have either of them there, listening, would make things impossibly difficult.

'Oh, talk!' She shrugged it off. 'A gift like mine is bound to draw talk, Mr Craddock. I am afraid I have got used to it. We plan to go back to the United States soon, my brother and I, and the Atlantic is a wide ocean. I doubt Portuguese tattle will follow me there. Or Anglo-Portuguese for that matter. So come, sit down here.' She gestured to a small and surprisingly comfortable-looking sofa. 'Now tell me what your trouble is.' She herself had sat down at a little writing table, and Jeremy was sorry. He had very much hoped that she would sit beside him. What in the world was happening to him?

'Miss Emerson,' he sat on the edge of the sofa, 'before we begin, should we not—forgive me—should we not discuss terms?'

'Terms?' She made it sound as vulgar as he felt. 'Forgive me, Mr Craddock, my brother is

70

not here at the moment, or he would have explained to you. Mine is a gift from God. It is not a question of terms, but one of healing. What you arrange with my brother is no concern of mine. Now, sit at your ease, Mr Craddock, and tell me about yourself.'

It was dangerously easy to talk to her. She had pen and paper beside her, but did not write, just sat quite still, the small, firm chin cupped in those siren's hands, holding him in the focus of amber-flecked grey eyes.

He stumbled through his prepared brief as well as he could, feeling ashamed of himself as he did so. How could he deceive this ethereal creature? And, more to the point, would he be able to?

Rachel Emerson listened in sympathetic silence as he told her about the childhood fall, the long spell of unconsciousness, and the increasingly frequent seizures that followed. 'It has made it impossible for me to serve in the army, as I wished,' he ended his tale, 'and of course marriage must be out of the question.' Now why had he said that? It was not in his brief.

'I see.' What did she see? She rose and for a moment he thought she had seen through his story and was about to order him to leave. But instead she moved across the room to stand behind him. 'No, no, don't get up. I am not a woman now, Mr Craddock, but a healer.' He felt her slim, strong hands at the back of his neck.

'Ah, yes,' she said. 'An absolute nest of vipers. Take off your jacket, Mr Craddock, and your cravat, please, while I close the shutters. You find the light trying, do you not? It is always better to work in twilight. Close your eyes, if you please, and think of some happy place where you have been. In your childhood, perhaps?'

'Mine was not a happy childhood.' He had shrugged himself out of the well-fitted jacket, glad that he had never risen to the services of a valet, and gladder still that he had put on a clean shirt that morning.

'I am sorry.' She had closed the shutters now and the room was more like a deep-sea cave than ever. 'But there must have been some happy times, some happy places.' She was behind him again, her hands finding tensions at the back of his neck that he had not known existed. They moved gently upwards and through the close-cropped hair to his temples. 'No, no,' she said. 'Don't think about your hair, Mr Craddock, think of that happy place, be quiet there.'

He had indeed been wishing he had washed his hair that morning and was deeply disconcerted. How long was he going to be able to keep up his pretence with this sorceress? A happy place? He found himself thinking of something Caterina had said that morning about their happy time at Falmouth. It was

72

true. It had been happy, that carefree walk along the cliffs, with the larks singing above. It had been a halcyon moment, the three of them easy together, good companions.

'That is better,' said the soothing voice from behind him. 'Keep your thoughts there, keep them calm, keep them gentle. Then I think I will be able to help you.' Her hands were quite still now, and, to his amazement, he began to feel something communicate itself from them to him, a warmth, a tingling ... He had studied Dr Mesmer's theories of animal magnetism and electrical currents for the purposes of this charade, and had dismissed the whole thing as charlatan's rubbish. So what was happening to him now?

'Don't fight it, Mr Craddock.' Her voice seemed to come from far away. 'I cannot help you if you fight me. And you do need help, though maybe not the help you thought you needed.' The gentle fingers moved down over his forehead and eyes. 'Calm now, quiet now, you might even sleep a little. Think of that faraway, happy place, rest there.'

He was nowhere now, or everywhere ... There was no time, no place, only a rhythm that might be the waves of the sea or the beating of his heart ... It went on for five minutes? For half an hour? An eternity?

'That's very good, Mr Craddock.' The hands lifted from his forehead and he opened his eyes slowly to the underwater dimness of the room. 'I'll leave you for a moment. When you feel able, open the shutters for me, would you?'

I would do anything for you. But he did not say it. He sat for a few moments after she left him, trying to recapture that deep quiet, to understand what it had meant, what had happened to him. He had seen something, understood something, but what was it? At last, he rose a little unsteadily to his feet and moved over to throw back the shutters and look down at the dazzling view of the river below, with its active tangle of small shipping, and, on the far side of the river, the *Anthea*, reloading now. She would sail for England soon and he must send a report by her, but what would he say?

He moved to a silver-framed looking glass and tied his cravat with hands that shook a little. Putting on the blue coat Stultz had made for him he tried again to recapture what it was he had understood.

He was back at the window, noticing the telescope on a balcony table, when the door from the staircase opened and a tall man came into the room.

'Ah, you have finished; I thought you would have. How do you do, Mr Craddock. I hope that clever sister of mine has done you some good.' Where his sister was slender and elegant, Ralph Emerson was tall and broad, with a rubicond complexion that suggested a

74

lavish style of life. His hand, too, clasping Jeremy's, was hot and moist, where hers had been cool and firm. He was handsome, Jeremy supposed, if you liked those florid kind of good looks.

But he returned Emerson's greeting civilly enough. 'Your sister has a great gift, sir.'

'That's what they all say.' Ralph Emerson rubbed his large hands. 'It's a funny thing, Mr Craddock, and I wouldn't say it to everyone, but my sister's gift means nothing to me. But in my view that makes me all the more fit to handle her affairs. Bless her heart, she would cure all the world for love, if I would let her. But the labourer is worthy of his hire, Mr Craddock, or hers as the case may be. Besides, we only value what we pay for. I am sure you, as a man of the world, will understand that.' And he proceeded to a brief, firm statement of terms that made Jeremy stare. 'In gold, of course,' he concluded. 'You and I know just what this Portuguese paper money they are so lavish with is worth. And a down payment for the first three treatments the next time you come, Mr Craddock? I am sorry to have to say it, but we have had some unpleasant experiences, my sister and I. And would you be so good as to make a neat little parcel of it, and hand it to me as inconspicuously as possible? My poor Rachel very much minds what she looks on as the sordid commercial aspect of her work, but man must live, Mr Craddock, and woman too. You will find out soon enough how the wretched mercenary Portuguese take advantage of the foreigners in their midst. I have heard stories of problems your gallant army is having just in getting supplied, and I have no doubt the captain of the *Anthea* down there at the quay is paying over the odds for the fast unloading job he has had. And a heavy enough lot of goods it looked too! Supplies for the army, I take it, since it all seemed to be going straight upstream.'

'Was it? I am afraid I was so busy getting my young companions and their baggage ashore I did not have time to notice anything else. I was glad to get on to land too, I can tell you.' He turned to look out across the balcony. 'You have such a good view from here I should think you could almost see for yourself. Specially with this splendid telescope. May I?' He picked it up and focused it on the *Anthea*, making a little business of it as if it was something he was not used to doing. 'No, I see what you mean. You can't really tell the detail at this distance, can you? It might be almost anything they are loading now, except that even I can tell it is not wine.'

'Nor will be for years to come, by what I hear. One army is as bad as another when it comes to ravaging the countryside. I suspect that the worthy wine merchants here in Porto pray nightly that wherever Lord Wellington turns when he has finally got rid of Masséna, it is not this way. They have had more than their share here. My sister and I arrived quite soon after Wellington's brilliant strike across the Douro. What a man! What a general! I cannot tell you how impatient I get with the moaners here who complain that he does not move fast enough. And you have them in England too, I believe. What is the word there? You will find us all eager for the latest news.'

'I can imagine so.' He must not seem too cautious. 'The uproar over the Convention of Cintra died down in the end, and Lord knows that bit of lunacy was no fault of Wellington's, but there are still plenty of Whigs in and out of parliament who run him down as a do-nothing Indian general.'

'I am sure you do not agree with them, Mr Craddock? You must feel, as I do, that he is working to some masterplan of his own.'

'I am sure of it. But as to what it is! I am neither a fighting man nor a strategist, to my sorrow.'

'You regret it? Then we must hope that my sister will be able to help you. We are agreed then. We had better ask my sister when she thinks she should see you next. Some people find themselves so fatigued after the first meeting that there needs to be quite an interval before the next one, but you look stout enough to me.'

'I do feel tired,' he said, and it was true. Something in him had been profoundly shaken, and it was hard to concentrate on parrying Emerson's carefully careless questions. Doing so, he was horribly afraid that he might have found the man he was sent to look for.

But here she was, holding out a friendly hand in farewell. 'I do hope I have not tired you too much, Mr Craddock. Some people do find my treatment quite disconcerting at first, and do you know, I often think that is a good sign. Do, please, go home and rest for a while. Your man is waiting for you with the servants downstairs. You are staying with Senhor Gomez of course?'

'Yes.' He had meant to ask the Emersons' advice about possible lodgings, now decided against it. If his suspicions were well founded that would simply land him in a nest of spies. 'When should I come to you again, Miss Emerson? I feel—' he paused, lost for words, 'I feel as if something had happened to me.'

'I hope it has.' She smiled at him, and his heart jumped. 'Take a day to find your way round Porto, Mr Craddock, and come to me at the same time the day after.'

'I shall look forward to it,' he told her, and meant it more than he liked.

*　　*　　*

Caterina had been showing Harriet the terraced garden, when a servant intercepted them by the fountain to announce a caller. 'Mr Ware? Ask him to join us in the loggia. And wine and cakes, of course. He's an old acquaintance,' she told Harriet as they started to move back up the series of terraces. 'They are a wine family too; we played together as children ... a long time ago; they sent him to England to school, well before the French invaded. I never much liked his mama. Funny, I remember her much better than I do him.'

'Then he's not the one—' Harriet started, and broke off, angry with herself.

'No, love, he's not the one. Must I remind you of your promise?'

'No, I'm sorry. I won't do it again. But, surely, Caterina, such an old friend—would you not like to be alone with Mr Ware, to talk about old times?'

'Nothing I would dislike more,' Caterina told her. 'You are my chaperone, love, remember. And you look less and less like one with every day in the sun, so, please, Harryo, some starchy airs at least, for my sake.'

Harriet laughed. 'I'll do my best, but it's hard to be starchy when I'm so happy. I just wish you were too, Cat dear. I know I mustn't ask—but is there no news at all?'

'None. And I love you for not asking.' With a quick kiss. 'But, come, we are keeping our gallant waiting, and he will tell his mother our manners are atrocious, and she will tell all Porto.'

They found Frank Ware standing in the vine-covered loggia, with a little posy in his hands. 'Welcome home, Miss Gomez,' he handed it to her. 'I remember how you used to love flowers. It seems a long time since I called you Caterina and pulled your hair.'

'It is a long time. You must meet my good friend Miss Brown. And thank you for these; it's good to see the Portuguese flowers again.' She handed them to the servant who was pouring wine. 'Put these in a vase for me, Sancho, would you? Now, sit down, Mr Ware and tell me everything that has happened here in Porto. I feel as strange as if I were just returned from the moon.'

'I know,' he said warmly. 'I felt just the same when I got back, but I promise you it soon wears off. My mother sends her love and asks you to name a day for her to give a little party for you at our house, to meet all your old friends.'

'How very kind of Mrs Ware.' But this was going altogether too fast for her. 'Tell her I would like it above all things, but not quite at once. I need to find my feet a little, and Harriet and I need to do some shopping. I caught some glances as we came up from the quay yesterday that made me think we are not quite in the Portuguese mode.'

'But then you never were much of a one for conforming, were you?' He was beginning to think none of this was going to be so bad as he had feared. 'I remember you as always the rebel. We were a fine lot of tearaways.' He turned to include Harriet in the conversation. 'And Miss Gomez always in the wicked lead.'

'I had no mother to make me mind my ways,' said Caterina. 'But they were good days just the same. I have hardly dared wonder what happened to the rest of us, Mr Ware.'

'No,' he said sadly. 'I was so sorry to hear about your dear Maria, Miss Gomez. I remember her well, how good she was to us all, and how patient.'

'Thank you.' She was surprisingly moved by the tribute. 'Was anyone else killed in the French invasion, any of our friends?' And when she saw him hesitate. 'Please, I have to know, and I would so much rather hear it from you.'

'I know just how you feel,' he said warmly. 'When I got back, there seemed to be almost a conspiracy of silence, as if it was too bad to be talked about. Well, it was. By a miracle, our house was spared, and all our servants survived, but other people in the Rua Nova dos Inglesas were less fortunate. There were the most shocking stories, which I will spare you, but in fact, of our little group of friends no one was hurt in the actual attack. Well, most of the English were safe away, of course, and the ones who were on board the ships that were caught in harbour were not molested. The worst was over by the time they were taken. It was only in the savagery of the first attack that people were hurt, like your poor Maria. The French claim that they discovered such evidence of atrocities by the mob before they took the town that there was no holding their men. Well, a sack is a terrible business. I am glad Wellington has managed to save Lisbon from that. What was the talk in England about what he is going to do next, Miss Gomez? You can imagine how anxious we are here lest he should choose this route to push on into Spain.'

'Goodness, don't ask me,' she said. 'I was shut up in a convent; no news of the war there, or of much else. But, tell me, our Portuguese friends, what of them?'

'Portuguese?' He thought for a moment. 'Did we have Portuguese friends? I hardly recollect—Forgive me.' He had remembered about her father. 'But you know how it has always been, here in Oporto.'

'I do indeed,' she told him. The subject was closed, and she changed it. 'Do you know an American brother and sister, the Emersons? My cousin is here in the hopes of a cure from Miss Emerson. He is seeing her now. Which reminds me, he is anxious to find somewhere to live nearer to the centre of town where they are. Can you think of anything, Mr Ware?'

'Your cousin?' He was thinking fast. 'As for the Emersons, I am sorry to tell you that my mother has had some treatment from Miss Emerson and does not feel it has done her

82

much good. But then her health is so precarious—'

'Yes, of course.' She was remembering his mother with more and more dislike. 'Perhaps Miss Emerson will be more lucky with my cousin. He is my mother's sister's son. I don't quite know what happened to her. She must be dead, I suppose. He certainly talks of a solitary childhood.'

'Poor fellow,' said Frank Ware perfunctorily. 'As to lodgings for him, Miss Gomez, would he perhaps like to come to us? My mother was saying just the other day how we rattle about in our big house, with only the two youngest still in the nursery. I am sure we could make a set of apartments available to him, if he fancied it. And it is only a step up the hill from our house to the Emersons'. I am sure my mother would be delighted to have him.' He was sure of nothing of the kind, but meant to see to it that she was. It was beginning to strike him that he could do a great deal worse than marry Caterina Gomez and her promised vineyards. She had grown to be a fine figure of a woman, and seemed to have quite lost the wildness that had made her formidable in their childhood days. And if it did nothing else, marriage with her would free him from his mother. He stayed ten minutes longer than the statutory length for a morning visit and pressed her hand so warmly when he took his leave at last that Harriet watched his retreating

83

figure with a look of amused comprehension. 'A suitor, no less.' She smiled at Caterina.

'I am afraid so.'

'You don't like him? He seemed well enough to me.'

'A nonentity; always has been. I am afraid I led him by the nose when we were children. And all he wants now is to get away from his dreadful gossip of a mother.'

'But, Caterina, love, have you thought—It might make him just the man for you.' It cost her a curious pang to say it. She had rather liked the diffident young man.

'Never!' said Caterina savagely. And then, 'Forgive me. I don't mean to be cross with you, Harriet dear, but I'd rather die an old maid than marry a cipher like that.'

'You'll hardly do that,' said Harriet.

CHAPTER FIVE

To her son's relieved surprise, Mrs Ware agreed readily enough to his suggestion that they take in Jeremy Craddock as a paying guest. 'It will help to keep the wolf from the door until you get things settled with Caterina,' she told her son. 'I am glad you find her tolerable.'

It did not strike him as at all the right word. 'She may not have me, mother,' he warned.

84

'Not have you? Ridiculous. She'll do as her father bids her. He's not a man I'd like to cross. And this first freak of hers is bound to have outraged him.'

'What's that, mother?'

'Just walking home up the hill from the ferry like a girl of the streets! I could hardly believe my ears when Mrs Bland told me this morning. But Mrs Sandeman saw them with her own eyes, the three of them, setting off up the lane by the Franciscans'. With not so much as a servant in attendance.'

'Much quicker than taking a sedan chair, mother.' He felt suddenly sorry for Caterina, and glad that she had that agreeable little Harriet Brown for company and support.

'What's that to the purpose? And the party? When shall that be?'

'Not quite yet. She was most grateful, but needs some time, she says, to get herself outfitted. It's true, she's not quite in the ordinary way ...'

'She never was. But she'll need help with that, advice; I'll call tomorrow.' Visions of the commission she would get from recommending her own dressmaker danced in her head.

'Do you think—' He could not imagine how to phrase the protest that leaped to his lips.

'Poor motherless child,' she went on as if he had not spoken. 'It will be a pleasure to guide her in her first difficult steps back into our little society.'

'She's Portuguese too, mother, don't forget. Something she said made me think it is very much on her mind.'

'I am glad she has so much good feeling. But all the more reason why I should launch her in our English circle. It's going to be hard enough for her, I think, after all the talk, but my countenance should just turn the scale, I am sure. And the money, of course. It may do very well yet, dear boy. And as to this Mr Craddock, tell him he is welcome to move in tomorrow.' The sooner her English cousin was removed from Caterina's side, the better. There was everything to be said for having him to live with them. 'I'm pleased with you for thinking to invite him, Frank. We will treat him quite like one of the family, tell him ...'

'Except for the little matter of his paying his way.'

'Well, that's of course.' Impatiently. 'I wonder how he is getting on with that dubious Miss Emerson. Naturally, we must hope that she can help him. It's the falling sickness, is it not? Poor young man! Impossible for him to lead any kind of a man's life—still less to marry. No wonder Senhor Gomez did not scruple to let him escort his daughter out from England.'

'You are well informed as always, mother.' Frank Ware thought he began to understand his mother's motives.

'I do my best to be, dear boy. For your sake.'
She watched him pick up his hat and gloves.
'You are going out?'

'I thought I'd stroll down to the Factory, take a look at the papers and see if Dickson is about.'

'You're surely not still thinking of that wild goose plan of going to work with him? Now that things are looking so promising—'

'Another string to my bow, mother. Here I am, able-bodied, unlike poor Mr Craddock. It sometimes makes me ashamed to be kicking my heels here in idleness while the future of Portugal may be being settled up there on the Spanish frontier.'

'You've heard something?' Sharply.

'Just a rumour going round town. You know how they come and go with the wind. There's talk that Marmont has taken over from Masséna and is on the move in Spain.'

'Coming this way?'

'Who can tell?' Shrugging. 'But let us hope that if he is, Wellington is ready for him. Of course he has the inner lines of communication and much better information than the French ever contrive to get, having made such enemies of the peasants, but it's a tricky enough business up there in the mountains.'

'I don't know what makes you think Wellington so well informed. Just think how Soult showed him a clean pair of heels after he retook this place.'

'That was quite different, mother. Pouring with rain, mountain roads, and the English troops had been marching for days. Some of them were without shoes, Dickson tells me. You can't get far through the mountains in that state.'

'Soult did.'

'He was running for his life. It makes a difference. I wish I knew the rights of what went on here when he was in control. Nobody seems to want to talk about it. Nobody who was here, that is. Caterina was asking about it...'

'Was she so? Well, dear boy, I think the less said on that head, the better. Specially to Caterina. Let bygones be bygones and all that. If you ask me, half the population, or at least half the ones who mattered, were standing eagerly in line to sign those fawning petitions in support of Soult. Oh, they tore them up quick enough when Wellington got across the Douro, but that didn't mean any more than signing them had. What with the democratic faction who don't much like being ruled from Lisbon, and the crusty old *fidalgos* who think only of their own comforts, I think there were plenty of people who quite liked Soult's idea of an independent Lusitanian kingdom.'

'With Soult as king? Mother, you cannot be serious!'

'Think a little, Frank. His own officers took it seriously enough to start that extraordinary negotiation with Wellington to join him in ousting Napoleon and replacing him by General Moreau.'

'You know about that?' Now she had surprised him.

'Of course I know about it. Everybody does. We just don't talk about it. I hope you contrived to make that clear to Caterina Gomez. Silence is golden. There's a lot goes on beneath the surface of things, here in Oporto. You have not been back so long as I have, of course, but I can see that you are beginning to find that out.'

'I am indeed.' But he was surprised his mother knew so much.

*　　*　　*

When Mrs Ware called at the Gomez house next day she found Caterina busy drawing her friend, and thought it a most suitable occupation for a young lady until she saw the picture.

'You've made a monster of poor little Miss Brown.' She looked in dismay at the savage black lines of the caricature.

'I've done my best to, but it's impossible. The sweetness of her nature will show through, try how I will.' Caterina was eyeing her guest as she spoke and Harriet read her thoughts and thought them dangerous. Her friend's gift for a brutal likeness had got her expelled from

ol; it might cause even more trouble here
isy Porto. She was relieved when Mrs
Ware turned from inspecting the picture to
look at her own irreproachable needlework.

'Beautiful fine stitching,' she approved.
'Which puts me in mind of the purpose of my
visit—aside from the pleasure of meeting you
again after all these years, dear Caterina. My
son tells me you are minded to replenish your
wardrobe, dear child, and I am come to offer
you the services of my own dressmaker,
Madame Feuillide. I know if I make a personal
favour of it she will find the time to make for
you at once, and I can promise, you will find
yourself in the very first stare of fashion.'
Looking down complacently at her own grey
silk.

'Madame Feuillide?' On a questioning note.
'A French modiste, Mrs Ware?'

'What else? Boney's a monster, we all know
that, but it doesn't stop Paris being the fashion
capital of the world. Even that dress you are
wearing, my dear, shows the influence of the
late lamented Empress Josephine.'

'She's not dead, is she, poor Josephine?'

'Not that I know of. But she might as well be,
now her Austrian supplanter has borne
Napoleon an heir. A sad enough life for
Josephine now, poor thing, mewed up at
Malmaison after all those years of glory.'

'Maybe she finds it a relief,' said Caterina.

'I very much doubt it. She liked to have a

90

hand in things, did the Empress Josephine. But now, tell me, child, when shall I ask Madame Feuillide to call on you? The sooner the better, don't you think? I do so much look forward to introducing you into our little society. You will find it very much the thing, I can promise you, quite like life at home.'

'But this is my home, Mrs Ware.'

'Well, of course, for the time being.' Mrs Ware looked momentarily taken aback, then made a quick recovery. 'I am sure you are getting a tremendous welcome from your father's *fidalgo* relatives,' she said. 'But you must not quite forget your dear mother's side of things. We are very much looking forward, Frank and I, to having your cousin as our house guest. I am sorry not to meet him here today. Frank saw him at the Factory last night and speaks most highly of him. A wretched shame about that illness of his. Poor young man, my heart quite bleeds for him. To know himself unfit to serve his country in these desperate times; unfit, poor fellow, to marry. We must just hope that Miss Emerson can do something for him, though I have to say that my experience of what she calls her treatment does not fill me with much hope on his behalf.' She began to pull on her gloves. 'Shall I tell Madame Feuillide to call on you tomorrow, my dear?'

'It is kind of you, Mrs Ware, but I am afraid I have already made my own arrangements.'

91

'That was a whopper if ever I heard one,' said Harriet when Mrs Ware had left, visibly fuming.

'Yes, wasn't it?' said Caterina cheerfully. 'And how I am going to make it good is more than I can see.'

'It's a pity about your father's relations,' said Harriet thoughtfully. 'Still not a word from them.'

'Yes, the old bitch had me there, didn't she? And didn't she just know it! I really am between the devil and the deep sea, am I not? But no need to look so anxious, love, I shall come about, I promise you.'

'I think you should let the old dragon give you that party,' said Harriet, surprising her.

'I'm afraid you are right, but first I must find myself a Portuguese dressmaker.'

'Who will sew better than a Frenchwoman. To give the devil her due, Mrs Ware was very elegantly turned out.'

'Yes, she was, wasn't she? It's a challenge, Harriet, and I do like a challenge.' She had reached for a new sheet of paper and was sketching idly as she spoke. 'Was the sleeve like this, or like that?'

'There wasn't much of it,' said Harriet looking over her friend's shoulder at the swift outline she had drawn of two fat arms in two elegantly draped sleeves. 'Like that, I think.' She pointed at the second one.

'And so do I. We are going to be busy for a

while, you and I, Harriet dear.'

'And a good thing too,' said Harriet robustly. 'I didn't think it possible, but I was really beginning to want some work to do.'

'Well, your holiday is over,' said her friend. 'We'll spend the evening in the Rua Santa Caterina—my street, love—where the silk merchants are, and with my design and your beautiful stitching, and the maids to do the rough work, I reckon we can contrive ourselves a wardrobe that will make the English tabbies green with envy. And, of course, you are right, Harryo, as usual. When Mrs Ware next calls, we will let her name a day for her party. We must have some friends, here in Porto.'

'Perhaps your father's kin don't know you are here yet?' suggested Harriet not very hopefully.

'With the whispers flying through the streets, as they do here in Porto? Impossible, and you know it. More likely they are waiting until I announce my engagement.'

'To an Englishman?' Harriet swallowed the question she had promised not to ask.

'It looks a bit like it, wouldn't you say?'

'And what are you going to do?'

'God knows,' said Caterina.

*   *   *

When it came to the point, Jeremy Craddock found himself oddly reluctant to leave the

93

dark, rambling Gomez mansion, with its odd hours and its army of inefficient, willing servants. Predictably enough, Senhor Gomez did not appear to say goodbye, but the two girls made up for this with their friendly thanks for his kindness on their journey. 'We shall miss you, cousin,' Caterina summed it up. 'And you must visit us very often and tell us how you go on at the Wares'—and with Miss Emerson.'

'I do hope she does you good,' said Harriet.

'And remember,' Caterina held out her hand in farewell, 'if you find Mrs Ware more than you can stand, you are always sure of a welcome here.'

'Thank you.' He nearly kissed her hand, shook it firmly instead. 'And you too must remember, Cousin Caterina, that I am yours to command if you should ever need my help.'

'On a voyage back to England?'

'In anything you should need.'

She thought he meant it, and was grateful. But she needed much more than Jeremy Craddock could offer. It was a relief to be interrupted by a servant ushering in Frank Ware, come to fetch his guest. 'My mother sends her kindest regards,' he held Caterina's hand for an extra minute. 'And asks you to name an early day for our party. It is good to have a pretext for one, in these anxious times.'

'Is there any more news of Marmont's movements?' asked Jeremy Craddock.

'Rumours, nothing more. And none of Wellington either. You would think there was a curtain of iron between us and the Spanish border, the silence is so absolute. It is making my mother quite anxious. She bade me urge you, Miss Gomez, to come to her at the least hint of danger. We are closer to the river for a quick escape to England, if that should prove necessary.'

'Please thank her for me,' said Caterina. 'But my place is here, with my father.'

'Miss Brown might not feel quite the same.' Turning to Harriet. 'Remember that the invitation is open to you too, Miss Brown. I know my mother would be glad to have your company on the voyage. And I hope you will think again, Miss Gomez.'

'We must hope that the need will not arise,' said Jeremy. 'I have more confidence in Wellington than you seem to have, Ware. I am sure the news, when it comes, will be good.'

'I just hope it comes soon.'

The two young men said their farewells and walked down to the Rua Nova together, leaving Jeremy's baggage to be brought down on the heads of a band of strapping Portuguese women porters. 'They are glad of the work,' Frank explained, when Jeremy protested at this. 'With trade so bad, and the vineyards upriver in ruins, they must grab what *scudos* they can get, poor creatures. I am afraid you have picked a sad time to come to Oporto,

95

Mr Craddock.'

'I find it all immensely interesting,' said Jeremy, with truth.

Introduced to Mrs Ware, he wondered if he had made a terrible mistake. The house, too, was an extraordinary contrast to the one he had left. English furniture and English chintzes filled airless rooms too full, and black American servants served English tea and English coffee at English hours. It was surprising how much he already missed the casual, friendly discomforts of the Gomez household.

He was due to pay his second visit to Miss Emerson next day and found himself looking forward to it more than he liked. He must not let himself fall under the spell of those magic hands in that strange sea-cave of a room. And, equally important, he must decide whether to pretend that she had improved his condition. He was uncomfortably sure that she had a keen eye for pretence. Altogether, it was perhaps a relief to find Ralph Emerson sitting with his sister.

'You are prompt to your hour,' Emerson greeted him. 'I thought you might have difficulty finding your way up through the lanes from your new home. You are happily settled with the Wares, I trust?'

'Yes, very happily, thank you.' Emerson's knowledge of his move confirmed everything Caterina had said about gossip-ridden Oporto.

'It's just like being at home in England.' This got him a wry, amused glance from Miss Emerson, who had so far smiled but not spoken.

'Where you may find yourself returning in haste any day now, if the latest tales are true,' said Ralph Emerson.

'And what are they?'

'I was sure you would have heard. Marmont is loose up on the border. They say he has thrown supplies into Ciudad Rodrigo, evaded Wellington and is ready to march either this way or down on Lisbon. With this way much more likely, of course, because of those bragged-about lines of Torres Vedras. And nothing but a parcel of guerrillas up in the mountains to stop him. You may find yourself packing up pretty smartly, Mr Craddock. But had you really not heard? I took it for granted that the Wares would keep themselves well posted. Young Frank spends a great deal of time at the English Factory, I believe. It is not a place to which I have had the honour of being invited, though my friend Joe Camo is sometimes allowed to darken its sacred doors. Do you believe that it is bound to end in war between our two countries?'

'Because of the friction at sea? I'm quite sure it will not; we all have more sense than that. Napoleon is the great enemy to peace after all. Your Mr Madison must see that as well as the rest of us; it would be madness to let Boney drive a wedge between us.'

'That is what you think he is trying to do?'

'Do not you?' This was not at all a conversation he wanted to be involved in.

'Who, me? I'm just an ignorant American from the backwoods. What should I know of world affairs? But I am keeping you two from your work. I trust my sister will do you great good, Mr Craddock. It seems to me that you are looking better already, but perhaps that is just the mild Portuguese air. I have a few errands to do in town so I doubt I'll be back before my dear Rachel has finished her ministrations, but I wish you well for them.' He rose, and it was Jeremy's cue to hand him the little bag of gold coins he had brought, while Rachel Emerson moved away to look out of the window. He found he disliked the whole business very much. And he was absolutely certain, for no good reason, that Ralph Emerson had made up or at least exaggerated the story about Marmont. Why? To spread alarm? Or to startle him into indiscretion? Probably both. He was glad to see him go.

'Sit down, Mr Craddock. But first take your jacket off.' Rachel Emerson closed the shutters and drew cool green curtains across the windows. Now she put gentle hands on the back of his neck. 'Oh dear! I should not have let you and my brother talk politics, Mr Craddock. You are worse than ever today. Did I do you no good at all?'

'Of course you did.' Was he sure of this? 'But it is quite true, I do feel anxious. If the tale your brother has heard is true, we are all in danger here. But I refuse to believe that Wellington could have let himself be out-generalled.'

'I am sure you are right.' Her voice was soothing. 'And now you will forget all about that, Mr Craddock, and think yourself back to that happy place where you were before.'

A happy place. Where had it been? It seemed a long time ago. Of course. He had imagined himself walking at Falmouth, with his cousin and her friend. But now, with those gentle hands soothing away thought, the happy place was here, in this cool, grey cave, with these magic hands gentling him. 'Yes,' he said, 'I am thinking of it, I am there.'

'That's good, that's right.' Her hands moved up to his forehead. 'Think of nothing, don't think at all, thought is your enemy, Mr Craddock. Or, think of water, and trees, and a cool calm.' Her hands were on his shoulders, now, quiet, resting there, binding him with her spell. He was calm, he was quiet, for the moment, but above and beyond all that, he knew himself entirely hers.

*   *   *

Caterina and Harriet had finished two dresses each, and Caterina was having trouble with the sketches for the next ones when the note came.

Old Tonio handed it to Caterina, very early one morning. She had gone down, before anyone else was about, to walk up and down the untended lower terraces and wonder what was going to become of her, and she was on the way back up the last flight of steps when he met her. 'For you, *minha senhora*, to be read when you are alone.'

'Thank you, Tonio.' The colour had drained from her face, and he thought, for a moment, that she looked like her mother on her deathbed.

'Father Pedro did not come back last night.' It was disconcerting to have him read her thoughts. Her father's confessor had been away for a few days and the whole household had breathed a secret, shared sigh of relief.

'It's early yet.' She looked up at the shuttered house. 'I'll stay out a while. Thank you, Tonio.'

'For nothing. We all love you, *senhora*, as we did your poor mother, God rest her soul. We'd do anything for you, remember that. Anything we can.'

She actually found herself fighting rare tears as she thanked him again and turned back down the terrace steps. There was something so touching about the characteristic peasant realism of his statement. They would do anything for her that did not risk their livelihood or her father's terrible anger.

She held the note clutched in her hand, not

daring even to make the giveaway gesture of tucking it down the front of her dress. The house looked sleepy enough, but there could so easily be a watchful eye behind one of those blind-looking shutters. Safe at last under the screen of rampant vines on the lowest terrace, she unfolded the note with hands that would shake. There had been no name on the outside; there was no signature; no need for either. She knew the handwriting, the way the note was folded; she had seen neither for more than three years, but how could she forget them? They were part of her heart's treasure.

Short and to the point, as always. No word of love. He knew, as well as she did, the savage need to keep the note small enough so that it could be concealed in a hand, in the fold of a dress. It had been always so between them. 'We must meet. If you can trust your friend, take her to see the sights. A picnic at the Fonsa Palace in the late afternoon. I'll be in the Temple of Venus. Waiting. Destroy this.'

She re-read the cramped, small hand quickly, kissed the note, almost ashamed of herself for doing so, and tore it into tiny shreds, letting them flutter, here and there, down towards the dry bed of the stream below. It was an ingenious plan; it would work. The Fonsa house, out beyond the Carrancas Palace, had been wrecked in the French advance of 1809 and nothing had been done yet about repairing it. There would just be one old, bribable caretaker camped in the ruins of the house. Its terraces had the best view in town of the whole course of the river down to Foz. She could perfectly well take Harriet there, and leave her on the upper terrace while she kept her assignation in the folly below. They had played hide-and-seek there as children; he had kissed her there, the very first time, finding her hidden in the cool darkness behind the statue of Venus. It was the right, the perfect place to meet. She could trust Harriet. But could she trust herself? She had thought about this meeting so often; dreamed about it; prayed for it and been ashamed of herself for doing so. And now it was upon her and every nerve tingled and thrummed with it. And yet she was afraid. What was she going to tell him? How much was she going to tell him? Why did the word 'folly' echo so in her mind? She had tried not to think about what Father Pedro had said about Luiz going off with the French. It could not be true, or, if it were true, Luiz would explain.

It was getting late; Harriet would be wondering where she was; she looked about her to make sure no betraying scrap of paper showed on the terrace and started back up to the house, repeating the words of the message in her head. Of course he could not speak of love, it was too dangerous; there would be time enough for that. Impossible to arrange the excursion for today; it would have to be tomorrow. Would he wait every day in the little temple, or had he, more likely, an informant in her house? Luiz had always been well informed about what went on in Porto; he used to boast of having a friend in every kitchen. She had loved him for his democratic spirit. Over and over again, since Father Pedro had told her about his throwing in his lot with the French, she had reminded herself how many other people had been deceived by their talk of liberty, equality and fraternity. It had amazed her to hear radical talk and read radical newspapers in England. Bowood House had been the nearest great house to her school, and the Marquess of Lansdowne and his family had been its benevolent patrons, much approved of by the nuns for their stand on Catholic Emancipation.

She had read Lord Lansdowne's speeches in the papers and they had astonished her. Brought up to think of Napoleon as practically the devil incarnate, she could hardly believe her eyes when she read of him as a great reformer, a man who had set France on its feet after years of misgovernment and tyranny. The odd thing was that, back in England, she had thought all this nonsense, another instance of English eccentricity carried almost to the point of madness. But now she was at home (or was it home?) in Portugal, with what she sadly recognised as misgovernment and tyranny all around her. Was everything different, or was she seeing it with different eyes? There must be something wrong with a system where a whole household held its breath in terror because of two men, her father and his confessor. She had thought the rule of her convent in England had been tyrannical; now she realised that she had had no idea what tyranny was. She had thought the poverty she had seen in Bath was abject and horrible, but that too was nothing compared to the deprivation here in her own country. If Luiz had taken sides with the French in the hope of giving the starving poor a voice, she could only sympathise with him, though she must think him wrong in trusting the French. Could she really be facing the possibility of thinking Luiz wrong?

But here was Harriet, waiting for her on the top terrace. 'I'm sorry, love, have I kept you waiting for breakfast?'

'It doesn't matter.' Harriet never lied. 'But, Caterina, there is horrid news. Poor Father Pedro was set upon on his way home last night. He was found in an alley, bleeding and unconscious. They have just brought him home; he looks terrible. Your father is out; the servants are getting him to bed; what should we do?'

'We must send for a doctor; I'll talk to Tonio; he will know who my father has not quarrelled with these days. But, it's extraordinary—you say he was attacked? A holy father?'

'I thought the servants were surprised too,' said Harriet, 'even though I could not altogether understand what they said.'

CHAPTER SIX

Senhor Gomez and Dr Blanco met on the doorstep, and Caterina's swift explanation of what had happened amazed them both. 'The reverend father attacked!' exclaimed Gomez. 'What is this country coming to? But I'll not keep you from him, doctor. Let me know how you find him.'

The patient was still unconscious, but breathing stertorously. Caterina, standing by while the doctor made his swift examination, thought his colour was beginning to come back, and the doctor confirmed her view.

'A terrible blow to the head,' he told her. 'A deep concussion. He will need absolute rest for a few days, but should be none the worse in the long run, please God.'

'Will he remember what happened do you think, doctor?'

'Very likely not. Don't question him, *minha senhora*, just look after him and see to it that he rests, absolutely, for several days. It's the strangest thing. We all know that Father Pedro never carried money. A holy father needs no money. So why should he be attacked?'

'A personal grudge, perhaps?' said Caterina, and wished she had not.

'Against a man of God?' The doctor sounded shocked. 'Most unlikely, *senhora*. But I must make my report to your father.'

'Of course. This way.' Ushering him into her father's study, she was glad to hear the doctor begin by praising the care his patient had received before he got there. 'Everything done just as it should have been, *senhor*, I am glad to say. You have good servants, and, if I may say so, a capable daughter.' With a civil bow for Caterina.

'I'm glad to hear it.' Without a glance for her. 'But, doctor, will Father Pedro be able to tell us what happened to him?'

'Perhaps.' The doctor shrugged. 'Perhaps not. But, for the love of God no questions, *senhor*. If he remembers and tells you, good, if not, let it go. Anxiety, searching his mind, would be the worst possible thing for him. Let your daughter and the women care for him, they will know what to do for the best. I would advise that you do not visit him for a few days, until his strength is re-established, in case the very sight of you should set him racking his brains as to what could have happened to him. I am sure you can have every confidence in your admirable daughter.'

'Good.' This got Caterina a long, thoughtful look from under the habitually frowning brows. 'Thank you, doctor. My steward will

106

settle your account.'

Father Pedro recovered consciousness that evening while Caterina was changing the dressing on his head. 'Where—' He looked about him. 'How did I get here?'

'You were brought here, father. Some wretch must have attacked you on your way home. You were found in an alley off the Cedofeita; of course they knew who you were, brought you home at once. Dr Blanco says there is no serious harm done, but you must rest, and not worry or try to remember what happened.'

'Rest! How can I rest, when there is so much to do!' He made as if to rise, but slumped back. 'I'm weak as a child.' He made it sound her fault.

'You have had nothing to eat, father, for I don't know how long. I will get you something at once, a little chicken broth perhaps?'

'A whole chicken would be better. I am starving, daughter. I begin to remember now, I had missed my dinner. I was on my way home...'

'Don't think about it.' She had finished dressing the wound. 'The doctor says you must not. I'll go to the kitchen and see what I can find for you.'

'Quickly,' he ordered.

'As quick as I can.' She had been amazed before at how much Father Pedro contrived to eat, fast and gluttonously, talking all the time, and still stay a gaunt wreck of a man. What did he do with it all? 'I'll ask Miss Brown to come and sit with you,' she told him. 'The doctor did not wish you to be alone today. Not until you feel more the thing.'

'Tell her to bring her bible,' he said. 'She can read aloud to me; I shall understand it well enough; I do not wish to converse with Miss Brown.'

Nor she with you, thought Caterina but did not say it. She was relieved when Father Pedro pronounced Harriet a surprisingly good reader and told her to stay and read to him while he dealt with the impromptu meal the cook sent up.

'He ate the lot,' said Harriet, awestruck, afterwards. 'And I truly thought he was going to ask for more. Soup, and some bacalhau, and a great plateful of that savoury stew, and sent the boy running back to the kitchen because there were no sweetmeats on the tray. And all the time I was reading the Epistles of St Paul to him, about the sins of the flesh. I do dislike St Paul, Caterina.'

'I don't suppose he understood a word of it,' said Caterina. 'His English is not nearly so good as your Portuguese is getting to be.'

'You're such a good teacher,' said Harriet. 'You make a game of it.'

'I enjoy it too.' Something had changed in Caterina, Harriet thought, but lovingly refrained from questioning her.

*   *   *

Calling early next morning, Dr Blanco pronounced the patient well on the way to recovery. 'No need for me to call again, unless you find any new cause for anxiety, *senhora*. And no need to stay with him all the time either. He says he would very much prefer to be alone with his thoughts.'

'I am sure he would.' She did not add that the feeling was mutual. 'In that case I think I will take Miss Brown for a well-earned outing this afternoon, doctor, if you think it is safe to leave Father Pedro. She has been reading to him devotedly and looks a little pale, I think.'

'A delightful young lady,' said Dr Blanco warmly. 'You are lucky to have her for a companion.'

'I know it. Perhaps you would be so good as to tell my father that you have given us leave to go out.'

It got her a sharp glance. 'I will most certainly do so, *minha senhora*. You, too, have earned your holiday, and I shall tell your father so. You could not have tended Father Pedro more devotedly if you had been his own child.'

Their eyes met in a glance of sympathy. The priest was not an easy patient.

Leaving the doctor at the door of her father's study, Caterina went straight to the cheerful chaos of the kitchen to order the nourishing food he had recommended for his patient. 'I

109

am taking the Senhora Brown out for a drive this afternoon; the doctor says she needs a breath of air, and I thought I'd take her to look at the view from the terrace of the Fonsa Palace, and maybe dine there *al fresco*. Could you put us together a little something?'

'With the greatest of pleasure, *minha senhora*. An afternoon out will do you both good. The Senhora Brown is not the only one who has been working hard and looks pale.'

It was a useful reminder to Caterina that everything one said was listened to, passed on and discussed. She just hoped that some useful pair of ears had picked up the news that she was going to the Fonsa Palace that afternoon and passed it in the right direction.

There was no need to go through the crowded centre of town, so she ordered the ponderous family carriage for their excursion. 'Sedan chairs are so stuffy,' she explained to Harriet, 'and anyway they only hold one person. One must use them for the opera, of course, but for today we will make old Francesco the coachman earn his keep. I want to talk to him anyway about getting a gentle mule for you to learn to ride on. It's much the best way to get about here, and it will be a good excuse to make a few excursions before the winter rains start. It will get us out of the house a bit.' No need to say more. The brief respite of Father Pedro's absence over, his brooding presence would soon be felt once more throughout the house. It was hard to tell which was the more oppressive, Caterina thought, her father's occasional rages, or the friar's habit of appearing, soft-footed, where he was least expected. But the doctor had told him to stay in bed for a few more days, and had also delighted Caterina by telling him he had suggested she and Harriet go out that afternoon.

The carriage smelled of damp and old leather, but the two girls' spirits rose as it lurched out of the stable yard and down the lane that led out of town. Their progress was slow at first as the coachman cursed and sweated and forced a way through the home-going tide of ox-carts and mules and market women. Despite the curses, it all seemed wonderfully good humoured, and Harriet remarked on this.

'Yes, they are a friendly lot, the Portuguese peasants, so long as you don't tread on their toes. And of course Francesco is one of them—and my family have a name for being good democrats, though you might not think it to meet my father.'

'Democrats?' asked Harriet doubtfully.

'Yes. Porto has always stood for liberty and the middle way. Our closest tie to the Braganzas is that Henry the Navigator was born here, but that was a long time ago. We Portonians have mostly preferred to keep royalty at arms' length. There is no royal

111

palace here in Porto, you know. The Barons of Nevogilde hold the Carrancas Palace on the understanding that the royal family have the use of it when they think fit to visit us. But that was all before that shameful royal flight to the Brazils. I doubt if they would get a welcome now, if they were to come back, and anyway the palace has been taken over as military headquarters. It's where Lord Wellington sat down to eat Soult's dinner the day he retook Porto. And there, at last, it is.' She pointed out of the carriage window at a solid-looking granite building on their right.

'It's vast,' said Harriet. And then, 'It didn't get damaged in the French attack?'

'No, they came in from the north, from Braga, though there was fighting all down the Foz road, I believe, as the defenders retreated. I suppose that was when the Fonsa Palace got attacked; someone must have made the mistake of holding out in it. There were pockets of resistance all over the city, sniping at the French from roofs and windows, and very savagely they were dealt with when they finally had to surrender. I've heard stories about that first day that I will spare you, Harriet. I think it does the servants good to tell me, so I let them. I cannot imagine how Soult ever thought he had a chance of becoming ruler here after the way his rabble of an army behaved.'

'I suppose soldiers always do behave badly,'

said Harriet. 'They're men, after all, men on the loose.'

It had been another very hot day but the air was beginning to cool when the carriage lumbered to a stop outside a solid granite building rather like the Carrancas Palace but on the river side of the road. Here, signs of devastation leapt to the eye. The walls were pitted with bullet holes, downstairs windows had been roughly boarded up, and the heavy front door hung askew from the hinges off which it must have been forced.

'But it's been more than two years—' said Harriet as the footman tugged at the heavy bell pull by the door. 'Why has nothing been done to repair the place?'

'The Fonsas have always been strong monarchists,' Caterina explained. 'They prefer life in Lisbon where the court is. They were there when Dom John the Prince Regent fled to Brazil with his poor mad mother, the Queen. Of course they went too. Nobody loves them much, here in Porto. Ah, here is old Tomas.' The big door had opened with some difficulty, just a foot or so, to reveal a ragged, white-haired old man with only one arm.

'Heaven preserve us.' He bowed low. 'It really is the Senhora Caterina. A happy day to make up for all the wretched ones! I could hardly believe it when the message came! But come in, *senhora*, you and your beautiful young friend like two saints straight from heaven. Come in and see what those French ruffians did to our house.' He tried in vain to push the door further open with his one arm.

'It's all right, Tomas, don't trouble yourself, we can manage well enough.' The two girls slipped past him into the cool damp of the front hall and looked about them, appalled. Even in the half light filtering through cracks in the boarded windows they could see the devastation around them. Oak banisters on the stone stairway hung drunkenly, this way and that. Great damp patches on the walls and sodden carpet underfoot suggested that it had been a long time before the windows had even been boarded up. There was no furniture, no pictures, the cord of a vanished chandelier hung limply from a central boss in the blackened ceiling.

'Oh, Tomas!' exclaimed Caterina. And then, 'What happened to your arm?'

'Those French bastards of course.' He swore and spat on the dirty floor. 'We held out for two hours, *senhora*, potting them like rabbits, Manuel and José and I—and a few others. All dead, all gone, tortured, horrible... I'd already got my wound, my right arm of course, when they broke down the door. *Senhora*, I'm ashamed! I hid—you remember the secret room? I couldn't fight; I hid. I heard it all; sometimes I wish I had died with the others. It would have been easier—'

'But you have looked after the house for the

family, Tomas. Who else could have done that?'

'Looked after! Call this looking after? And much they care!' A despairing gesture led their eyes from the ruined staircase and a few broken bits of furniture to a pile of sodden tapestries in a corner. 'What could I do? Not a word; not a *scudo* from that day to this. At first I waited for orders, for help. In the end, we did what we could, my friends and I. I know how shocked you must be, *senhora*, after all those happy times when you were children here . . . But what more could we do? And just you wait until you see the gardens—' He turned to lead them to the back of the house, down a corridor which showed more signs of systematic looting. 'The French called them enemies of the people,' he explained, 'the masters. Because they had gone to the Brazils with the poor old Queen, God bless and keep her. They took everything that had not been destroyed. The pictures—all the family pictures that had not gone to the Lisbon house. Anything they fancied, they took. And now it is all lying rotting, somewhere in the mountains on the way to the border. They had to abandon everything, *senhora*, all their loot, even their treasure chests, some people say. There, look at that!' He had thrown open a door at the end of the corridor to reveal a terrace crazily overgrown by vines. 'I'm ashamed to let you see it.'

'Well, at least it is cool for us, Tomas.' She

115

moved over to a marble table where Gomez servants, sent on in advance, had set out a lavish cold collation. 'And I hope you have somewhere fairly snug of your own where you can entertain my people. You are to be our guest, of course. And no need to trouble yourselves about us. My friend and I will wait on ourselves.' Desperate, now to be rid of him, she concealed her impatience as best she might as he made her a long speech of thanks.

'Harriet, dear,' she plunged straight in when they were alone at last. 'Will you forgive me if I leave you here, to keep watch for me? If someone comes for orders, pretend I'm just gone for a moment—on a necessary errand. That will silence them.'

'Of course,' said Harriet. 'He's here, is he? Waiting for you?'

'Oh, God, I do hope so. Harryo, I'm ashamed. I know I should have told you more, but how could I? I promised, you see. I have to talk to him first.'

'And get his permission?' asked Harriet, putting her finger on it as usual. 'Caterina, love, I do beg you to be careful. What kind of an assignation is this he has summoned you to? You are walking a knife edge already, here in Porto, and he asks you to put your reputation still further on the line for him? What would your father say?'

'I don't even dare think about that. But I have to see him, you know that as well as I do.

To tell him, if nothing else—'

'Think hard before you do,' said Harriet. 'Listen to him first, let him explain. I'm not entirely in the dark; of course I know who it is, why we are here, of all places, why he has to meet you in secret like this. He risks his life as you do your reputation. Fair enough. But if he is a traitor, Caterina, as they say, sold out to the French—what are you going to do?'

'I won't believe it,' said Caterina. 'I don't for a minute believe it. Of course he will explain; that is what I am giving him the chance to do. Oh dear, if only I had known you knew ... I promised him. I solemnly promised I would never tell.'

'And you have kept your word,' said Harriet. 'Well, now, love, promise me you will listen to him before you tell him anything.'

'I promise.' Caterina snatched up some food from the loaded platters and started down the vine-hung steps. Harriet watched her go in silence, then loaded food on to two plates, filled two glasses with wine, drank a little out of each and began philosophically to eat.

Caterina, emerging on to the next terrace down, had made a discovery. The wilderness ended here, but instead of the formal knot garden where she had played as a child, she had come out on to a well-tended vegetable patch. Onions, aubergines and tomatoes grew in neat rows dominated by a scarecrow in what she recognised as tattered French uniform. But

117

there was no time to waste on admiring Tomas's peasant practicalness that was making the house pay its way. She hurried on down to the next terrace where the old vines and olive trees also showed signs of careful tending. The folly was one more level down, and her heart beat hard as she hurried down the last crumbling flight of steps. 'Luiz?' Very softly. 'Are you here?'

'At last!' He came cautiously out from the shadows of the little temple and her first thought was how unlike him it was to be cautious. Her next was that he looked much older. 'You're alone?' He hesitated, watching her, and she had time to see that his uniform was shabby, his dark hair ill-cut. But the deep-set black eyes held the old magic.

'Of course I'm alone. Oh, Luiz!' The food she had brought was a nuisance now; she put it down on the temple steps and moved towards him, hands outstretched.

'Provident as always, my little Caterina.' He took them, pulled her to him for a long, hungry kiss. 'It's been so long, so desperately long. I began to be afraid I would never see you again.'

'I too.' Her body trembled against his. 'But, Luiz, we haven't much time; tell me quickly, what has happened to you? Why do they call you traitor?'

'Straight to the heart of the matter!' He put her away a little to look down at her lovingly. 'And I'm glad. I'm playing the most dangerous of games, my love. I can't tell you much; I'm not allowed to. They didn't want me to get in touch with you at first, but I showed them what a help you could be to us.'

'They? Us?' She looked up at him, puzzled. 'Who, Luiz?'

'How should you know, my little darling? And the less I tell you, the safer for you. But there are deep, dangerous currents here in Porto. Have you heard of d'Argenton?'

'Yes—something—I know, wasn't he in a plot against Soult?'

'You are well informed.' Was he more surprised than pleased? 'Yes, he and his friends were plotting to get rid of Napoleon himself. They thought that the army would mutiny when Soult declared himself King of Lusitania, as he meant to do. That would be their chance. D'Argenton risked his life to visit Wellington at Coimbra, to ask for his help, but the French caught him on his way back across the lines.'

'But didn't he escape when the French retreated?'

'Yes, that's why I went with the French. To contrive his escape on that wild flight through the mountains. A brave man, that, a French patriot, and a good friend to us.'

'Us?' she asked again.

'The Friends of Democracy, here in Porto. D'Argenton and his fellow conspirators wanted France for the French, not an Empire forged in blood. They were glad to let us

Portonians plan for the future of our city, for our own free Kingdom of Lusitania. Free from both the French and Lisbon. No one but us gives a thought to what will happen here when the war is over. Your friend the Bishop has gone off to be a great man on the Council of Regency in Lisbon. As for the Prince Regent, the word is he is very happy in the Brazils; they'll have the devil's own job to get him back across the Atlantic. It's going to be the great chance for a free independent state of Lusitania, and we mean to be ready for it. But to be ready, we must be informed. That is where you come in, Caterina, my little love. I cannot clear my own name without implicating my friends; I've resigned myself to that; I am happy to work in the shadows until the day of freedom comes. I'm promised great things then. So, you are to be my eyes and ears, here in Porto.' His arms were round her now, his hands tracing familiar, thrilling paths about her body. 'Caterina! It's been so long. Come—' He was urging her towards the shadows of the temple.

'Luiz, I can't.' She held back, against her will. 'There's no time. Harriet—you know about Miss Brown, of course—she is up at the house, keeping guard for me; I can't stay.' Did she want to? Of course she wanted to. 'How do you mean, your eyes and ears?'

'There is so much we need to know. The boat you came on: what was on it? And the rest of

120

the news. Is it true that Marmont has given Wellington the slip and is on the march this way? Old Tomas does his best, but he's not in the position you are for gathering information.'

'Tomas is in it?' This was a relief; Tomas would be keeping her own servants busy eating and drinking.

'Of course. He has good cause to hate the French, and not much reason to love his employers, come to that, left here alone to fend for himself as he has been. He welcomed me with open arms, a great weight lifted from his shoulders, poor faithful, stupid fellow. If any disaster were to befall my cousins the Fonsas I am the next heir, you know. It gives me some authority with him, and he is glad of it. And glad to run my errands, in so far as he is able. But, Caterina, my questions, they are important.' His busy hands were telling her a more important tale.

She made herself concentrate on what he had asked her. 'The ship's cargo? Heavy stuff; I didn't take much notice of it; it was hidden under tarpaulins and they didn't start unloading until we were all on shore.'

'But you could find out. That cousin of yours who brought you over, he would know. And which way did it go?'

'Oh, I know that,' she said. 'Upstream. I watched from the terrace.'

'But you can't see the landing stage from
121

your terrace.'

'No.' Surprised. 'But I could see the whole downstream reach, and there was no extra traffic there, so whatever it was must have gone upriver.'

'My clever little love! I am sure you are right. How I longed to be there, that day, in our secret place, to greet you. But I am under orders, just as much as any soldier. Only they are deadly dangerous ones, never forget that. My life is in your little hands.' He kissed them, one after the other.

'Harriet knows.'

'The devil she does!' She had forgotten his sudden frightening rages.

'You're hurting me.' She pulled away the hand that was savaging her breast. 'I didn't tell. I kept my promise. Harriet worked it out for herself. She's no fool, and safe as houses; a friend in a million. She'll help. She is helping, up there, this minute.' It reminded her. 'I must go back.' She had been relieved to feel the dangerous tide of fury ebb away in him as she talked. For a moment, she had been frightened. For herself? For Harriet? 'We've been away as long as I dare. Father Pedro has been hurt. He likes Harriet to read to him.'

'He is conscious then?'

'Oh yes, the doctor said he was lucky; it might have been much worse. But he is lying there, in bed, listening to everything that goes on in the house.'

'Damnation! Too soft a blow! But, Caterina, my other question. Marmont.'

'I know nothing about that. I've been tied to the house, looking after Father Pedro. And my cousin has left us, he is staying with the Wares now.' She was talking almost desperately as his hands became more insistent and she felt her body begin to betray her, melting towards him. So easy to give way, to lose herself in the old ecstasy. 'Mrs Ware's giving a party for me; there will be talk there, but how shall I see you? I can't come here again. Will a message to your house reach you?'

'No!' Explosively. 'The old bitch, my grandmother, is in her dotage, believes everything they say against me. The servants love me, of course, would do anything for me, but it's not safe. I dare not go near the place.'

So that was the real reason why he had not been able to come to their old meeting place. Disconcerting to realise this. 'Oh, Luiz, she loved you so much. I am so sorry. She must really be out of her mind.'

'Oh, she is that all right, and dangerous with it. I'm told she seems to make sense some of the time, poor old hag. But you won't be seeing her, that's one thing certain. I hear you've not exactly been welcomed with open arms by the nobility and gentry of Porto. Never mind it, my little love, it will all be changed when we come into our own. In the mean time, I've found a dressmaker for you.'

123

'A dressmaker?' She was amazed at the sudden change of subject.

'Where we can meet, child. A safe house, on the edge of town. She is a true friend of liberty. Here's her direction.' His questing hands left her body at last and she shivered with a strange mixture of disappointment and relief. 'Here. Put it away safe and be sure and visit her tomorrow with news for me. Late afternoon, like this. I'll try to be there, but I'm not entirely my own master. The cause I serve is greater than any of us. Hush!' He put a finger to her lips, but all she heard was a bird's cry. 'That's Tomas. We must part, my darling. It breaks my heart.'

CHAPTER SEVEN

'Did you tell him?' asked Harriet when they were safe in the carriage, rumbling back towards town.

'There was no time. So much to say ...' She was sorting through their brief, tense talk in her mind, trying to make sense of it all.

'And now you have to decide how much to tell me,' said Harriet, startling her. 'Not a word more than you want to; there's no need; I'm your friend whatever happens. You know that. And what I don't know, I can't betray. Are you going to see him again?'

'Oh, *yes*! He's found us a dressmaker.' She pulled out the scrap of paper and read it for the first time. 'Good gracious. It's Madame Feuillide! Now, how in the world am I going to manage about that?'

'Easy,' said Harriet. 'Tell Mrs Ware you have changed your mind. A woman's privilege. No need to say more; she'll be delighted. I have no doubt she'll be getting commission from Madame Feuillide.'

'Yes, but I don't like it.' She could not think why it made her uneasy, but it did. 'He wants me to go tomorrow; I'll have to send a note to Mrs Ware as soon as we get back. And I think maybe I'll suggest a date for the party at the same time.' It would be a chance to get the information about the *Anthea*'s cargo that Luiz wanted.

'Why not?' said Harriet. But it was with a sharp look for her friend.

The streets were emptier now and they got back more quickly than they had come, but the servant who opened the big front door told Harriet that Father Pedro had been asking for her impatiently. 'And the Senhor Ware is on the terrace waiting for you, *minha senhora*.'

'Tell him I'll be with him directly,' said Caterina, exchanging a quick glance with Harriet. This at least made things easier. He could take a message to his mother.

Frank Ware was standing at the edge of the terrace, watching the busy traffic on the river.

'There's talk of a ship at the bar, in from England,' he told her. 'The first since you arrived; I wonder what news she will bring.'

'Will she bring mail?' Eagerly.

'Oh, bound to. Do you find yourself missing your friends at home, Miss Gomez?'

'I'm afraid I haven't many. It is Miss Brown who longs for news of her mother, who was not well when we left. I do hope there is something for her.' Here was a chance. 'I wonder if this ship is as heavily loaded as the *Anthea* was. Do you know, someone was asking me what she carried, and I was ashamed to have to admit that I had no idea.' And, oddly, as she said this, she remembered for the first time that Jeremy had told her it was war material.

'I'm glad of that,' said Frank Ware. 'If I may give you a piece of advice, Miss Gomez, don't ever dream of answering that kind of question, and look a little askance at the people who ask them. This is a military base, remember, and information like that might be invaluable to the enemy. Who was it asked you, I wonder?'

'Oh, nobody. A stranger. We got talking at the linen drapers.' Harriet and I had thought we would try our hand at our own dressmaking, but I am afraid we have made a sad botch of it. I'm so glad to find you here, Mr Ware. I had been meaning to write a note to your mother to ask if I might take her up on her kind offer of her own dressmaker's services. A French lady, I believe. I had not much liked the

126

idea, but I am afraid needs must . . .'

'When fashion drives? I know my mother will be delighted to let you have her direction,' he said. 'And she told me to ask if you were ready to name a day for the party.'

'Just as soon as I have made my arrangements with the dressmaker,' she told him. 'And my kindest regards to your mother, Mr Ware. And say something friendly to my cousin for me. How is he getting on with Miss Emerson, I wonder.'

'He comes back from visiting her with a spring in his step,' said Frank Ware, surprising her. He turned back to look at the river. 'Look, there comes the ship now, she'll just make it with the tide.'

'And heavy loaded,' said Caterina.

'Like the *Anthea*.' He smiled at her. 'And remember, Miss Gomez, if any other friendly ladies start asking you questions in the shops, get their names and tell me about them.'

'You?'

'I'd know where to report it. And how to keep your name out of it. I mean it, Miss Gomez.'

'I know you do, and I'm grateful. It's hard to believe, with everything seeming so ordinary here, that blood is being shed up on the border. I can't tell you how glad I am to have your mother's assurance that you will let me know if there should come a time to think of escaping to England. Even if I should feel it my duty to stay with my father, I think I would have to take up your kind offer and send Harriet home with you. But I take it there is no need to be thinking of that yet?'

'Not the least in the world, and I am sure there won't be. I have the greatest confidence in Lord Wellington. I am sure this talk that Marmont has outmanoeuvred him will turn out to be just that, talk. And seditious talk at that. But where is your friend Miss Brown? Not worn out, I hope, with attendance on Father Pedro?'

'She is reading aloud to him at this very moment, poor Harriet. I'm afraid she has been altogether too successful and now he says he can't do without her.'

'Oh, poor Miss Brown. But I am sure I can count on you not to let him bully her, Miss Gomez.'

'I hope so. Should I write a note to your mother, Mr Ware?' She thought it time to come back to the matter in hand.

'No need. I will bring you the dressmaker's direction first thing in the morning, but I do beg you, Miss Gomez, don't let her turn you out in black, like the Portuguese ladies. I can't tell you how depressing it is when they all come to the opera looking like a funeral party. And black would quite quench Miss Brown's delicate good looks.'

'Yes, it would, wouldn't it?' said Caterina, amused. She rather liked the idea of herself in black. 'It is sad don't you think, Mr Ware, that even in dress there is a division between Portuguese and British society. I'm grateful to you for reminding me.'

'And you must belong to us, Miss Gomez. I am sure you will find that all the ladies begin to call on you, once our party has taken place. My mother says they have been hanging back a little ...' He stammered to an awkward halt, was silent for a moment, and made a new start: 'Miss Gomez, as an old friend, may I give you a word of friendly advice?'

'Of course.'

'You are so awkwardly placed, you and Miss Brown, between our two societies here in Porto, you need, perhaps, to be a little extra careful of censorious eyes. Please, don't go walking about the town again unattended.'

'Oh dear.' She smiled at him ruefully. 'We were seen then? I should have known it. And I did enjoy it so.'

'Miss Sandeman was looking out of her window. She usually is. And of course she told her mother. And she told Mrs Bland, her best friend.'

'And Mrs Bland told your mother? And a man with us, too, even if he is a cousin.'

'He's not Miss Brown's cousin. My mother was wondering if Miss Brown is perhaps connected with her friends the Cavendish-Browns of Bath.'

'I very much doubt it. But I do thank you for

129

your words of warning, Mr Ware. I had forgotten just what things were like here in Porto.' She smiled what she hoped was a dismissal, but he lingered for a while and she wondered if he was hoping that Harriet would escape from Father Pedro and join them. It began to look as if here was one battle she would not have to fight with her father. Frank Ware might have planned a union between their vineyards, but that was before he met Harriet. She liked him too well to imagine for a moment that, whatever the advantages of the match, he would propose to her once he had realised that it was her friend he cared for. His mother would be furious, of course. But it was certainly one problem the less for her. She just hoped it would be a long time before her father realised what was happening. Or rather before Father Pedro did.

* * *

Frank Ware found his mother and Jeremy Craddock sitting over a cup of tea in her stuffy, chintzy sitting room. There was a glow about Jeremy, and Frank was not surprised to learn that he had just returned from a session with Miss Emerson. 'She dismissed me early today,' he said. For him there was only one 'she'. 'Her brother needed her services as a secretary. There's a ship due to dock this evening and promising a quick return to England, if you have mail for home.'

'No, but I hope she brings some.' Frank was remembering what Caterina had told him about Herriet's mother, and wishing he could go and enquire about mail for her. But it would automatically be collected by the Gomez servants. 'I have a message for you, mother.' He accepted a cup of tea. 'From Miss Gomez. She has decided she needs your dressmaker after all and I promised I would take her the address in the morning.'

'How wise of her. And our party?'

'As soon as she has seen—I couldn't remember the name at the time but it is Madame Feuillide, is it not?'

'Yes. I'll write it down for you.' She poured more tea for herself. 'A little more for you, Mr Craddock?'

'No, thank you. I think I'll just step down to the quay and see what's doing there.'

'And I will come with you,' said Frank. 'I wish you wouldn't interrupt my sessions.' Rachel Emerson had finished writing to Ralph's dictation. 'It is so bad for the treatment.'

'And you were getting along so beautifully! I could have laughed when I came in and saw the young fool making those great eyes at you. You've got him properly to rights, my dear. I hope he is singing like a canary.'

'It's a funny thing,' she said thoughtfully. 'He talks a great deal, but it is all about the deep past, about his mother, his wretched childhood...'

'Well you had better apply your mind to bringing him up to date.' He took the finished letter from her and signed it with a flourish. 'I'll take this down myself; there's no trusting the servants not to dally on the way.' He was looking past her out of the window. 'Yes, as I thought, she is docking on the south bank as the *Anthea* did.' He picked up his tall hat, turned back in the doorway. 'Should you not call on Miss Gomez? You are the older inhabitant, after all, by the ridiculous rules of the British visiting game.'

'Oh, should I?' Doubtfully. 'I wonder if she would see me.'

'Surely she would, and be grateful. By all accounts her Portuguese *fidalgo* kin are turning her the coldest of cold shoulders, and the British ladies hanging back too. I wish I could get the full tale of what happened before she was sent away, but they're close as oysters about that.' He looked at his watch. 'Too late for today, but run along tomorrow, there's a good girl, turn on that charm of yours, get her talking and see what you can find out. I reckon she'll greet you with open arms, with no company but that little shrimp of a Miss Brown who don't look as if she had two ideas to put together. You'll be best friends in no time!' He clapped his hat on his head. 'Don't wait up for me. I'll get something to eat at the

132

coffee house.'

'Can we afford it?'

'Whose fault is it if we can't?' He slammed the door behind him.

*   *   *

Madame Feuillide turned out to live on the fringe of the city in the direction of Braga, so once again it would be possible to take the carriage for their late afternoon appointment. This way, the traces of the French assault two years before were all too apparent. Some houses still stood as burned and blackened ruins, others were in the slow process of repair, while broken-down walls revealed ravaged gardens where the fighting must have been heaviest. Madame Feuillide had apparently been lucky. Her little house was outside the defences that had been hurriedly thrown up at the news of the French advance, in a little hollow screened from the road by a wall and trees.

'Yes, they missed me completely.' Madame Feuillide was tiny, dark and sharp-featured and still spoke with a strong French accent. 'Was it not a blessed thing? I cowered here, like a mouse, listening to the shouts, the screams, the savage sounds of the battle, praying that my little house would be spared. I was lucky.'

'You did not think of running away?' asked Caterina, admiring her courage.

'*Mademoiselle*, I did not dare. The mob were tearing French prisoners to pieces. And I am French, after all, and still sound it, though I have lived happily here in Porto for more than twenty years. I was one of the lucky ones when our terrible revolution happened in France. Our chateau was in the south, near Bayonne. I got away with my faithful Marie, over the border into Spain with so many wretched others, but again I was lucky: I had friends here in Porto. I came to them; they were wonderful to me, kindness itself, helped me to turn my skill as a needlewoman into something that would support us, me and my Marie, God rest her soul, and theirs. All dead, Mademoiselle Gomez. I am alone now, but, thank the good God, I am able to support myself, and give a little to charity in memory of those who have been so good to me. But why am I wasting time in talk? My friend Mrs Ware says I am to outfit you for your début in English society, and I can see that it will be the greatest of pleasures. And your charming young friend. With whom am I to begin? You will have to respect my little habits. I am an artiste, as I am sure you will understand; I cannot bear an audience at my work. I must concentrate entirely. The lady I am not working on will have to retire to the shade of my little garden. I hope it will not be too tedious for you?' to Harriet. 'I will begin with Mademoiselle Gomez.'

As easy as that, thought Caterina,

submitting herself to be measured by the voluble little Frenchwoman who must be more than the thirty or so years she looked, if she had been old enough to make her escape from revolutionary France back in the early nineties, when blood began to flow. She tried a question about the escape, but Madame Feuillide had her answer ready. 'Forgive me, *mademoiselle*, but I need all my energies for the problems of design. If you will bear with me, we will work in silence.'

She was altogether a perfectionist, Caterina thought, almost an hour later, when she in her turn was despatched to the secluded garden and Harriet took her place in the workroom. 'I am afraid I may have to take a little more time with your charming young friend,' Madame Feuillide had warned. 'Her figure is not perhaps quite such an ideal one for modern fashions as yours, but I promise I will do my very best by her, if it takes the rest of the afternoon.'

'Thank you.' It could hardly have been made more clear, Caterina thought, taking Harriet's place on the rustic bench in the little summerhouse between yew hedges at the far end of the shady garden. It was not really surprising, though it had surprised her, that the French had not found this secluded spot. But how did Luiz know of it, and how soon would he appear?'

She sat there in the quiet garden for a little
135

while, waiting for him, dreaming about him, wondering what dangers he was risking to come to her.

'At last!' He emerged suddenly from behind one of the thick yew hedges. 'Have you had to wait long, my little love?' He swept her at once into a strong embrace and she felt the old exultant tide sweep through her. 'Is not this well planned?' He was glowing with satisfaction. 'Madame Feuillide is a true friend of our cause and will see to it that she keeps your worthy companion out of our way as long as possible. I am only sorry I cannot offer you greater comfort.' He let her go and took off his all-enveloping brown cloak to reveal the blue jacket and plush breeches of a peasant in his holiday best. 'I am the maid's cousin in from the country for the day,' he told her. 'You should just see the big eyes she makes at me, but I have none for her, I can tell you.' He had spread the cloak on the paved terrace, now held out his hand to her. 'I've missed you with every bone in my body—' His hand was warm on hers, persuasive. Possessive?

'But, Luiz—' The blood seethed in her veins. Her body yearned towards him, to submit, to let go, to be at last entirely his again. So, why was she still standing there, her eyes locked with his, resisting that imperious hand? Instinct battled with instinct. And then, the shriek of an ox-cart's wheels on the road beyond the garden wall came as a reminder of how risky their position was. 'I can't,' she said. 'Not here, not like this. Besides, we must talk, I have so much to tell you.'

'My splendid girl. Business first.' She had hit on the one thing that could distract him. He sat down on the bench and put a warm arm round her waist. 'So, you have managed to get news for me; I knew you wouldn't fail me.'

'But I *have* failed you, Luiz, that's just what I need to tell you. I found Frank Ware at the house when I got back the other day; that's why I was able to make my appointment here so quickly. But when I asked him, very casually, about the *Anthea*'s cargo, he gave me a great scold about military secrets. I shall have to be very careful, I can see. But there's good news too,' she went on eagerly. 'He is sure that Lord Wellington is holding his own at the border. I pretended to be afraid and wondering whether to go back to England and he promised me there was no need: Wellington is bound to outmanoeuvre Marmont.'

'Bound to?' She had his full attention now. 'But he did not know for sure?'

'No.' Reluctantly. 'I suppose not. There's another ship in, did you know?'

'Yes, the *Chloe*, unloading on the south bank as the *Anthea* did.'

'She left England in a great hurry,' Caterina told him. 'We had hoped for mail, Harriet and I, but she caught a wind and came away without it.'

'Too bad.' He did not sound much concerned. Well, how should he know what a bitter disappointment it had been to them? 'But what is she carrying, my own, that's the important thing. Why was she in such a hurry?'

'Nobody knows,' she told him. 'But it looked very much like what the *Anthea* was carrying. And it's all going upstream as her cargo did. On small boats because the river is so low.'

'For what that's worth.' His hand had found its way, distractingly, to her breast. She was dizzy for a moment with all the memories, all the confusing passion it aroused. 'Did you name the day for this great British party of yours?'

'It's to be just as soon as Madame Feuillide sends our clothes home. She promises them in a week or so.'

'Good.' With an approving touch to her nipple that made her catch a quick breath. 'There's an odd couple in Porto I'd like you to see are invited. The Emersons, brother and sister; do you know of them?'

'Of course. My cousin Jeremy Craddock came out for treatment from Miss Emerson; I'm told she is doing him a great deal of good.'

'Who told you that?'

'Frank Ware.'

'I'd forgotten about him.' Dismissively. 'And that mother of his. But they will be useful to you, my angel, as sources of information.

138

'Has Ware made you an offer yet?'

'Good gracious no!' How did he know about that? It was on the tip of her tongue to tell him about Frank and Harriet, but he gave her no chance.

'That's good.' He approved. 'Keep him at arms' length just as long as you can, like the clever child you are. He'll be much more useful that way. There will be nothing but trouble when the time comes for you to refuse him. How is Father Pedro by the way?'

'Much better. The doctor says he can get up tomorrow.'

'I'm sure no one is looking forward to that.' He pulled her round for a sudden, fierce kiss. 'And that's enough talk, my girl. We have better things to do than talk. Devil take these buttons!'

'No!' Suddenly furious, she pushed his hand away. 'You take too much for granted, Luiz! I'm not your strumpet!'

'What?' He looked suddenly the angry boy she remembered, brown cheeks flushed, the bright dark eyes losing their sparkle, turning dangerous. Then he took a deep breath: 'Caterina, my own, you misunderstand me! We are one, you and I. Nothing can change that.'

'Can it not?' She had the most extraordinary feeling that something had. But this was not the time to tell him about that. 'Luiz.' She pulled a little away so that she could meet his eyes. 'There's something I wanted to ask you.

I've been thinking about you so much, and your Friends of Democracy, but there is something I don't quite understand ... What has the *Anthea*'s cargo, or the *Chloe*'s, come to that, to do with your plans?'

'I should have explained better, my own.' He put out a loving hand to stroke a strand of hair away from her forehead. 'We need to know when the moment of crisis is coming. That is our chance, don't you see, and we must be ready for it.'

'You mean you hope the French attack again? Oh, Luiz—'

'Not hope, love, just mean to be ready. For that chance or for any other. We have been slaves to Lisbon and those absentee Braganzas for long enough. Imagine a democratic state of Lusitania, backed by our British friends...'

'And an end to all the corruption and beggary.' She took him up on it eagerly. 'It's wonderful, Luiz, of course I'll help.'

'I knew you would.' His arms were round her again, compelling. And then, 'One more thing. Have you met an English Major called Dickson?'

'No, I've not met any of the English except Frank Ware, but, do you know, I think he has mentioned him. I am sure the name is familiar.'

'Then see to it that the Wares ask him to this famous party of yours, there's a good child, and flash your pretty little eyes at him. My friends say he's working closely with

140

Wellington, probably knows more about what is going on upriver than anyone, but he's said to be close as an oyster. I'm sure you could open him up, my clever darling.'

'I'll certainly try. No, Luiz, we can't, we mustn't—' She detached the hand that was at work again on the buttons of her dress. 'It's getting late, Madame Feuillide must be about done with Harriet.'

'What's the matter with you, Caterina? Why have you changed so?' His eyes were dangerous. 'Don't tell me they have turned you into an English miss among them!'

'They could hardly do that, could they?' Now was the time to tell him. But he was kissing her hands again, in farewell this time.

He put a finger under her chin and gazed into her eyes. 'If I have offended you, my own, remember it was love that did so, and forgive me. We will understand each other better next time we meet. Mind you make an early date to come again, and for the party. Be very sure I will risk anything to meet you here. Deuce take it, here she comes.' He picked up his cloak and vanished round the corner of the yew hedge as Harriet came down the steps from the house.

*   *   *

Father Pedro left his room for the first time next morning, and the whole house seemed darker for his presence. He moved so silently,

141

on his sandalled feet, that no conversation in any of the public rooms was safe from him. 'We must not seem to huddle in our own rooms.' Caterina summed it up, safe for a moment at the far end of the terrace with Harriet. 'Nor appear to have secrets.'

'Everyone has secrets,' protested Harriet. 'Oh, I do wish we had heard from England.'

'I begin to think I made a great mistake in coming,' said Caterina. 'But how was I to know things had changed so in this house? Oh dear, this must mean a caller.' A servant had appeared from the house, and announced that the Senhora Emerson had called.

'Jeremy's wonderful Miss Emerson,' exclaimed Caterina. 'Bring her out here, Sancho. And wine and cakes, please.' Both girls watched with interest for the appearance of the young woman who had been described as putting a spring into Jeremy Craddock's step, and both were faintly disappointed with what they saw. The bright sunshine of the open terrace was hard on Rachel Emerson's pale good looks. Her broad-brimmed hat concealed the flaxen hair and cast unkind shadows on the smiling face.

'I hope you do not think I am taking a liberty in calling.' She held out a friendly hand to Caterina. 'I was so desperately lonely here in Porto when my brother and I first arrived, and I have been thinking a great deal about you two, tucked away here so far out of town. And your cousin talks about you so much. He is a most delightful young man, is he not, and quite devoted to you, Miss Gomez. Such a sad life as his has been, poor young fellow. I do so hope that I may be able to help him a little.' She paused in her flow of talk to be introduced to Harriet. 'Delighted to meet you, Miss Brown. Such a fortunate thing that you were able to accompany Miss Gomez on her voyage home. That is, if you feel it is home, Miss Gomez?' Dismissing Harriet, she turned back to Caterina. 'The Portonians strike my brother and me as an unfriendly enough set of people, but I suppose you feel yourself one of them. And at least you are part of English society too, which seems to have quite its own rules and customs. I have never been lucky enough to visit England, and quite long to do so. My father came from a little English village called Barnstaple. He was pressed into the British navy during the struggle for American independence, captured and ended up a better American than most, my mother always used to say. Have you perhaps been to Barnstaple, Miss Gomez?'

'No, I am afraid not. Bath is the furthest west we have been, Miss Brown and I.'

'A beautiful city, I believe. My brother has suggested that I might care to go there to practise my healing arts among the invalids who take the waters, but I confess to you young ladies that I quite long to be back home in our

United States. Foreign parts are all very well for a while, but between you and I, there is no place in the end like home. But how I am running on. My brother says I am a terrible talker, and I am afraid that when I feel at ease in society it is quite true. I can tell right now that we three are going to be the greatest friends. We have so much in common, don't you think? Distant homes and homesickness, and, of course, the charming young fellow we all know, your agreeable cousin, Miss Gomez. Such a tragedy that his complaint puts marriage out of the question for him, otherwise we might see ourselves as rivals, might we not? Tell me,' to Caterina, 'what is young Ware like? I have never had the pleasure of meeting him, though his mother has long been one of my most valued clients. I can't tell you the flattering things she has said to me. I miss her sadly now she is so busy with the arrangements for the party she is giving for you, Miss Gomez. I am sure we all look forward to that. With the news so gloomy we must take our pleasures where we find them, must we not?'

'Is there bad news today?' asked Caterina.

'I was sure you would have heard. Poor Wellington's beat, they say. Marmont has thrown supplies into Ciudad Rodrigo, enough to last all winter, shown the great general a clean pair of heels and is on the quick march for Lisbon.'

'For Lisbon?'

'A surprise, is it not? He must have thought of a way to deal with those lines of Torres Vedras we heard so much about last year. But at least we don't have to be worrying here in Porto, a great relief to me, I can tell you. I tremble to think what would happen to me and my brother if the French should come here. That tyrant Bonaparte had me thrown out of France, neck and crop, for standing up in defence of his poor wife Josephine. She was my good friend and patroness, you know. Many's the time I have soothed away her miseries for her, poor lady. Magic, she used to call my hands, pure magic. If I may say so, Miss Gomez, you look as if you could do with a touch of my magic; I can always tell when I am needed, though I do not always have the presumption to say so. But I feel so comfortable here; it is because we are going to be friends; the only unattached young ladies in our little society. We must be friends or rivals, and friends is much better, is it not so?'

Caterina and Harriet exchanged one quick glance. 'I'm sure—' Caterina began, and stopped. Father Pedro was bearing down the terrace upon them and she could not have believed she would ever have been so pleased to see him.

Introduced to Miss Emerson, he lost no time in making his displeasure felt. 'You practise some kind of healing, I believe, here in Porto?'

'I do my poor best to soothe away the

anxieties of these terrible times, father. It's a little gift God gave me, and I thank Him for it every day of my life. I truly believe that I am helping the *senhora*'s cousin a little; he is certainly so good as to say so. I was just saying to her that I thought she might benefit from my services, if she would let me try. Purely for love, of course, because we are all young people together.'

'It's very good of you—' Caterina was trying to think how to phrase her instinctive rejection of the idea, but Father Pedro interrupted her.

'Ridiculous,' he said. 'An absurd notion. What has the *senhora* to be anxious about, at home with her loving father? And if she were to think herself in any difficulty, she knows well in what direction it is her duty to turn. We'll have no talk of your mumbo-jumbo healing practices in this house, if you please, Miss Emerson.'

'I beg your pardon.' She was obviously used to being rebuffed. 'I only meant if for the best. Surely you must agree with me, father, that we are all in this world to help each other. I am sure Miss Brown thinks so.'

'Why, yes, of course.' Harriet was surprised to be suddenly included in the conversation. 'Only sometimes it's hard to know just what one should do for the best. I often wonder if leaving people alone isn't the kindest thing one can do for them.'

'There's my cue to take myself off,' said

146

Rachel Emerson, putting down her glass with a sharp little click on the marble table. 'It has been good of you to be so kind to me, Senhora Gomez, and I do thank you a thousand times for inviting me to Mrs Ware's party. I shall very much look forward to seeing you there, and introducing my beloved brother to you. You will find him quite out of the usual way.' She leaned forward to plant an apparently impulsive kiss on Caterina's cheek. 'My heart tells me we are going to be the very best of friends. Goodbye, Miss Brown, Father—' With a cool nod for Harriet and a deep, graceful curtsey for Father Pedro.

'But I never invited her to the party,' said Caterina, when she had gone.

'No. What an odd performance.' Harriet turned to watch Father Pedro move solemnly away from them down the terrace towards the house.

'Performance?'

'Didn't you think so? She was putting on the act of a silly young American woman. All that talk about Barnstaple and had we been there. I don't like her, Cat.'

'No more do I. But she made me remember those happy days at Falmouth. Oh, Harryo, I wish we would hear from your mother.'

'So do I,' said Harriet. 'But I am sure no news is good news.'

CHAPTER EIGHT

Frank Ware was getting anxious about his mother's increasingly ambitious plans for her party. 'Mother, you are absolutely outrunning the constable,' he protested one mild September evening when he had found her in her boudoir giving lavish orders to an obsequious wine merchant. 'We will have all the duns in town descending on us if you go on at this rate. And I am sure Miss Gomez would much prefer the kind of quiet little affair you first planned.'

'Nonsense, Frank, you see it all the wrong way round. This party is to be at once an endorsement of Miss Gomez's position in our society and a statement of our own. It is just the way to re-establish our credit, and, frankly, I blame you more than anyone for the damage that has suffered. All this absurd talk of getting a job, going to work for Major Dickson ... Naturally people are beginning to talk, to wonder if things are not quite right with us. Good name is everything in these troubled times, and I do beg you to remember that.'

'Good name won't be much use if we have Marmont down on us like a whirlwind,' he told her.

'I thought he was heading for Lisbon?'

'Nobody knows for sure. Dickson went

upriver the other day with the last of the *Chloe*'s supplies, and I just hope he will be back soon with real news. This state of uncertainty is hard on everyone. I thought Miss Gomez and Miss Brown were in a suppressed state of nerves when I called on them yesterday, and there was not much I could say to comfort them, except to renew your invitation to join us if there should have to be another flight to England.'

'I'm sure there won't,' she said comfortably. 'But I'm sorry the poor girls are anxious; all the more reason for diverting them with plans for the party. I am glad you are such a faithful visitor to their house, Frank. Can I hope that there will be an interesting announcement to make to our friends at the party?'

'Oh, mother, impossible! It's outrageously too soon. How can I ask the girl to marry me when I have only known her for a few weeks?'

'Don't be absurd, Frank. She's half-Portuguese, remember, and must have been brought up to the idea of an arranged marriage. Besides, you were childhood friends; everything's on your side. I expect if the truth were known she is impatiently waiting for your proposal. And I am sure her father is.'

'If she is, mother, she conceals it admirably. She is a most self-possessed young lady, and of course I hardly ever see her alone. She and Miss Brown are quite inseparable and Senhor Gomez never shows himself.'

'That Miss Brown.' Something in his tone had alerted her. 'What do we know of her, Frank? I have been wondering a great deal about her, a nobody from God knows where. Can I safely introduce her to my friends? I wish you would try and find out something about her for me.'

'She is Miss Gomez's friend, mother. Surely that must be enough for us.'

'It's all so awkward,' grumbled his mother. 'At home in England it would be easy enough to find out, but here—I'm sure I don't know what to do for the best.'

'Welcome her to your house!' He felt himself getting angry and knew he must fight it. 'What are we, after all, but honest wine merchants? I hope I am as good a gentleman as the next man, but to more than that I will not pretend. My grandfather was a sugar baker in Hull, remember.'

'On your father's side.' Impatiently. 'But my mother—'

'Was Lady Susan, an earl's daughter. Mother, how could I forget it? But she's long gone now, and I would much rather stand on my own two feet as an honest business man.'

'If you still had a business.'

'Well, there's the rub, isn't it? If only father had thought to diversify, to put some of his money into salt cod, or shipping, but it was vines all the way with him, and now look at us.'

'That's right, blame your poor father.' She

put a lace-trimmed handkerchief to dry eyes. 'I knew it would come to that, it always does in the end.'

He nearly said, better than blaming your extravagance, but restrained himself. Quarrels with her always ended in hysterics, recriminations, and abject apologies on his part. He picked up his hat. 'I think I'll just step down to the quay and see if there is any news.'

* * *

Caterina, too, was beginning to be a little anxious about the plans for Mrs Ware's party. What had originally been described as a little meeting of the English colony now seemed to have burgeoned into a formal affair, with dancing. 'Not that I don't love to dance,' she said to Harriet. 'And I know you do too, but it's not at all what I had reckoned on.'

'No, it is odd, isn't it? Specially when they are supposed to be so hard up. Mr Ware was telling me the other day how very much he hoped that when Major Dickson returns from upriver he will have work for him to do. He hates his idle life, he says, now with the future of the world at stake.'

'What kind of work, I wonder?' Caterina did not like questioning her friend under false pretences, but it must be done, for Luiz.

'He's not sure, but he says Major Dickson was very encouraging before he went away. His

151

is a Portuguese rank, you know, and he finds it hard to get the help he needs from his English subordinates. I think maybe his plan is for Mr Ware to act as some kind of assistant. His knowledge of Porto and the Portonians could be very useful.'

'Yes indeed. I hope Major Dickson is back in time for the party; I do so look forward to meeting him. He sounds a most interesting man.'

'If the party is put off again, I should think he is bound to be,' said Harriet. 'Mr Ware says his mother is being driven quite to distraction by all the delays; there's no getting a sense of urgency into the heads of the Portuguese, she finds. If it's not the wine, it's the musicians causing delay, or the problem of getting the floors ready for dancing.'

'Oh well,' said Caterina philosophically, 'the more delay the better, if you ask me. I can't say that I absolutely look forward to that party.' She was minding more and more that she had not told Harriet about her father's plans for her and Frank Ware. At first it had seemed unnecessary, since she knew she was going to refuse Frank, but now, as she watched him and Harriet together, she did wish that she had mentioned it casually, as an impossibility, in the first place. Too late now, but it would make things extra difficult if, as she sometimes feared, Mrs Ware intended the party for an occasion to try and precipitate an engagement between herself and Frank. Father Pedro had said nothing more about the plan, and his very silence made her anxious. Was he taking her acquiescence for granted? And to make matters worse, Madame Feuillide had twice postponed her and Harriet's fittings on one pretext or another. Since there had been no word from Luiz either she felt she must assume that he was out of town on some secret business for his group of conspirators. She very much wished he would come back. She had things to tell him, and things to ask.

And yet, in another way, it was a halcyon time, with the September days getting cooler and Harriet proving a fearless rider on the gentle mule that had been found for her. As her confidence increased, they rode further everyday, often down past the fishermen's quarter to the sea at Foz, where Caterina had happy memories of rare childhood outings with the Gomez cousins who now ignored her.

A worse worry than social ostracism was a very basic one. Anything she asked for, she got, except money. Her father's credit was good everywhere. There was no problem about Madame Feuillide's account, or the yards of material and the gloves and shoes that she and Harriet had bought in town. The bills went to her father's steward and were paid without question. But when she asked him for some money of her own, the steward referred her to her father. 'I am afraid I have no instructions about that, *minha senhora.*'

'Not even a *scudo* to throw to a beggar?'

'I am afraid not, *minha senhora.* I have no orders.'

Useless to plead with him. They both knew that her father's decisions were irrevocable.

'What am I going to do?' She and Harriet had ridden out to their favourite view of the sea at Foz, and were sitting in the shade of a wild vine that grew riotously up a neglected cork tree. 'I must have money to send home. Your mother won't wait for ever; why should she?'

'I'm sure she won't do anything rash.' But Harriet did not sound entirely certain. 'Do you think your cousin would help?'

'How could I explain?' She looked unseeingly at the distant view of the castle at Foz and the blue horizon beyond. 'I know he said he would help if I needed it, but, Harryo, how could I ask him for money?' They sat silent for a few minutes, sharing the thought of Jeremy's friendly visits and the way he talked about Rachel Emerson.

'He's beglamoured,' said Harriet at last.

'If only I liked her.'

'How could you?'

'How can he?'

'It's not liking with him.'

'No.' Why did she mind it so much? 'Time we turned back,' she said, more cheerfully than she felt. 'The grooms are getting restless.'

'Yes.' Harriet laughed. 'Views are just not in

154

their line. But what a beautiful country yours is, Cat. No wonder you care about it so.'

'Do I?' said Caterina thoughtfully. 'I suppose I do, but, Harryo, it may be beautiful, but don't you feel it's cruel too, and stupid.' She longed to tell Harriet about Luiz's plans for a happier country.

'Oh dear, yes.' Harriet was thinking of something else. 'Had you thought of trying to sell your pictures?'

'My pictures?' She had been about to kick her mule into movement, but paused.

'Not the people.' Laughing. 'We all know about those. But the little pictures of places and things that you do so well. Might not there be a market for them?'

'Goodness, I wonder. Harriet, I'll think about it.'

'Give it a try,' said Harriet.

'It would have to be to the British.'

'An argument for Mrs Ware's party.'

'Well, I am glad there is one.'

'Oh, I think there are several,' said Harriet cheerfully.

*   *   *

Frank Ware had been across the river at Villa Nova de Gaia for a gloomy look at the disused family wine vaults that should have been a scene of so much activity at this time of year. Built into the slope of the hill close under the

155

Serra Monastery, the wine lodges had been used as barracks by the French during the short time they had held Porto in 1809, and repairing the damage they had caused had broken his father's heart, he thought, as well as going near to bankrupting him. But at least Mr Ware senior was not alive now to realise what a serious mistake he had made in selling the vineyards he held near Porto in order to invest extensively in the new lands that had been opened up by the clearing of the dangerous rapids at Cachao de Valeira on the Upper Douro. The land up near the border had been cheap, the conditions for growing the port grape admirable; how was his father to know that the area would be a battlefield one day? But now it meant that whereas other firms that had kept their vineyards on the Lower Douro were still in business in a small way, his own company was at a complete standstill, with maintenance of the huge, cool cellars in the hillside slowly eating away at what capital remained.

And today the old caretaker had pointed out a new leak that would be a disaster when the autumn rains began in earnest. It must be repaired, and here was his mother running him into debt with this elaborate party. Ridiculous. He had neither been facing facts himself nor making her do so. He was not going to propose to Caterina Gomez. He did not love her, and, he was increasingly sure, she would not have him if he were to ask her. Without a word spoken, she had told him this in all kinds of friendly, quiet ways. It would not be the act of the gentleman he hoped he was to propose and put the burden of refusal on to her. Her father seldom appeared, but his shadow lay heavy on the house. He did not like to think how very uncomfortable Caterina's life would be if she offended him. And then there was Father Pedro, whose silent approach so often broke up the brief *tête à têtes* he managed to secure with Harriet Brown. He rather thought it was Father Pedro's constant intrusions that had made him realise he loved Harriet. And what a wife she would make for a working man. There was not an ounce of pretension or snobbery about Harriet. How long had he been thinking of her by her Christian name? I must get work, he thought. I must start earning my way. And came down to the river to see Major Dickson on the quay.

'You're back! I am so very glad to see you.' He hurried forward to wring his friend's hand. 'But what's the news?' Dickson looked exhausted, he thought, as if he had not slept for days, but cheerful just the same.

'Good, thank God. But it was a near run thing. Some of the rumours we've been hearing were true enough. Marmont did manage to give Wellington the slip up there in the mountains and throw supplies into Ciudad Rodrigo, and there was a moment when it

157

looked as if he had Wellington just where he wanted him, but by a miracle old Hooky escaped. He's good at miracles, is Lord Wellington. I can tell you, my friend, it was touch and go up there for a day or so, but trust Wellington to smell his way out of danger. Now it's to be winter quarters, and a little pleasure for us all. And the best of it is, Marmont's men had eaten up most of the rations that were meant for Ciudad Rodrigo. They only got in supplies for a month or so. They'll be hungry in that fortress when we come on them in the spring.' And then: 'Forget I said that, Frank. Or rather, remember that, if you agree, I want to take you on the strength. I don't need to read you a lecture about official secrets first, do I?'

'Of course not. You really want me? I can't tell you what good news that is.'

'I don't just want you, I need you and your local knowledge. It's like this—' He took Frank's arm and walked him a little downstream, away from the crowded quay, to a place where a convent stood a little back from the river. Its landing stage was deserted and they sat down there on a baulk of timber. Dickson was silent for a moment, looking at the busy scene on the river, marshalling his thoughts. Then: 'I probably don't need to tell you that Wellington plans ahead. He's not going to find himself short of big guns again. He ordered a siege train out from England,

158

back last winter, and when it reached Lisbon in July he had it shipped up here at once. It is upriver from here that he plans to make his next move. In fact, there is no need any more to be secret about that. Marmont learned about it early this month; that's why he went to the relief of Ciudad Rodrigo. He must have an informer here in Oporto, Frank, and I want you to keep your eyes and ears open as to who it may be.'

'I certainly will. But that's hardly the work you mean?' Frank was at once flattered and disappointed.

'No, no. That's just a sideline. You must have shared the general curiosity about the heavy loads that came out from England on the *Anthea* and the *Chloe*.'

'There has been talk, of course. Mainly because they were so very swiftly and efficiently trans-shipped.'

'Yes, that was efficient enough!' Savagely. 'Wait till I tell you the rest. When the first shipments of the siege train got upriver to Lamego and were unloaded, they discovered that there were no block carriages for the guns. Would you believe it, Frank? Guns and no carriages for them. They've been getting them across the mountains—you could hardly call them roads—on their own carriages or on makeshift sledges, but the result has been all kinds of damage to their wheels. We need wheelwrights, Frank, urgently, at Lamego.

And carpenters.' He laughed angrily. 'The minute Wellington heard of the lack of stock carriages he sent off an urgent appeal to London. They came out on the *Anthea* and the *Chloe*. Only they are the wrong size! Each one will have to be altered. Wheelwrights and carpenters. That's your job, Frank. As many as you can find, the best of their kind, ready for a hard winter's work upriver. The pay will be good, the conditions hard, tell them. I rely on your local knowledge to help me on this. I don't need to tell you how important it is.'

'No. I can see that. But where will they be working? Will it be at Lamego or further on? They will want to know that.'

'I suppose they will.' Reluctantly. 'And, yes, it may well be further on. There are broken-down gun carriages lying by the roads all the way up to Villa da Ponte. They must be ready for anything. And no women, Frank, no wives, no followers. This is serious, secret work.'

'Yes, I can see. Am I allowed to ask what the guns are for?'

'Of course you may ask, and I shall tell you what everyone is being told, and the obvious answer at that. They are to reinforce the fortress at Almeida. It's vital to the defence of the border, and I am sure you remember how the French garrison there managed to give our people the slip, destroyed the defences and got clean away in the night, thanks to some appalling incompetence on our part. It

160

wouldn't have happened if Wellington had been there. He means to refurbish it and have it solid at his back before he moves.'

'Defence is the best mode of attack,' said Frank thoughtfully.

Dickson laughed. 'That's it, my boy, that's just it. But let's take my good news across the river; it's just the tonic Oporto needs, I'm sure.'

'It certainly is,' agreed Frank. 'And, Dickson, I am more grateful to you than I can say. I'll start work at once.' They had got up and were moving back upriver to where the ferry crossed. 'I hope this means you will be in town for a while now. My mother is having a party next week; I know she would wish me to invite you.'

'I'll certainly try to be here, but of course it depends on Lord Wellington's plans; we shall be busy enough for a while before the men are fixed in winter quarters.'

'Upriver?'

'Most certainly. Out of mischief's way. But the officers will be another matter, naturally. Your mother may find herself with more distinguished company than she had expected if she is entertaining next week. There was talk, when I came away, that Lord Wellington himself was thinking of making a bolt for it down here for a few days of business and pleasure, and you know what a one he is for sniffing out a private party with ladies present.'

'My mother would be immensely honoured.'

For the first time, Frank thought with satisfaction of his mother's lavish preparations.

'There will be a dinner at the Factory, of course,' said Dickson, as they approached the landing stage. 'Men only, naturally. Not the same thing at all. And not a word to a soul till I give you leave. Not even your mother. You know the ladies, God bless 'em.' And he turned the conversation to indifferent topics as they boarded the boat.

*   *   *

'Major Dickson is back.' Ralph Emerson came in from the balcony to join Rachel. 'Chatting away like an old friend with young Ware. Have you heard anything from the old lady, by the way?'

'Not a word. I did try and give a hint to Miss Gomez, but I'm not at all sure that she took it. She's a close one, that girl, there is no getting to her. And Miss Brown nothing but her dutiful echo. That's a terrible house, Ralph, I'm glad I don't live there. There is a feeling of listening in the air.'

'You and your feelings! I wish you would feel us out an invitation to the Wares' party; I don't need to tell you how badly we need it.'

'No. I wonder if Mr Craddock ... But it's hard to see just how to set about it...'

'He'd give you the sun and the moon and the

stars if he could, poor young fool.'

'Yes, I believe he would, but he can't, can he? And the odd thing is I'm not quite sure that he would get me an invitation to Mrs Ware's party, even if he could, and knew I wanted it. There is something about him that I don't quite understand, some corner he keeps to himself. It worries me a little.'

'You had better step up the pressure a little had you not?'

'It's too soon, Ralph. This is a difficult one; I'm feeling my way; you must leave me alone to handle it as I think best.'

'That's all very well, but what about the Wares' party? We have to be there. What's that?' Irritably, as a servant knocked and entered with a note for Rachel. 'A *billet doux?*'

'No.' She was looking at it with amazement. 'It is an invitation to Mrs Ware's party.'

*   *   *

Caterina and Harriet were discussing the party too. 'We shall look a proper pair of fools if Madame Feuillide doesn't finish our dresses in time,' said Caterina impatiently. The continued silence of both Luiz and the dressmaker was beginning to tell on her nerves.

'I have been doing some work on the ones we started for ourselves,' said Harriet. 'They would be quite out of the ordinary, you know.'

'Yes, but is that what the English colony expects?'

'Do we care what they expect?'

'I wish I knew.' Caterina thought about it for a moment. 'Nothing has worked out as we planned, has it?'

'Nothing ever does, it seems to me.' Harriet was looking over Caterina's shoulder at the picture she was working on. 'I think you have got it just right now. They'll love them!'

'But will they buy them?'

'I was thinking about that,' said Harriet. 'Had it struck you, Cat, that in a way you can't lose.'

'What in the world do you mean?'

'You aren't thinking, Cat. How long, as things go here in Porto, will it take for your father to hear that you are selling pictures to your lady friends? And how will he like it?'

'Oh,' said Caterina.

'Precisely. And if he wants you to stop, he will have to pay you to. Either way, you get the money you need. And we do need to send it by the next boat, love, or I would indeed be worried. Mother is not a patient woman.'

'I almost wish we hadn't come,' said Caterina.

'What else could we do? Don't look so desperate, Cat. Mother is not wicked, she is just hard-headed. Well, she has to be. It's a woman's lot. Specially a poor woman's. Don't ever forget that when times are hard for the likes of us they are really hard. It's not just inconvenience, it's starvation. Sometimes I look at myself in the glass, here in the luxury of your father's house, and can hardly believe what I see.'

'Do you think he is hungry?' asked Caterina.

'Oh, Cat, I do hope not.' It was the best she could do for her friend, and she was almost relieved when a servant appeared with an unusual summons for Caterina to her father's study.

'At once?' asked Caterina, with a quick glance for Harriet.

'If you will, *minha senhora*. The holy father is with him.'

'Oh.' This was not good news. 'I'll come, of course.'

* * *

The two men were seated on either side of Senhor Gomez's huge writing desk. Both made token gestures towards rising when she entered the room, and the friar muttered a statutory blessing.

She curtseyed, bowed her head for the blessing, took the upright chair that had been placed facing the desk. 'You sent for me, father?'

'Yes. Father Pedro has heard a rumour that we find disquieting.'

'Porto is full of rumours, always.'

165

'You will not bandy words with us, Caterina. You have been here for almost a month now. Father Pedro made your position entirely clear to you when you arrived and we had thought, by your behaviour, that you had understood it. We had expected an announcement at Mrs Ware's party next week, and now what do we learn?' He paused impressively for the question she would not ask.

'You appear to have lost your cavalier,' Father Pedro spoke into the little silence. 'Why would Mr Ware seek work with the British army if he was expecting to make an advantageous match?'

'Is he?' Now she was forced to the question.

'You did not know?' This was Senhor Gomez.

'He has not called for a few days.'

'Because he is busy recruiting labour for the British. And you did not know?'

'Nor that he had been making chances to see Miss Brown alone?' asked Father Pedro inexorably.

'Which leaves your other gallant,' said her father. 'And we do not get the impression that he has been exactly punctilious in his attentions.'

'Everyone knows he is making a fool of himself over that imposter of a clairvoyante,' said Father Pedro. 'You seem not to have been applying your mind to the matter in hand,

166

daughter. You will hardly get a husband by riding about the countryside with Miss Brown. Even if there had been a chance of it, no respectable Portuguese gentleman would think of you after the hoydenish way you have been carrying on since you got back here to Porto. So your father has decided, in his great goodness, to give you one last warning. His house has been turned upside down for quite long enough. Female frills and female talk. You have until after this party—there is so much talk about. Find yourself a suitable husband, English or Portuguese, one your father need not be ashamed to have as his heir, and you shall be married as the daughter of this house should be. Or it will be the Little Sisters of St Seraphina. And this house quiet again.'

'But—so soon?' It was the first of the protests that thronged in her mind.

'You had your warning. It is not good for your father's health, still less for his spiritual well-being, to have so much disturbance in his house. Talk and laughter in the hallways, guests coming and going ... And besides, there is the burden of the estate. You have not thought to notice, I think, that your father is not a well man, not fit to bear the burden of all his business affairs. It is time for him to compose his mind for the life hereafter. Give him a son-in-law who will bear his burdens and the problem is solved. Or you know your alternative. Take yourself—and that Miss

Brown—off to the Sisters of St Seraphina and I and my brothers can step in and take the burden of his affairs off his hands.'

'No!' Now she saw it all. Idiotic not to have done so sooner. Of course Father Pedro had left her alone, he had hoped for just this outcome, this rich estate for his brotherhood.

'Father—' She turned to her real father, hands outstretched, to say ... to say what?

But he was already rising to leave the room.

CHAPTER NINE

'It's all my fault,' said Harriet. 'If you hadn't brought me, Cat, they might have been able to bear it, those two cross old men.'

'There was no way I could have come without you. Never think that. But what are we going to do, Harryo? If only I would hear from Luiz!'

'Your father would never accept him. You're not thinking, Cat. A proclaimed traitor.'

'If I told my father what he told me? About the free Kingdom of Lusitania?'

'He wouldn't listen, or believe you. And would your Luiz let him tell Father Pedro? He'd be bound to, you know.'

'No. Never. He is deeply sworn to secrecy, and so am I! I didn't mean to tell you, Harryo dear.'

'I know.' Smiling. 'I wormed it out of you, didn't I? And I'm glad I did. I long to meet your Luiz.'

'I long to see him,' said Caterina. 'Or at least hear something. But you're right, of course. He would never agree to my telling my father. How could he, when he has resigned himself to waiting until the war is over to clear his name.'

'All very well for him,' said Harriet. 'But it hardly helps you, does it?'

'Nothing seems to help me. But the first thing is money for your mother. Next time Jeremy Craddock comes, I will ask him for a loan. There's no one else to turn to. If I tell him about my pictures, show them to him, perhaps he will believe that I will be able to repay him presently.'

'If your father has not shut you up in that convent,' said Harriet. 'I think you should tell your cousin about that threat. He did promise to help, after all.'

'And might feel forced to offer me marriage if he thought me hard pressed enough. And we both know how he talks of Rachel Emerson. Never, Harryo!'

'Oh, very well.' Harriet looked at her friend with surprise, and some interest.

It was a relief to both of them when a summons arrived, for the day after next, from Madame Feuillide. 'It must mean Luiz is back,' said Caterina. 'I think I have to tell him everything, don't you?'

'I wish I could meet him,' said Harriet.

Caterina received another summons that same afternoon, one that amazed her. 'It's from Luiz's grandmother,' she told Harriet after a swift look at the signature. 'Father Pedro told me she was mad, but her note doesn't read like that.'

'When did you start believing what Father Pedro told you?'

'You're quite right. I'm a fool, Harriet, she wants to see me. It reads like a royal command.' She handed over the brief note.

'It does, doesn't it? "Tomorrow, first thing. Ask for my son. You will be brought to me." Will you go, Cat?'

'Of course. She is his grandmother.'

'"Alone," she says.' Harriet had been re-reading the note. 'How will you manage it, Cat?' They were out on the terrace, quite alone, and she was glad of it.

Caterina had been thinking about this too. It was unthinkable that a young unmarried lady should call on an older widowed man, but that was what the old lady told her to do. Strange suddenly to remember her so clearly. She had been a formidable old autocrat who kept to her own wing, sending out, from time to time, a sharp instruction that the children should play more quietly. It was an order that was always obeyed, but the old lady had been loved as well as feared, she remembered. Well, she was going

170

to obey her now. But how? Father Pedro had told her the Sanchez house was a fortress, and it had looked like one when she and Harriet had driven by: closed, shuttered, lifeless. Impossible to drive up to that forbidding entrance and demand admission. She made up her mind. 'You will help me, Harryo?'

'You know I will.'

'We'll take our sewing and a cold collation down to the second terrace early in the morning, before the hour of visits, the time when Father Pedro prays with my father. I shall go on down and cross the ravine—don't look so anxious, there is a path, it's just a long stride. The servants do it all the time so there must be a way up on the other side. And you will sit and sew and look as if butter wouldn't melt in your mouth, and if a servant should bring a note, which is the worst that could happen, you'll blush a bit and suggest I am off on a natural errand.'

'But are you sure you will be able to get across?' Less active than Caterina, Harriet had only been down to the bottom of the garden once. 'That gap looks too wide to me. I am sure it's only menservants who cross.'

'I'll wear my fullest skirt and take my scissors, slit it if necessary. I have to go, Harriet, and this is the only way. Think! She may have news of Luiz, something may have happened to him. They were always devoted to each other.'

'Then of course you must go,' agreed Harriet. 'Don't worry, I'll keep guard for you. I just hope the weather doesn't choose to break.'

'No, all we need is the first autumn rainstorm and God knows what I would do. There is no way I can use the front door without causing a storm of talk in the town.'

But the next day dawned fine and clear and the servants showed no more than their usual amazement at the young *senhora*'s odd habits when Caterina announced that she and Harriet were going to breakfast in the garden.

'Time to go.' Caterina stood up when the last dish had been removed. 'Now, you must stay here, Harriet, and hold the fort for me.'

'Do be careful, Cat.'

'Believe me, I will.'

No water was running yet down in the crevasse, though it looked very deep and alarmingly wider than she had remembered. But the signs that other people had crossed were obvious enough. Men in breeches or women in skirts? Now she looked at it with a calculating eye, she thought it must only have been men. She looked down at her muslin skirts, took out her scissors, changed her mind. It was going to be odd enough to appear from the bottom of the Sanchez's garden without compounding the offence by doing so in a slit skirt. It was only one long stride, she told herself, and not a soul in sight. She hitched her skirts to her waist, took a deep breath, and

172

strode it.

How strange to find herself once more in these gardens where she had played so happily as a child, and to think of all the later times when Luiz had come hurrying down this path to stride across the chasm and meet her in the little summerhouse. Strange too to think that she had never even paused to look at the ruins of the little building where all her life had been changed. No time now to look back, she started up the long series of terraces to the house that was set much further back from the river than her own.

It was all very quiet. The grapes had already been picked on the terraces that faced the sun, and the vines pruned back for the autumn. It was only when she got up to the top terrace of all that she saw an old gardener she remembered raking gravel between yew hedges, and summoned him imperiously. This must be carried off with a high hand. 'You there, tell Senhor Sanchez that the Senhora Gomez has called on him.'

He gaped at her for a moment, then swept off his battered straw hat in salute. 'The Senhora Gomez! A sight for sore eyes if ever there was one. I'll tell them in the house, *minha senhora*.' And he hurried away towards a servants' entrance, leaving her to stand and look at the view upriver towards the Serra and remind herself that there was no way she could be seen from the terraces of her own house.

She did not have long to wait. A small black-clad woman came bustling out of the house, hands outstretched. 'The Senhora Caterina, I thank the good God and all his angels. My lady said you would be sure to come, but I could hardly see how you would manage. But, come, she longs to see you.'

'How is she, Carlotta?' It had taken her a moment to recognise the woman, so aged and thin and anxious was she.

'Old, *minha senhora*. Old and so brave. She is holding this household together with her two hands, her two poor hands. But you will see. Come! No, this way.' Caterina had turned automatically to the remote wing where the old lady used to live. 'The master is there now. It is better so.' And before Caterina could ask the next question she had thrown open the door of the house's main salon, a room Caterina could never remember entering before.

'Caterina, dear child!' The old lady sat enthroned in a massive straight-backed chair. 'I won't get up. It is too painful. Come and kiss me, child, and say you forgive us.' She held out hands knotted into hard lumps, and Caterina took them very gently and bent to kiss the cold, white cheek.

'Forgive?' she asked.

'For what we have done to you between us. My fool of a son told me nothing at the time, thought he was sheltering me. He shelter me! It's a sad joke now. By the time I found out

174

from the servants it was too late. Your father had sent you off to England, and Luiz— Caterina, I have sent for you to talk about Luiz.'

'I'm so glad,' said Caterina

'You won't be. Sit down, child, here where I can touch you.' One of the gnarled hands pressed Caterina gently down on to the stool set ready by the big chair, and rested lovingly on her shoulder. 'Do they still call you Cat?'

'My friend Miss Brown does.'

'I am glad you have her. A true friend. Yes?'

'Yes.'

'Your father has not changed.'

It was not really a question, but Caterina answered it just the same. 'No, and now he has Father Pedro.'

'I have heard about him. I may live shut up here, but I know what is going on. It just takes a little longer. I thought there was plenty of time. I am afraid I was wrong. You have seen my grandson, have you not?'

'Yes.' What was it about the old lady's tone that chilled her so?

'And believed his lies?'

'Lies?'

'Yes, lies. It hurts me as much to tell you, Caterina, as it will you to hear, but I must. I owe it to you for having failed you before, when you were sent off to England. My grandson has sold out to the French.'

'Oh, no, ma'am, you're wrong!' Caterina

175

breathed a deep sigh of relief. 'That's just what he is letting people think. He explained it all to me, but it is the deepest of secrets. If he did not feel he could tell you, I must not.'

'You believed him?'

'Of course I believed him.'

'But should you have?' The hand was moving gently, lovingly on her shoulder. 'Think hard about it, and listen to what I must tell you. There are two sides to it, and I don't know which is the worst.' She took an audible, hard breath. 'Yes, I do. When your father found the two of you, down in that summerhouse, it was Romeo and Juliet, was it not? Whoever loved that loved not at first sight?'

'I'm glad you understand—'

'It's you who don't understand, Caterina. Forgive me, but I have to tell you. Did you ever notice that all our maids were ugly, here in this house?'

'We used to laugh about it.'

'A pity you never thought about it, but why should you have, the child that you were. Now, you must. We hired ugly maids, my daughter and I, because if they were pretty, Luiz seduced them. We had sent two home, pregnant, to their families—What is it?' Her hand had felt the shock in Caterina.

'I can't believe it.'

'You must, child, because it is true. I do passionately hope that nothing has happened

176

between you and Luiz this time, that at least Madame Feuillide was there to protect you from that.' She did not quite make it a question.

'Madame Feuillide! You know about her?' It was all too much to take in at once.

'To my cost. I have no doubt she told you her romantic tale of flight from the French revolutionaries, and safe asylum here in Portugal. Did she tell you who gave her that asylum?'

'No.'

'I did. We had been at school together in Paris. She was one of the little ones, but of course, when she came to me here I helped her. She rewarded me by seducing my son-in-law. Luiz was just a baby then. Perhaps my daughter was too wrapped up in him. God knows he was a beautiful child, one to warm your heart. They never had another. Things were never the same between them after I got rid of Madame Feuillide. Just as well. She had made him unfit to father a child. I am sorry to have to tell you this, but you need to know. He's mad now, shut up. I let it be thought that it is I who am out of my mind, for very shame at his condition, and its cause. I regret that now. It was a mistake. One of the many mistakes I have made. And now I have to save you from paying my reckoning. You met Luiz at Madame Feuillide's did you not? No breach of secrecy in admitting it; I have had a watch kept on her for many years. I know you did.'

'But why?'

'Because I did not trust her. Well, I had cause enough for that. How did she manage for money after we turned her out, my daughter and I? She has had no more help from us. That's not what she told you?'

'No.' She had to admit it.

'And I have no doubt that she told you the French missed her poor little house when they advanced on Porto.'

'Yes. By a miracle, she said.'

'A well-arranged one! But I have no proof that she is acting as a French agent. It's been so difficult, shut up here as I am, thought to be crazy. Nobody would believe a word I said, they'd just call me an old madwoman and probably shut me up in a convent, and then what would happen to my son-in-law and the estate? I can't risk it. I'm counting on you, Caterina.'

'On me?' Caterina was numbly trying to grapple with all the horrors she had heard. The unspeakable thing was that they made sense. Older, wiser and sadder now, she looked back on that brief passionate romance with Luiz and realised that the inexperience had been all on her side. How should she have known it then? And if he had been false in this, why believe anything he had told her?

'Did he ask you questions?'

'Yes.' She had to face it. 'Yes, he did. He

178

wanted me to find things out for him. But, you see—It's not what you think ...' She stumbled to a halt. Was she sure of this? Was she sure of anything? 'I think I have to tell you,' she said at last. 'He made me promise not to say a word, but I think I have to tell you.'

'I think so too, child. I promise it shall go no further. Perhaps I am doing him a grave injustice, just because of my suspicions of Madame Feuillide. God knows how much I hope that I am. We loved him so much, my daughter and I. Too much, I sometimes think, poor Luiz.'

'Me too,' said Caterina, horribly aware of the old lady's use of the past tense. But she too was a lifetime away from the passionate child who had run down the long terraces to lose herself in her lover's arms. 'It was wonderful,' she said. 'We were so happy. We really were, ma'am, both of us. It was real. It was right. I am sure of that. Why didn't they let us marry? I think it would have worked if we had been allowed to marry.' Was she really putting it all in the past?

'Perhaps,' said the old lady sadly. 'I don't know, child, about that. What's bred in the bone, you know. But that is just what I asked, when I heard about it, so much too late, after I got back from visiting my other daughter in Lisbon. The two houses, the two wine lodges, what could have been more suitable? I have no doubt that was what Luiz had in mind, and if I had been there that is what would have happened. I wonder if you would be grateful to me now? But I was away. Your father came storming around to the house, my daughter fainted and took to her bed—she was like that, poor Joaquina—and the two men came to blows. Fatal. There was no hope of rational discussion after that. Your father sent you off to England without another word, my son-in-law and Luiz said things to each other that neither of them ever forgot or forgave. I think Luiz found out about Madame Feuillide around then, his father had gone on seeing her, you see. No wonder she managed to infect him so fatally. I'm sorry, child. I am speaking to you as the grown-up woman you have to be.'

'I am,' said Caterina. 'Poor Luiz, I do begin to understand a little. And then the French came—'

'Yes, the French came, with their fine talk. You can have no idea, Caterina, how strange, how dangerous things were here in Porto, those two months that Soult was here. There was wrong on both sides during the fighting, remember. I think there always is. Innocent prisoners in the Porto gaols were dragged out by the mob and slaughtered in the streets. One of them was Luiz's best friend. They had joined the Loyal Lusitanian Legion together; he had been arrested on some idiotic charge; it was all a mistake; you know what the law is like here in Portugal. But I don't think even that was the worst of it for Luiz. You remember that my other daughter and her family went to the Brazils with the royal family?'

'No, I had quite forgotten.'

'A terrible mistake,' said the old lady. 'If a Braganza were to enter this room tomorrow, I would not stand up and curtsey. Of course Luiz was tormented about it in the Lusitanian Legion; you know how men torment each other. Worse than women, I think. He was all at odds with everything when he met that French Captain d'Argenton who led the conspiracy against Soult. Can you blame him for believing the promise of an independent kingdom of Lusitania under the benevolent auspices of a reformed French republic, free from Napoleon?'

'But that's just it!' Caterina was delighted not to have to betray Luiz's secret. 'That is what he believes, what he and his friends are working for.'

'How I wish I thought you were right. I'm sure he did at first. He went with the French, when they had to run for it from Porto, in the hopes of helping to engineer d'Argenton's escape.'

'And d'Argenton did escape.' Eagerly.

'Yes. Up in the mountains, in the rain. Whether Luiz had much to do with it I rather doubt. He wouldn't have been trusted very far, then, such a recent renegade from our side. But now, two years later, he turns up again under

181

the auspices of Madame Feuillide. What are we to think of that?'

'You are so sure she is a French agent?'

'Short of proof, yes. That is where I am counting on you, Caterina. What did he want from you? It wasn't just to talk of old times, was it?' The hand on the back of her neck managed to be wonderfully friendly.

'No. He wanted information. Asked me a lot of questions. I have been trying to find the answers to them.'

'Such as—'

'The cargo of our ship; Lord Wellington's plans; the news from upriver. He said it was for his friends, the Friends of Democracy. So they would be ready when their chance came.'

'And so it could have been, I'd almost believe it, were it not for Madame Feuillide. And for what I now feel about my grandson. Don't trust him, Caterina, I do beg that you will not trust him. And for God's sake, don't yield to him. I feel that you haven't?'

'You are right.' It was an odd relief to have that clear between them.

'And now I hope you understand why I feel that we have a duty, you and I, to find out what he is really doing. Whether these "Friends of Democracy" really exist. And you are the one who can do it. When are you next seeing him?'

'Tomorrow, I hope. But, ma'am, you can't be asking me to spy on Luiz?'

'Why not, if he is a spy himself? And if he is

not, we will see to it that you do him no harm. But I am afraid I should be very much surprised. For me, the connection with Madame Feuillide is damning. And, I have to say this. She is an attractive woman still, they tell me.'

'In a sort of a way—' For a moment she did not understand. Then, 'You can't mean ... after his father ... impossible!'

'I wish I was sure of that. I wish now that I had told him she was the cause of his father's illness, but at the time it seemed impossible ... Oh, Caterina, so many mistakes I have made...'

'You mean, he knows of the association—'

'But not the infection. And, I'm afraid, being Luiz, he might have felt it a challenge. I do beg you, Caterina, harden your heart against him.'

'And spy on him?' asked Caterina bleakly.

'At least, don't let him make you a spy. Which you will be, Caterina, if you take him answers to his questions.'

'If you are right. But, ma'am, suppose this really is his chance to prove himself with these Friends of Democracy. To rehabilitate himself. And I spoil it for him. I'd never forgive myself.'

'No,' said the old lady. 'But on the other hand, Caterina, would you forgive yourself if your information led to the defeat of Wellington and the fall of Porto?'

'Never. But how can we be sure?'

183

'I am sure, Caterina, and he is my grandson, the only hope of my house. I am so sure that if only I had proof I would hand him over to the British tomorrow.'

'The British?'

'He'd be safer with them than with the Portuguese. He may be a traitor, Caterina, but he is the sole heir to two great houses. I want him to live, and repent, and get a son.'

'But he has a son.' It was out, irrevocably.

'What?' The cherishing hand was suddenly still.

'My son.' Caterina's voice was steady. 'When I got to England. I didn't understand what was happening to me, but the nuns did. They recognized it quite soon after I got to the convent. I owe them a great debt. It has taken me a while to realise just how great. They told no one, those good nuns. Just sent me to a woman with a house outside Bath who made a living out of such cases. She was good to me in her way, and there were companions in misfortune. Harriet, my friend Miss Brown, was one of them, but her baby died, poor thing. That made me realise, for the first time, how lucky I was. He's everything I have in the world, ma'am, my Lewis.'

'But how? Where is he? He must be almost three years old.'

'Yes, walking and talking, a fine boy, beautiful ... I thought my heart would break when they took him away and made me go

184

back to the convent. He was given to Harriet to suckle. It's a great bond between us. I think she loves him almost as much as I do. The nuns put it about that I had been visiting my grandmother in Wales. And they were kind, they let me see him sometimes, and they let me teach the little ones so I could pay for his keep. And then I did an idiotic thing. I can take a likeness, ma'am, I enjoy doing it. But they are not always flattering. Mother Superior found one I had done of her. I can't blame her for being furious, after all she had done for me. She said I must go at once; I was a bad influence. I was to go to my grandmother in Wales, but my cousin Jeremy Craddock arrived just then with my father's summons. I thought there was more hope in coming here, that perhaps I would be able to tell my father, that he would help. Or that Luiz...'

'Have you told Luiz?'

'No. Somehow, I didn't, I'm not quite sure why; I meant to tomorrow.' She found herself yet again slipping into the past tense.

'Don't,' said the old lady. 'Don't trust him with that. At least, not yet. But, Caterina, this changes everything. I have an heir.' The hand had resumed its gentle stroking as she almost chanted the words.

'But, ma'am, you're forgetting. Poor little Lewis, he's not ... He's got no name.'

'He shall have mine. Not Sanchez but Fonsa. You'll be surprised, child, what money can buy.'

'Money? I don't understand.'

'You don't, do you, and I love you for it. It's my money keeps this place going. We were cousins, my husband and I, both Fonsas. But I had the money. My family's lawyers did not trust my husband—they were right, by the way—they tied it up so tight he never got his hands on the capital. Money is power, Caterina. If you don't know that already you will soon learn. Oh, there is so much to be thought of, so splendidly much! We must put our heads together and think how we are going to manage things. I'll talk to my lawyers. They will work out a story for me. He must come out here, of course, be baptised in the cathedral, brought up as the *fidalgo* he will be. Oh, what a happy day.'

Caterina opened her mouth to say, 'But he is *my* son,' and closed it again. Overriding instinct warned her to go very carefully here. The old lady might not be mad, but was she entirely sane? Instead of the instinctive protest, she framed a practical question. 'How shall I get in touch with you, ma'am, to tell you about Luiz?'

'Best not come here again.' The old lady thought about it. 'The lawyers are bound to take their time. We don't want any rumours until it is all settled. Your father might so easily do something crazy.' And so might you, thought Caterina. 'I have it,' the old lady went

186

on. 'You'll write to me. Carlotta's grandson is courting your poor Maria's daughter. They go to and fro across the gorge all the time. I pretend not to know, but it will be useful now. Give your letter to Tonio; it will reach me in a day and I'll answer by the same route until everything is clear for us. But, oh, what a happy day.' She folded Caterina in her arms for a long, stifling, almost frightening kiss.

CHAPTER TEN

Harriet was beginning to think that Caterina had been gone a very long time when Sancho appeared with Frank Ware following close on his heels. 'I know it is shockingly early, but I had to be the first to tell you the news.' If he noticed Caterina's absence it was only to be glad of it. 'It's the deepest of secrets, of course.' With a glance for the man.

'That will be all, Sancho.' She managed a good imitation of Caterina's tone, and decided as she did so that she would simply say nothing about her friend's absence. Why should she? She sat down again and picked up her needlework. 'What is this splendid secret news? Or should you be telling me?'

'Of course I should. In fact, my mother asked me to, she said it was only right that you two young ladies should know. It's about our party next week; we have hopes of a very distinguished guest indeed. Mother hopes Miss Gomez will not mind if she finds herself not exactly the guest of honour after all. I know you won't.'

'Well I never was,' said Harriet cheerfully. 'I am just grateful to your mother for asking me at all. I can't tell you how much I am looking forward to it. It will be my first dress party and I only hope I won't do anything silly because of not knowing how to go on.'

'I shall look after you,' he promised. 'And I know you will behave just like the lady you are. And because you are, you won't mind if some of my mother's friends seem a little stiff; it's a curious ingrown society we British have here in Oporto. I didn't mind it when I was young but sometimes now I do find myself wondering if this is where I want to spend the rest of my life.'

'But have you much choice?' asked Harriet.

'I am beginning to hope that perhaps I may have. My friend Major Dickson has offered me worthwhile work to do, here in Oporto, and seems to think that it might even lead on to something back in England, if I make a job of it. Which reminds me that I had hoped for some help and advice from Miss Gomez.' For the first time he looked around as if wondering where she was.

Harriet was still casting around for an explanation, when to her relief Caterina came sauntering up from the lower terrace, with a bunch of grapes in her hand. 'Good morning Mr Ware. See what I found! My favourite vine run made all over the summerhouse. Have some, they are delicious.' She handed the bunch to Harriet, smiled at Frank. 'You are an early caller. I hope it means you are the bearer of good, not bad news.'

'It's good.' Harriet was aware of coiled tension in her friend. 'Tell her, Mr Ware.'

'My mother sent me, Miss Gomez.' He came to a halt. What had been easy to say to Harriet seemed surprisingly difficult now.

'They are expecting an immensely important guest at their party.' Harriet came to his help. 'So we are to put on our very best dresses and smiles, Cat, and not mind too much if we don't seem to be quite the guests of honour we thought to be.'

'Goodness,' said Caterina. 'Who can it be that is to take the wind so out of our sails?'

'It's a deadly secret,' Harriet told her. 'Mr Ware has not named the important guest, but I can make a guess, cannot you? I do hope I am right.'

'I expect you are,' said Frank Ware. 'There is really only one man, here in Portugal just now, is there not? But Miss Gomez, I am also come to ask your help.'

'Mine?' Surprised.

'Yes. Once again, this is entirely between ourselves, but my friend Major Dickson has asked me to do a job of work for him. He needs

189

wheelwrights and carpenters, urgently, and has asked me to use my local knowledge to find them for him. I thought it would be easy, with times so hard here in Oporto, but the trouble is, the work is upriver, at Pinhel and even further, and it is turning out more difficult than I expected. I was wondering if you, with your local knowledge, could perhaps help me in this?'

'I am sure I can. Old Antonio was telling me the other day about a cousin of his, a carpenter, who is desperate for work. And he will very likely have friends ... But Mr Ware, it is all very well to say it is a secret affair, but one will have to give the men some idea of what they are to be doing.'

'Repairing gun carriages,' he told her. 'That's the wheelwrights, of course. And the carpenters are to alter the ones that came out on the *Anthea* with you, Miss Gomez. They are the wrong size, would you believe it, for the guns Lord Wellington has got up on the border.'

'So that's what we brought,' said Caterina.

'Oh yes, everyone knows that now. Even the French. That is why Masséna made that last effort to get supplies into Ciudad Rodrigo. His spies had told him that Wellington's next move would be up there on the border. And Wellington is busy re-arming the fortress at Almeida as a base for such a move. That is what I am allowed to tell the men I hire, but I

190

have to say it surprised me to find the Beau thinking in such defensive terms.'

'The Beau?' asked Harriet.

'That's what his officers call Wellington, because he is always so neat in his appearance. Well, you'll see—' And then, 'Forget I said that.'

'We didn't hear it,' said Caterina, smiling at him. 'How can I help you if you will not relax?' Rachel Emerson's room was cool and shady as usual, her gentle hands were at the back of Jeremy's neck, her voice was soft, soothing. 'Forget your troubles, forget your illness, remember happiness and a quiet place ... You are quiet, you are calm, you are almost asleep ...' There was a rhythm to her words now, a kind of lullaby effect and he felt his eyes begin to close ...

Fight it. He must fight it. He had known, from the moment he arrived, that something was different today. There had been tension in the air. He thought he must have interrupted a quarrel between the Emersons. And Ralph Emerson had been in a hurry to be off. He had an engagement, he said, to sample some new wine over in Villa Nova de Gaia. He had accepted the little package of gold coins Jeremy had brought and left almost at once, warning Rachel that he would not be home till late. 'Don't wait up for me.'

Here was a chance, or a trap, or both. How to use it? The soothing incantation continued,

191

the hands were gentle on his neck ... How easy to let go, to float with the tide ... 'Rachel!' He stood up suddenly, turned to face her, took both her hands in his. 'We can't go on like this, fencing with each other, pretending ... I love you! You must know I love you, helplessly, passionately, beyond myself. I'm in your thrall. I don't know who you are spying for. The French? The Americans? I don't care. It's not your fault, I know that, it's that brother of yours, compelling you. Let me take you away from it all. I'm not a rich man. I only wish I were, so that I could pour my gold at your feet, make your life easy for you at last. But I will work for you. I have friends, I have influence in England. When they know what an inducement I have to work, they will find me a livelihood. We will be married at once, here in Oporto, if you wish it. Then I shall have the right to look after you, to take you away from that bullying brother of yours. He makes a mockery of your gift, makes you use it for his own ends. With me, you shall use it as it should be used, for the good of mankind. Rachel, why don't you speak? Answer me.'

She had stood all this time, silent, head bowed, the fair hair falling to screen her face, her hands quiet in his. Now she looked up at him, the grey eyes brimming with tears. 'You knew all the time?'

'I was sent to find out. But how could I help loving you? I have told them nothing yet. I am

192

ashamed, but it is true. I love you too much to let harm come to a hair of your head. I shall have to resign, of course. But I have friends; I shall come about. We will be happy you and I. Together against the world . . .'

'You are so sweet.' Slowly, almost langorously, she raised her lips to his.

'Rachel!' He was devouring her, lips, cheeks, hair, the delicate body clasped against his. And getting a message he could not mistake. 'Rachel?'

'I enjoyed that.' She pulled away from him at last, smiling like a contented cat. 'Very much. But we must be practical, you and I. Love in a cottage would not suit either of us. And besides you don't love me, dear creature, though it is kind of you to say so. Were you perhaps brought up to think you must love every woman you fancied? Now, we have not much time!' With a quick practical look at the clock ticking away on the mantel-piece. 'Ralph will break in and surprise us in just half an hour. He thinks I have been going too slowly with you; it was to be blackmail from now on. But I like you too well to let that happen to you, my little Jeremy. So, what are we to do? You knew— they knew in England all the time, you say?'

'Suspected. We knew there was a leak here in Oporto; I was sent to find it.'

'Looking for just one, my poor friend? The place leaks like a sieve.' Another glance at the clock. 'I'll make a bargain with you, Jeremy

Craddock. Safe passage home to America for me and Ralph and I'll find out for you who the others are. Now I can't say prettier than that, can I?' Disconcertingly, as she talked her voice had coarsened, taken on an accent he did not recognise, except as alien.

For some reason he did not understand it made him feel he must repeat his offer. 'I meant it,' he said. 'I meant every word of it. If that is what you want, Rachel, I'll take you to America, marry you and work for you there. Why are you laughing?' It felt like a slap in the face.

'Nice Jeremy, you understand nothing. If only I could, I really believe I might be tempted to chance it. Lord knows, you are an infinitely better prospect than my poor Ralph, but I can't, you see. He's not my brother, Jeremy Craddock, he's my husband. And here he comes. Leave this to me.' She turned to face the door as Ralph Emerson threw it open, then stopped on the threshold, surprised at the tableau he did not see.

'In the nick of time, my dear,' said Rachel coolly. 'We are playing this scene quite differently, as things turn out. Mr Craddock knew about us all the time. Indeed, he was sent here to track us down, and has succeeded.' She turned, smiling, to Jeremy. 'How satisfying to think that all that gold you have poured into my husband's hands is British government gold after all. I was really hating to take it from you, my poor young friend. Little did I know! The case is,' back to the man Jeremy was furiously recognising as in fact her husband, 'Mr Craddock is in the process of agreeing to arrange our passage to America in exchange for a little information in his turn. Now, don't lose your temper, Ralph, this is no time for a scene.' She laid a restraining hand on his arm. 'The goose that laid the golden eggs is dead; you'll get no more little packets of sovereigns from Mr Craddock. And, frankly, the sooner I am away from this place the happier I shall be. I don't a bit like the feel of things here; it's blowing up for a tempest, and I'd rather be clear away before it starts.'

'What do you mean?'

'I don't know what I mean, but I know what I feel. Do you remember, Ralph, back in the spring of 1803, before war broke out again, how nervous I felt, how I urged that we take the first boat back to America? How I wish we had. This time, I tell you, I shall go even if you do not. I'd rather scrub floors for a living back in New England than live the shabby kind of life we have here. I mean it, Ralph, believe that I mean it. And I know Mr Craddock will help me.'

'Of course I will.' What else could he say? 'Mr Camo has a ship sailing for the States in ten days or so,' he told her. 'I'm sure he will arrange passages for you two, if I ask him. And if you keep your side of the bargain.' It struck

195

him that there would be some satisfaction in using his secret service funds for their passages.

'And what, pray, is that?' Ralph Emerson still looked close to explosion point.

'I'll tell you later, Ralph, but I will tell you now, with Mr Craddock as witness, that this worm has turned. I wonder why I have let you browbeat me for so long, and make so many mistakes for us both. You know perfectly well that your French masters (yes, it is the French, Mr Craddock) have never taken you quite seriously; the pay has been miserable; the conditions wretched; I've misused the gift God gave me to no purpose. Whatever you decide to do, Ralph Emerson, I am going back to America on Mr Camo's ship. And if you so much as lay a finger on me, I will report you to the police here. Mr Craddock will back me, and with a bit of luck I will leave you to rot in a Portuguese gaol.'

'You really mean it.' He looked suddenly abject, a bully exploded.

'I really mean it. I'm glad you believe me.' She turned to Jeremy. 'Goodbye, Mr Craddock. I thank you with all my heart for what you have done for me today. And you shall have your information when we have our passages. And, Mr Craddock—Jeremy—don't mind too much.'

*　　*　　*

It was pouring with rain when Jeremy got outside into the stinking alley and he was glad, it suited his mood. Fool, idiot, fool. Hardly aware what he was doing he began to climb the steep slope towards the cathedral, and then beyond, up to the ruins of the seminary where Wellington had made his landing two years before. It was deserted up there, the rain bucketing down, he could stand unnoticed and curse his own folly. He had let her make a lovesick fool of him, he who had sworn long ago that he would never trust a woman. It was good to feel the rain wash the taste of her off his lips, the feel of her from his body. Gradually, beginning to feel colder, damper and somehow purged, he began to think about it all again, differently. She had not mocked him, not really. When she had said she enjoyed his kisses, she had meant it. And so had he. I've lost a love, he thought, and maybe found a friend. How very odd. And he walked five miles upriver and back through the drenching rain without thinking of anything at all.

'Mr Craddock, where in the world have you been?' Mrs Ware exclaimed in horror when he finally returned and unfortunately met her in the hall as he came dripping in from the sodden outdoors.

'Walking,' he told her. 'I'm sorry to flood your house, ma'am. I'll go straight to my room.' He knew she was thinking of her Axminster and her chintzes.

'I trust you have dined, Mr Ware. We waited for you as long as we could.'

'I'm so sorry—'

'You'll take tea with us, I hope. In half an hour? I'll have hot water sent up.'

'Thank you. It's more than I deserve.' He looked at the little pool of water forming at his feet on the marble floor of her cold hall.

Changing swiftly into dry clothes, he had the strangest feeling that he was recovering from an illness. He felt free, clear-headed, his own man again. He ought to be broken-hearted and instead he was relieved. And, best of all, it looked as if he was going to get the information he had been sent for, just for the price of two passages to America. He would be able to stop pretending to be an invalid; he would be able to leave this gossipy town where Rachel Emerson felt disaster looming, and return to England, a step taken forward in his career.

He was knotting his cravat, met his own eyes in the looking glass. He did not want to go back to England and take up his career. If Rachel Emerson was right, if disaster was really imminent here in this dangerous town, how could he leave? And did he want to go on with work that involved him in such shabby pretences? It suddenly struck him that he could hardly go to his cousin Caterina, and tell her that he was not a sick man at all, had merely been feigning sickness in order to advance his career. He remembered how kind, how considerate of him the two girls had been on the voyage out and thought he would rather die than admit it had all been pretence. So, best go at once? And leave them to the dangers Rachel felt threatened here in Oporto with no protector but that old curmudgeon of a father and his attendant priest?

His half hour was almost up. He must not be late again. He retied his cravat with ruthless efficiency, shrugged into his best jacket, ran a comb through damp hair and hurried downstairs.

'That looks better, Mr Craddock. I do hope you have not taken cold.' Mrs Ware was alone, enthroned behind her elaborate tea equipage. 'Frank has gone to see Miss Gomez,' she went on. 'He quite haunts that house these days. He says it is something to do with this mysterious new work of his, but I think you and I know better, do not we?' With a roguish look. 'It's a little difficult to imagine how a charming young thing like Caterina Gomez could be associated with Major Dickson and his material of war.' She handed him his tea cup. 'Just as you like it, I fancy. Now, Mr Craddock, I am hoping for a word of advice from you.'

'I should be delighted. Thank you.' He took the cup and put it down on the gilt-legged table beside him. 'Anything I can do—' He looked as puzzled as he felt.

'You're thinking I should ask Frank!' She

gave one of her braying laughs. 'A boy, Mr Craddock, a charming boy. I flatter myself, but a boy for all that. Now, I recognised you from the start as quite the man of the world, for all your unfortunate illness. I am sure you can give me just the advice I need. The case is this: I have been approached, on the very highest level, but the less said about that, perhaps, the better. All most flattering, most civil ... Who would have thought when I planned my modest little party that it would come to this? If only my poor husband were alive, how happy it would make him. And then, of course, I would not need anyone's advice but his. But as it is—a poor widow woman with no one to turn to ... I know I can trust you with a secret, Mr Craddock.'

'Of course. You said a high-level approach—' He could not help but be interested.

'About my party. Yes. It seems that a very important person indeed is planning a bolt to Oporto, as he calls it, for next week. When he heard about my party, he most graciously said he would like to drop in on it. No pomp, no circumstance and above all no talk, just a friendly visit and a dance or two with some elegant company. He's being dined at the Factory that day, you see, and means just to walk over and give us a look in. All very fine, but what I need to know is when. My Frank has never been to one of their formal dinners,

200

so he's no help at all.'

'I'm sorry to disappoint you, ma'am, but nor have I. And anyway, does it matter if it is indeed to be a surprise visit?'

'Of course it matters. Why do you think I was warned of the "surprise" if it was not so that I could make suitable arrangements? I am sure you can find out for me, Mr Craddock. But tactfully, of course, so that no one has any idea...'

'I am sure I can,' he told her. And so could your son. But he did not say that.

CHAPTER ELEVEN

Calling at the Gomez house, Frank Ware found the two girls on the point of leaving to visit their dressmaker. 'I am so sorry, Mr Ware,' Caterina apologised. 'But if we are not to disgrace your mother next week we must keep our engagement with Madame Feuillide.'

'And we want to look our very best, now we know who is coming,' said Harriet. 'I could hardly sleep last night for thinking of it.'

'You won't forget that it is a deep secret,' he warned. 'Madame Feuillide has lived here for ever, I know, but the fact remains that she is French. Don't for goodness sake let anything drop about why you want to look your best.'

'Our lips are sealed,' Harriet promised him.

'You would be surprised how well women can keep a secret if they really want to.' Was it his imagination or did she and Caterina Gomez exchange a quick glance?

Caterina had risen as a servant appeared to announce that the carriage was ready. She picked up a paper from the table beside her. 'Here is a list of names and directions I got from old Tonio.' She handed it to him. 'He says he is sure most of them will be happy to find work under almost any conditions. I had not realised quite how bad things are here in Porto. It all looks the same on the surface, or not much different, but Tonio says there is real despair, real hunger, in the back alleys and out in the country. He actually asked me to be careful where we went, Harriet and I. Me, a Gomez! It's hard to believe.'

'But I beg you to take the man seriously,' he urged. 'I have heard tales of highway robberies on the road to Braga, of desperate men who would risk their lives for a few *scudos*. You do always take an armed escort, I trust, when you go riding down at Foz?'

'We take a groom,' she said. 'If you like I'll make sure he is armed. And in return I suggest that you do not take any sidealley short cuts on the way home from here, Mr Ware. Tonio said something that made me a little anxious— about feelings towards the British. You do rather keep yourselves to yourselves, don't you, and behave as if the world were your oyster.'

'You are talking as if you were not half British yourself, Cat,' protested Harriet.

'Why, so I am. How very strange.'

*   *   *

The two girls sat silent for a while as the carriage lurched forward through rain-sodden lanes. Caterina had told Harriet everything that had passed between her and Luiz's grandmother, and they had discussed it upside down, backwards, and sideways, in the day that had passed since she met the old lady. And at the end of it all, they seemed to be back where they had started. Caterina could not bring herself to believe that Luiz was as bad as his grandmother had painted him. Or was it, Harriet wondered, that she could not bring herself to admit that she believed it? She had promised to be infinitely careful in what she said to him, but felt she must suspend judgement until she had talked to him. 'After all,' she said in the carriage, as she had said before, several times, 'Madame Feuillide is a clever woman. She has deceived the Portonions easily enough, maybe she has fooled Luiz too.'

'Maybe,' said Harriet, not for the first time. 'But, Cat, whatever you do, don't tell him about little Lewis. I think his grandmother's plans for the poor baby sound alarming

203

enough, without his father's getting involved.'

'I'm sure you are right about that,' agreed Caterina. 'It frightens me. She means to have him. She was going to send for her attorney today, she told me. I just hope nothing too drastic comes of that.'

'What a blessing Lewis is safe in England,' said Harriet.

'If he is safe.'

'He may be hungry,' said Harriet, 'if money is tight. But he will be safe enough, I am sure. Mother has got the sense to take the long view. He won't be in clover, poor little duck, but he won't be in actual danger either. Not so long as you are alive to ask after him.' A shiver ran down her spine as she said it. 'Cat, do you not think you should tell your father?'

'I don't dare.' She leaned forward to peer out of the carriage window. 'If only it would stop raining! How am I going to meet Luiz if it goes on like this?'

'You won't be able to meet him outside anyway,' said practical Harriet. 'Your shoes and skirts would be drenched; it would be bound to cause comment you cannot afford. I think you have to assume that Madame Feuillide and your Luiz will have worked something out between them.' Privately, she thought she was glad of the rain, which might force the two conspirators to make their position clear to Caterina. 'I wish you would let me stay with you this time.' She had urged this before. 'It would give me a chance to make up my own mind about him.'

'Your unprejudiced mind? I do see what you mean ... Oh, Harryo, if only I knew what to do for the best.'

'Whose best?' asked Harriet. And went on to answer herself: 'It seems to me, love, that it has to be little Lewis's. If you hold on to that, I don't think you can go far wrong.'

'Oh, Harryo, I do thank God for you!' Caterina turned quickly to hug her friend. 'And here we are!'

'You are prompt to your hour,' Madame Feuillide greeted them with her usual subtle distinction between rich girl and poor girl. 'I was afraid this terrible weather might keep you at home.'

'With the great party only six days off?' said Caterina. 'Impossible. To tell truth, ma'am, we had been getting a little anxious at not hearing from you.'

'Oh well, all's for the best now.' The Frenchwoman was bustling about, doing things with damp shawls. 'We'll begin with you today, I think, Miss Brown. If you wouldn't mind stepping into my humble little salon while we work, Miss Gomez? You know how I need to concentrate. You may find a young relative of mine there, I hope you won't mind it. And the less said about him the better.' With a conspiratorial smile for the two girls. 'His father went to the United States with the

Marquis of Lafayette years ago, but when the Marquis came back, my cousin stayed on and went into business there. Young Louis is on his first voyage to Europe and made a point of coming to see his old cousin. Isn't it the most touching thing? But what with the French connection and this dreadful threat of war between the United States and England, I thought it best for him to lie as low as possible in the few days he is with me. Such a pity! I would so like to show him off here in Porto, but we all know that one cannot afford to set tongues wagging here of all places. Try to cheer him up, Miss Gomez? I am afraid he is finding life sadly dull here with me. Not what he expected at all. And not a word to anyone.'

*   *   *

'At last!' Luiz had been out in the rain and his normally curly black hair was plastered close to his skull. It made him look quite different. Older. Dangerous? He held out his arms. 'My little love—' And then, 'No need to look so scared. Madame the dressmaker has given the strictest orders that we are not to be disturbed. And so have I, which is more to the point. They know better than to cross me here. But, what is it, my own?' As she still hung back, facing him across the little room with its platoon of upright gilt chairs. 'You want to make your report first, like the admirable colleague you are? Quite right,' he approved. 'But I've been travelling all day, through this foul weather. Come, love, let's sit here and be comfortable while you tell me your tale.' He stepped forward, took her hand and led her to a stiff little sofa that matched the gilt chairs. 'I could curse this weather,' he told her as he seated her and took his place too close beside her. 'You have no idea what luxurious arrangements I had ordered to be made for us in the garden here. Never mind.' He put a proprietorial arm round her shoulder. 'Privacy will be all the sweeter when we achieve it at last. What a devilish clever girl you are to tease and tantalise a man so. I'd never have thought it possible, but I am as mad for you now as I was that first day, so long ago. How am I to bear thinking of you, surrounded by those stolid Englishmen at the Factory? I have been teasing madame the dressmaker with the notion that I will smuggle myself into this party next week, just to keep an eye on you, my little witch.'

'But, Luiz, it would be madness.' If only the hand that held her would keep still.

'Oh, not as myself, love. I'm not so crazy as that. But if you suddenly feel a warm breath on your beautiful bare shoulder from one of the flunkeys, don't look round, for it will be I.'

'Luiz—' She pulled a little away to look him in the face, and felt that he did not like it. 'We have to talk, you and I. You must see that I cannot answer your questions unless I know

207

more about why you are asking them. Porto is full of whispers. I've been warned again about careless talk by Frank Ware. You remember, he scolded me before because I asked him about the *Anthea*'s cargo.'

'Young busybody. I must certainly come to that party. But the *Anthea* is an old story now—no longer important, though of course I am infinitely grateful to you for trying to find out for me, my precious one. And the same goes for Marmont's movements, though I am sure you have a great tale to tell me about them too. Everyone knows now that he got supplies into Ciudad Rodrigo and nearly got Wellington too, I believe. And now they are all going snug into winter quarters and we have to wait until spring for our next move. At least I hope it will mean a chance for us to be together, my sweet love. I am hoping my friends will agree that I am the obvious person to watch the course of events through the winter, here in Porto, and then I can find myself a place of my own, somewhere we can safely meet.' His arm was close round her again now, telling its own urgent tale. Half of her yearned towards him; the other half thought of Lewis, her son, and what Harriet had said. And, suddenly, she knew just what Luiz was planning. Why had she not seen it before? He wanted her pregnant. That way, he thought he could force her father into letting them marry. He was wrong, of course. Her father would simply cast her out.

Deep in her heart, she thanked God for the rain.

Did he feel her instinctive, momentary withdrawal? 'You are absolutely right, my angel, as usual. That Miss Brown of yours will be upon us any moment. We must seem the mere acquaintances she thinks us. I shall put on a Yankee accent and ask you Yankee questions! So—tell me about this great party you are going to look so splendid at next week! You will be guest of honour, Madame Feuillide tells me. I think I really must get myself a flunkey's livery just to watch over you among all those pompous young Englishmen, my angel. I'd like to see you queening it there—'

The habit of confidence dies hard. It was on the tip of her tongue to tell him that she was not to be guest of honour after all. 'I'm not—' and then remembering Harriet's warnings and Frank Ware's, she turned the sentence in a new direction: 'I'm not letting myself look forward to it too much,' she told him, 'for fear that my father should suddenly get into one of his passions and forbid us to go, Harriet and I.'

'And why in the world should he do that?'

'He's very strange these days.' It occurred to her that in their two meetings he had asked her nothing about her own life. Did she only exist for him as someone to be made use of? It was dangerous to think like this, sitting here, alone with him, his arm around her. Her coachman

209

and groom were far away in the back parts of this isolated house. Suppose he were to sense that she was no longer the willing, ignorant tool he thought her? Could she really be imagining the possibility of being kidnapped by Luiz, held to ransom? And then what would happen to little Lewis? She made herself lean a little closer to him, look up at him confidingly: 'It would be entirely too dangerous for you. She is inviting mainly English people, of course, who would not know you, but think of the servants, Luiz. Your face is not one to be easily forgotten. Promise me you won't think of it. I expect it will be deadly dull really, and I will tell you all about it afterwards. Do you think you will have your own house by then? How in the world will I manage about coming to see you?'

'No need to worry your pretty little head about that; I shall manage for you. So you don't think I need to be at Mrs Ware's to forbid the banns?'

'To—oh!' This was disconcerting. 'You have heard of that crazy plan of my father's? I told you he is strange these days. He really did seem to think he was going to marry me off to Frank Ware, and get himself a son-in-law who would do as he was told.' She laughed, infinitely relieved to have hit on this safe subject. 'Of course I don't mean to marry him. You should know me better than that, Luiz. Anyway, I think Frank Ware has quite other plans.' She heard the sound of movement in the next room, and disengaged herself gently. 'We are going to be interrupted. Promise me you will be very careful, Luiz.'

'I'll be careful, and lie low here, so long as you promise to be my eyes and ears. We need to know who comes down from up-river, and all the news they bring.'

'Yes, of course.' Yesterday, she would have told him at once about Major Dickson and his wheelwrights. Today, she answered with a question of her own: 'How shall I let you know?'

'I've worked it all out; can't go on being dependent on madame the dressmaker.' Lowering his voice. 'I don't entirely trust her, to tell you the truth. I begin to think that she has fish of her own to fry. So I have been working at alternatives. My father's house is too dangerous for me. You are quite right, alas, mine is not a face that is easily forgotten. But I have found a friend there. I knew someone must still be faithful to me, and looking forward a little too. I'm the heir, remember, when those two old wrecks drop dead at last. What a joyful day that will be! For both of us. In the meanwhile, write me all you hear, tuck your little love letter under a stone in our summerhouse. Never fear, I shall have it within twenty-four hours at the longest. And answer with all my heart.'

His callous tone chilled her heart. How

211

could she ever have loved him? Thought she loved him? 'Here you are at last, Harriet,' she turned with relief to greet her friend. 'Monsieur Feuillide has been telling me the most interesting stories about life in the United States.'

*   *   *

Madame Feuillide wanted to know about Mrs Ware's party too, but after fending off Luiz's questions, Caterina found the dressmaker's easy enough to parry and responded with some of her own as the dressmaker pinned, and fitted, and admired her admirable handiwork. Caterina longed for the fitting to be over. There was so much to think about, so much to face.

'There,' said Madame Feuillide at last. 'You will be the belle of the ball my dear. I'll send the dresses to you in good time, two days before the party. I mean to come into town the day before it,' she told Caterina, 'so that I can make any final adjustments my clients may chance to need. I do not usually do so, but something tells me that this is to be a very special occasion. There are all kinds of interesting rumours flying round the town, you must have heard some of them, surely?'

'I try my best not to listen to them,' Caterina told her. 'Where should I get in touch with you, madame, if Miss Brown or I should need your assistance?'

'It is not entirely settled yet, but I am rather letting myself hope that Mrs Ware herself may contrive to find some tiny attic where I can tuck myself away and make myself useful to her and to her guests. Just think what a chance for a country mouse like me. To be actually there in the house; to hear the music, maybe contrive to peer out of my attic window to see the honoured guests arriving. If Mr Ware should chance to call on you, as a little bird tells me he frequently does, perhaps you would be so good as to say a word in my favour? It would be such a convenience for you young ladies to have me right there in the house to pin up your hem for you if you should chance to need it.'

'I don't suppose I shall,' said Caterina. 'So well as you make, madame. But of course I will say a word if Mr Ware should call. I can imagine it might be a great comfort to his mother to have you in the house. Does it rain still?' She wanted this fitting over.

'Harder than ever, I am afraid. Will you not let me give you a cup of tea, and wait until it slackens? It is no weather for young ladies to be out in.'

'I think not, thank you kindly just the same. The nights are drawing in and my father does not like me to be out after dark.'

'I am glad to hear he takes such good care of you.' She might as well have said: 'I don't believe a word of it.'

It made Caterina more anxious than ever to

213

be gone. She opened the door into the salon and found Harriet alone. 'Time to be going,' she said, and then: 'What happened to Monsieur Feuillide?'

'I am afraid he found my company vastly tedious, though he was too polite to show it.' Harriet, too, seemed eager to be off, and they were both relieved at the speed with which the coachman brought his horses round.

He bundled them unceremoniously into the carriage, shouted something to the groom, whipped up his horses and drove off at such speed over the rough road that the two girls could do nothing but cling to each other and set their teeth against the jolting they were getting.

'What in the world?' gasped Caterina. It would have been funny, she thought, if it had not been so frightening.

'Something has scared him,' said Harriet.

'Yes. I wish I knew what.'

'He'll tell you when we get safe home,' Harriet said confidently. They had got on to the Braga road now, the going was a little smoother and the pace slightly less desperate. She turned to look at her friend in the gathering dusk. 'What happened between you and Luiz, Cat? I didn't think it had gone quite as he expected. He was edgy as the devil with me, couldn't get away fast enough, not a civil young man, your Luiz.'

'Not my Luiz,' said Caterina bleakly and

found that the tears were streaming down her face. 'I've been such a fool, such a blind, besotted fool. He's been using me, all the time; he loves no one but himself. How could I not have seen it? If it hadn't been for his grandmother—' She was sobbing helplessly now, but Harriet's arms were warm around her.

'It's so easy to see what one expects to see,' said Harriet. 'Don't mind it so much, love. At least you saw through him in time.' She did not let it be a question.

'Yes.' Caterina answered it just the same. 'Just. When he expected me to walk into his arms today, and I didn't, and I saw his face... It's odd how different he looked with his hair wet,' she said irrelevantly. 'I saw it all suddenly, Harryo. He meant to get me pregnant; thought he would be able to force my father into letting us marry. How little he knows of anything. And then, when I held back, wouldn't let him! I was frightened, suddenly. I found myself thinking of a kidnapping, of demands for ransom.'

'Not ransom,' said Harriet soberly. 'Rape, more likely. What a good thing Francesco spotted something was wrong. I wonder what it was. But, Cat, you didn't tell him about Lewis?'

'I didn't tell him anything.' This at least was satisfactory. 'It was on the tip of my tongue to tell him about the distinguished guest at the

215

party, but I managed to stop myself. It's so hard to stop trusting someone.' She was crying more quietly now, to Harriet's relief.

'Thank goodness you stopped yourself,' she said. 'There are altogether too many questions in that house, if you ask me. I'm sure the old lady is right about Madame Feuillide, but what are we going to do about it, Cat?'

'I don't know,' said Caterina slowly. 'I just don't know. If only the Bishop were still in charge here, I would go to him. He knows me, he wouldn't treat me like a silly female with romantic terrors. I never met Dom Antonio, the acting Governor ... I don't think I dare try him.'

'Could you go to the English maybe?' asked Harriet. 'Frank Ware is a very sensible young man, I think.'

'So is Jeremy Craddock, come to that, if only he wasn't besotted with that Rachel Emerson. But who would listen to either of them, with a tale of a young lady's fears? The one comfort is that we do know nothing is set to happen till spring; there's plenty of time, and of course I shall tell old Madame Fonsa all of it, she may well feel she can go to the Governor.'

'About her own grandson? Oh, Cat—'

'All the more reason why I feel it must be her decision, do not you? Mind you, she has turned all her attention on to her great-grandson now, and Lord knows what is going to come of that. How long do you think Lewis will be my secret

216

now? Oh, look, we're home, thank God.' The carriage had just turned in at the courtyard gates. 'Lend me your handkerchief, love. I don't want to look an absolute fright to the servants.'

'They love you too much to notice,' said Harriet as Caterina dried her eyes.

'*Senhora!*' Francesco himself had leapt down from the box to open the carriage door for them. 'Forgive me for giving you such a rough ride home. I saw a man back there in that Frenchwoman's kitchen I had never feared to see again. A bad one and a friend of bad ones. Kidnappers ... murderers ... I am glad to have you safe home.'

'So am I, Francesco, and I do thank you.'

'Luiz?' asked Harriet, under her breath, as they moved indoors.

'Oh, no,' said Caterina confidently. 'He would never be found in anyone's kitchen.'

'So, a friend of his, or of Madame Feuillide's?'

'Or both,' said Caterina.

CHAPTER TWELVE

'So what the deuce are we going to tell him?' After Jeremy Craddock had left, Rachel Emerson had let the storm of her husband's rage blow itself out over her bowed head. Now, at last, he was beginning to sound rational.

'The truth, I think, or some of it, though I know it is not a course that appeals to you. But think about it a little.' She reached behind her into a corner cupboard, pulled out a squat bottle and poured him a liberal dram. 'The English and Americans are at daggers drawn over all this trouble between their ships. Get ourselves thrown out of here as having spied on the British for the French and if we are lucky we'll get home to find war has broken out, and get a heroes' welcome.'

'Oh.' He had not thought of this. 'You mean, we tell him—?' He took a long draught from the glass.

'Some of the truth. A doleful tale of ungrateful clients in Paris, and the bailiffs after us ... And then being approached by Fouché's secret police and offered the chance to come here, all expenses paid, and that fine cover story of my standing up for my good friend Josephine. As if she hadn't been one of the worst of all when it came to paying her bills, but never mind that! And then coming here and finding a skinflint paymistress in Madame Feuillide—I have no qualms about her. I'm sure she has cheated us all along, kept back funds that were meant for us and feathered her own nest with them. What she sent us after you told her about the *Anthea*'s cargo was an insult—'

'She said someone else had got in first,' he

reminded her. 'Are we going to tell Craddock that?'

'No. Why should we? When did he say Camo's boat sailed?'

'In ten days or so, I think.'

'I wish it were sooner. Step down to the harbour, would you, and ask around, tactfully, for an earlier sailing. I don't know about you, but with the chances of war as they are I'd as soon not be on a boat belonging to so good a friend of the British as Joe Camo.'

'Oh?' This was another new idea for him to cope with. 'But would Craddock pay for our passages on a different boat?'

'I think he'll be glad to be rid of us at any price, don't you? Such an embarrassment to him, poor man, a constant reminder of what a fool he has made of himself.'

'I sometimes think you are a devil, Rachel.' But he said it with admiration. 'What a pity we can't tell him who is behind Madame Feuillide. That really would get us gold-plated treatment, if we only knew.'

'It is a pity, isn't it, but she's a very clever woman, that one. You would have to get up very early to outgeneral her.'

'But we have not done too badly, after all,' he said, and went off to do her bidding.

*　　*　　*

After what seemed a night entirely without

sleep, Jeremy Craddock was waked by the army of chattering workmen who were making the Ware house ready for the party that was supposed to be such a casual affair. Shaving himself glumly in the subdued light of another day of drenching rain he faced the fact that nothing had solved itself during his wretched night. He had gone to bed wondering to whom it was his duty to tell his tale of idiocy and betrayal, and woken with no answer. His instructions had been ruthlessly clear on this point. 'You are on your own, Craddock. Get into trouble, and we disown you. We cannot afford any kind of friction with our gallant allies the Portuguese.'

So that was that. He cut himself, and swore. His obvious duty was to take the next boat home and explain himself to his superiors there. Why was he so reluctant to do this? Surely he could not be taking Rachel Emerson's forebodings of trouble seriously? Why should he ever again believe a word she said? He wished now that he had made it clear that he would require proof positive about the other spies she named, but she was no fool, she would understand that.

Anyway, the first thing, this morning, was obviously to go down to the quay and talk to Joseph Camo about passages for the Emersons. And at the same time he must find out when the next ship would sail for England, and book his own passage. And granted the speed with which information flew up and down the alleys of Oporto, he had better prepare the ground with Mrs Ware first. He was glad to find her presiding over the tea and coffee urns at her lavish breakfast table.

'I trust you are none the worse for your wetting, Mr Craddock.' She handed him his coffee, made just as he liked it.

'Not the least in the world, but feeling a bit of a fool,' he told her. 'The case is, ma'am, I have to admit you were quite right about Miss Emerson. A shameless charlatan! I'm not entirely an idiot, though she must have thought so. I caught her at her tricks yesterday—I'll spare you the details . . . We parted not the best of friends, I'm afraid, but she has undertaken to go home to America if I do not shame her publicly. I know I can count on your discretion, ma'am.'

'Of course you can, and I won't even say I told you so. I am only sorry for your disappointment, Mr Craddock. I had really been flattering myself that perhaps she had been doing you a little good, despite my own doubts about her. I suppose this means that you will be leaving us?'

'Yes, it has been a fool's errand if ever there was one. I am off to the quay this morning to enquire about passages both for myself and for the Emersons.'

'Handsome of you to take the trouble on their behalf.'

'I want to make sure they keep their word.' He had finished a rapid breakfast and rose to his feet. 'If you will excuse me?'

'But you won't think of leaving before my party, Mr Craddock?'

'I should be desolated to miss it, ma'am, but I think I must take the first sailing that offers itself. I have wasted quite enough time playing the invalid here in Oporto.' And that was all too true, he thought, as he walked the short distance to the Rua das Cangostas behind the Factory House, where the firm of Webb, Campbell, Gray and Camo had its office. He found Joseph Camo just putting on his hat to go to the quay, and they walked down through the crowded alleys together.

'The Emersons,' said Camo in reply to Jeremy's first question. 'Oh, yes, he was asking about passages last night, I believe. On the *Washington*, sailing Saturday. It seems that our *Anna* does not sail soon enough for them. They are in a great hurry to get out of town all of a sudden. It surprised me a little. I would have thought that having succeeded in getting invited to Mrs Ware's famous party next week, Miss Emerson would be mad keen to stay for it, but from what her brother said, she is just as keen to go. What are you laughing at?'

'I was wondering what goes on in Oporto that you don't know about.'

'Not a great deal,' agreed Camo. 'That's why this snap decision of the Emersons' makes me a trifle uneasy. I really can't fathom it.'

It was almost a question and Jeremy answered it as such, telling his story of Rachel's charlatanism with apparent reluctance, and, of course, in deepest confidence.

'But I still don't see why she wants to go before the great party,' said Camo at last. 'And I hope you don't intend to, Craddock. I think it is going to be an occasion not to be missed, if there is any truth in the stories that are going round. Of course, you must know all about it, living with the Wares as you do.'

'I can tell you the house is almost uninhabitable,' said Jeremy. 'And of course I have heard talk of the very distinguished, highly anonymous guest, just like everyone else. All Porto must know about that by now.'

'Yes', said Camo. 'It's what all Porto is going to do about it that interests me.'

'A hero's welcome, and oxen roasted whole in the streets?'

'I wonder,' said Joseph Camo and turned away to greet an acquaintance on the busy quay.

The note of doubt in his voice helped to make up Jeremy's mind. If Joseph Camo scented danger, it was no time to leave. When he found that a ship was in fact sailing for Plymouth just the day before Mrs Ware's party, he did nothing about a passage, planning instead to send a full report by her. It would undoubtedly be easier to do it in writing,

223

he told himself, and was ashamed. But he could not even start to write it until he had his information from Rachel Emerson. From the way she had spoken he was convinced that she knew perfectly well who their employers were, but she would no doubt make a mystery of it, as she did everything, and not tell him until the last moment, just in time to get their passage money. But how odd it was that Rachel Emerson should be planning to leave before the party. He remembered, all too vividly, an early session with her in which she had tried to suggest to him that he should apply to Mrs Ware for an invitation for her and her 'brother'. He had played stupid and shrugged it off, but had thought at the time she had no chance of getting one, considering what Mrs Ware habitually said about her. And now, having actually got her invitation, she was planning to leave before the day.

But here was Ralph Emerson looming down on him full of such rubicond goodwill that it was hard to believe in yesterday's scene. 'The very man,' he said. 'I am just on my way home to tell Rachel the good news. We are booked on the *Washington*, sailing Saturday. We shall have to bustle about to be ready in time, but my Rachel is a devil of an organiser when her heart is in it.' He had contrived to nudge Jeremy into a quiet corner by a fountain where chattering women were drawing water. 'The passages were expensive, of course, bound to be.' He named a figure that made Jeremy whistle. 'But I knew we could count on you. So—tomorrow morning?'

'You will have the information I want?'

'Naturally.'

'Very well then. Ten o'clock.' He held out his hand to seal the bargain and was surprised how much he disliked doing so. 'One thing does puzzle me.' He resisted the temptation to wipe his hand on his sleeve after Emerson's moist grasp. 'I would have thought the two of you would have wanted to stay for the Ware party; that's why I suggested Camo's boat in the first place.'

'You're not thinking, Craddock. Or have you been too busy with your own affairs to pay attention to the news? Or maybe our American affairs are not worth your notice? That would be just like you English. But my Rachel is a wonderful correspondent and keeps us in close touch with all that goes on at home, and I can tell you the chances of war between our countries grow stronger every day. It needs just one more outrage like your navy's attacks on the *Chesapeake* and *Little Belt* and our hawkish Congress will cast the die. You know how long news takes to cross the Atlantic; it could have happened already. And whose side would your friend Joseph Camo's captain be on if he were to learn of it on the high seas? Rachel and I would be bundled back to England in chains. No, thank you, we are for the *Washington*, which belongs to Jefferson himself. We should be safe on her if there is safety anywhere.' He raised his hat. 'Tomorrow at ten then,' and walked away.

*   *   *

Caterina found writing to Madame Fonsa one of the most difficult things she had ever done, but the letter was written at last and consigned to old Tonio. 'There will be an answer for you tomorrow morning I am sure, *minha senhora*,' he promised.

It seemed a long time to wait, and Caterina's spirits were not raised by an encounter with Father Pedro who waylaid her as she returned from her regular visit to the kitchen to give the day's orders.

'A word with you, if you please, daughter.' He blessed her perfunctorily as he spoke. 'Alone.'

'Very well.' She led the way into the disused library of some long-dead ancestor, where crumbling volumes mouldered on the shelves and an acrid smell of decaying leather hung in the air. What a pleasure it would be to spring clean this house, she thought, and turned an obedient, listening face to Father Pedro.

'It is only five days now till this party of Mrs Ware's,' he said.

'Yes, father.'

'And you have no news for your father and

me?'

'No, father.' What else could she say?

'I called on the Little Sisters of Saint Seraphina yesterday, at your father's request. They need a little notice, they say, of new entrants. Am I to give it to them?'

She raised her head to look him full in the face. 'No, father. We will not discuss this again, if you please, until the day after the party. That was the understanding, and I intend to stick to it. And now, if you will excuse me, I have my duties about the house to attend to.'

*　　*　　*

'And he'll do it, too.' She had told Harriet the whole story. 'Bundle us out, neck and crop, on Wednesday morning, and no one would lift a finger to prevent it.'

'Madame Fonsa would, surely?'

'Do you know, Harryo, that was my first thought too, and the horrid truth is that I'm not sure. It's not me she wants, it's Lewis. I told her enough so she could find him if she were to set those lawyers of hers at work. Let the doors of silence close on you and me and he would be all hers, to bring up as she chose.'

'That must not happen,' said Harriet soberly. 'All we need is a little time, Cat. I suppose nothing will change your father's mind?'

'You know it won't, not with Father Pedro

227

beside him, egging him on. Harryo,' she reached out to take her friend's hand, 'I hardly like to ask it, but do you think Frank Ware would help us? Could we go and stay there, perhaps, until things sort themselves out?'

'I'm sure he would want to help.' Harriet had flushed crimson. 'But, Cat, I can't ask him! It would be asking him to—' She stammered to a halt. 'How can I? I confess I had thought ... I had hoped ... Maybe when this party is over, but don't you see, I might easily have been imagining it all ...'

'If you have, then so have I.'

'But that's not the point, is it? If he were to ask me, I would have to tell him all about myself. It would be bad enough anyway, I can't believe it won't make a difference ...' She was crying now.

'Not if he really loves you,' said her friend staunchly, 'but I do see the difficulty. If you did something, said something to plump him into it, you'd always remember—'

'And so would he. Things would never be right between us. Oh, Cat, I am so very sorry, but I can't.'

'No, I can see you can't.' Caterina hugged her lovingly. 'So we have to think of something else. Yes—?' To Tonio.

'The Senhor Craddock has called, *minha senhora*. He is in the small salon.'

'Jeremy Craddock.' The two girls exchanged a long, thoughtful look. 'He did offer to help,'

228

Caterina said at last. 'Maybe I will see him alone, Harryo, if you'll excuse me.'

'Gladly,' said Harriet. 'I need to wash my face. I can only wish you luck, love.'

'I need it.'

*   *   *

Caterina was startled out of her own worries by Jeremy Craddock's appearance. He looked wretched, as if he had not slept for nights or eaten much either. Constant wetting had turned his elegant short crop into an unruly thatch of curls, and a little blood had seeped out from under a dressing on his cheek.

'You're not well, Mr Craddock, I am so sorry. What can I do for you?' She held out an impulsive, friendly hand.

'You can let me tell you what a fool I have made of myself!' He had not known quite what impulse had brought him calling here today, now he understood. 'Oh, thank you,' he said vaguely, as she poured him the statutory glass of sweet wine and handed him a plate of the cook's macaroons. 'That's good,' he said, and reached out for another one. 'I'm afraid I have bored you and Miss Brown often enough with singing Miss Emerson's praises,' he plunged right in. 'Oh, you were too kind, too polite to say anything, but looking back I realise how little you agreed with me.'

'Well,' she said temperately. 'A woman's

view of another woman is always different, you know. And Harriet and I like you so very much, Mr Craddock, that maybe we did wonder a little if she was good enough for you.'

'Good enough! She's not Emerson's sister, Miss Gomez, she's his wife.' He had not meant to tell her this.

'His wife?' She gasped. 'Oh, poor Mr Craddock.'

'It's so sad.' It was a relief to talk about it. 'In fact her gift is real enough. She was actually doing me good, more good than I had imagined. I feel differently about things.' He had not realised this before. 'And yet it's all false,' he groaned. 'Used for false ends, for money.'

'There's nothing wrong with money, Mr Craddock. If you ask me, there's a lot to be said for it. Try having none and you'll see. And if she has really done you good, why not be grateful and let it go?'

'And let them go on deceiving people? I can't do that. I have insisted they leave for America by the next boat. And promised my silence if they do so. I know I can count on you, Miss Gomez.'

'Of course. So I suppose you will be leaving us too?'

'Yes, but not until after the party, I thought.' He had been absent-mindedly sipping at the Madeira wine as he talked, and was beginning to look better as colour returned to his haggard face. 'I don't want to miss that after all the preparations I have seen being made for it.'

'Oh, that party! There's been so much talk of it, I sometimes find myself wondering whether it will ever really take place.' She was talking almost automatically, hardly aware of what she was saying, while a new idea grew in her head. 'Mr Craddock—'

'Yes?' Something in her tone made him forget his own troubles and really look at her for the first time. 'Miss Gomez, I'm a selfish fool, too full of my own affairs. Something's the matter, isn't it? Is he being impossible, that father of yours? We are cousins, remember, and I feel extra responsibility because I brought you here, you and Miss Brown. You promised you would let me know if you should need my help.'

'Oh, thank you, Cousin Jeremy.' The offer made up her mind. 'We were at our wits' end, Harriet and I, when you called, and I truly believe you could help us, if only you would.'

'Of course I will.'

'Wait till you hear. You won't much like it, I'm afraid. Well, I don't myself.' He was amazed to see that she was blushing, something he had never seen before. 'It is my father. You are quite right about that. He sent for me because he wants a son-in-law to come into the firm, to take his name, I imagine. Do you see?'

'I think I begin to.'

231

'I am sure you have heard the stories about me, here in Porto.' She ploughed steadily on. 'No Portuguese gentleman would have me, so they gave me a choice, he and Father Pedro: you or Frank Ware. Wait—' She put up a hand to silence him. 'That was when we got here; now they are getting impatient. Father Pedro told me this morning that I must announce my engagement the day after the party, or they will send me off to join the Little Sisters of Saint Seraphina.'

'The silent order!' Now she had truly horrified him. 'Both of you? But, once there—'

'Exactly. We might as well be dead. I rather think Father Pedro has gone off to make the arrangements today. Can you guess what it is I am finding so hard to ask you, Mr Craddock?'

'Of course, we must marry.' He had never thought to hear himself say it. 'What is it, Miss Gomez?' She was actually laughing, of all things.

'Oh, *kind* Mr Craddock.' She put her hand to her mouth to quell another irresistible bubble of nervous laughter. 'I shall never forget that to my dying day. But the situation is not so desperate as that. All we need is a little time.' How long would Madame Fonsa's lawyers take, she wondered. 'Then I truly think things may come about for us. Forgive me if I don't explain—it is not entirely my secret ... So the case is, would you terribly mind pretending to be engaged to me? Just for a few weeks. If you are really going back to England it would make it all much easier, would it not? We could break it off at leisure, by post, and no harm done.'

Now, oddly, he did want to protest, but raised another point. 'Why don't you come back with me, you and Miss Brown? If it is a question of the fare, I would be only too happy to help.'

'Kinder and kinder! But, no, I am more grateful than I can say, but there are things I have to do, here in Porto, before I can think of leaving.'

'Will you be safe when I am gone?'

'Engaged to you? Yes, I am sure of it.' Had he tacitly agreed to the scheme?

'Then let us by all means be engaged.' He ate the last macaroon and rose to his feet. 'Miss Gomez, will you do me the honour—What is it?'

'You mustn't.' Were those tears in her eyes? 'It's not real, remember.' She held out her hand. 'And I am more grateful to you than I can say. Oh—' He had bent to kiss it.

'I think you are the bravest woman I know, Miss Gomez. Now, do you not think that I should go straight to your father?'

CHAPTER THIRTEEN

'But what will Luiz do when he hears?' While Jeremy was with her father, Caterina had told her tale to Harriet and was taken aback by her reaction.

'Oh, my God, I had forgotten all about Luiz!'

And that was interesting in itself, thought Harriet. 'Well, you had better start remembering him now,' she said. 'And warn Jeremy Craddock about him too.'

'Warn—'

'You're not thinking, love. That's a violent man, that Luiz. I've seen some and I know. And associated with violence too. I do hope that grandmother of his does something quickly when she gets your letter about him. You did tell it her straight, didn't you?'

'As straight as I could. But, you know, there's not that much to go on. Just my instinct, really. And how can she report her own grandson to the authorities?'

'You think she is more likely to use her suspicions to blackmail him into going away? That's not very pretty either, is it?'

'No, it's not, but it would be a great relief.'

'I should just about think so, and I am glad you do too. But it's what he might attempt before he goes that worries me. Hearing about you and Craddock is going to be a terrible blow to his pride, Cat. Did you ever wonder how Father Pedro came to be attacked that time?'

'A footpad, surely?'

'You've been too busy to think, that's your trouble,' said her friend. 'Did it not strike you how very convenient it was for your Luiz to have the holy inquisitive father out of action for a few days just then?'

'Oh!' Caterina put a hand to her mouth. Suddenly, blindingly, a casual phrase of Luiz's came back to her. She had told him that Father Pedro was conscious, and he had said, 'Damnation! Too soft a blow!' It had chimed in so with her own feelings about the detestable father that it had not struck her until now what it implied. Idiot that she had been. Had Luiz struck that blow himself, or merely arranged for it to be struck? 'I'm the world's fool!' She told Harriet about it and was surprised at her lack of surprise.

'Just so,' she said. 'I wonder how long it will take for the news of your "engagement" to reach him. It's going to spread like wildfire, you know.'

'Oh dear, I suppose it is.'

'You hadn't thought of that either, had you, love? What is the old lady going to say, for instance?'

'Do you know, I had thought of that,' said Caterina. 'I think it will strengthen my hand in dealing with her. To have a man apparently behind me, do you see?'

'Oh yes I do,' said Harriet. 'There's a lot to be said for it! I suppose you could send a note to Luiz to say that the engagement is a pretence?'

'No,' said Caterina. 'No, I don't think I could do that.'

'Then you must most certainly warn Mr Craddock.'

'But it will mean telling him—'

'Yes, it will. I think you owe him that, don't you? And after all, Cat, face it: everyone is going to know about little Lewis soon enough. When the old lady and her lawyers go into action they are bound to name you as his mother. I do think it would be civil to tell Jeremy Craddock first.'

'Of course I must.' She remembered that he had begun by asking her in all earnest to marry him. 'You're right; I've not had time to think.' She raised her voice to summon a servant. 'When Mr Craddock leaves my father's study bring him in here please.'

'But he has already left, *minha senhora*. And your father wishes to see you.'

* * *

The interview had gone badly from the start. Senhor Gomez had been closeted with Father Pedro and had refused to see Jeremy alone. He had then listened to the young man's rather stilted proposal in stony silence, and had exchanged a long, questioning look with Father Pedro before he spoke. 'It is usual, I believe, for the young lady to say that a proposal of marriage has surprised her, but this time I am the one who is amazed. What will Miss Emerson have to say about it? You may think that I live isolated here, but this does not mean that I am quite unaware of what is going on in town.'

'I am sure you are well informed.' With a speaking glance for Father Pedro. 'And by tomorrow you will know that the Emersons are booked to leave for the United States on the *Washington* this Saturday. I plead guilty to some folly in that quarter, but it is over, *senhor.*'

'And more profitable councils have prevailed? A pity Miss Emerson did not manage to cure you before she decided to leave us. I need a man for a son-in-law, Mr Craddock, not a cripple with the falling sickness.'

'But—' What could he say? He was caught in his own net. 'I have been perfectly well since I have been here in Oporto.' Which was true enough.

'Under the tender ministrations of Miss Emerson? And you think, now it suits you, to come straight from her arms to my daughter's. I hope I am too good a father to permit that, Mr Craddock. I have quite other plans for

Caterina.'

'I know,' said Jeremy. 'She told me. And they are monstrous, sir. That is why I made bold to offer myself sooner than I would otherwise have dared to do, after what I confess was my folly over Miss Emerson.'

'And that is why she took you.' Father Pedro spoke for the first time, though Jeremy had felt him in implicit control of the conversation throughout.

'Maybe,' said Jeremy. 'But what is that to the purpose? You gave her the choice of marriage or the silent order, sir.' He spoke directly to Gomez. 'And this is her answer. Do you propose to go back on your given word?'

'It was I, not Senhor Gomez, who put the proposition to his daughter,' said Father Pedro.

'And that lets Senhor Gomez out? What kind of sophistry is that? And do you, I wonder, stand to gain from it?' He looked from one man to the other and saw that he was right. 'I tell you both that I consider myself engaged to Miss Gomez, with or without your consent, sir. As her fiancé, I will fight any attempt to incarcerate her with the silent sisters. The Bishop of Oporto, I know, is her godfather... I mean to return to England shortly, and should be proud and happy to take her with me, as my affianced bride, to stay with our mutual grandmother, until I can provide a fitting home for her.'

'Brave words,' said Father Pedro.

'Believe that I mean them.' And the odd thing was that it was true.

'I have listened to enough of this ranting.' Gomez's hand was on the bell-pull. 'Tonio, show Mr Craddock out. He will not be admitted again.'

The great door slammed behind him. Too late, Jeremy wished he had insisted on seeing Caterina again, but he had been too angry to think straight. He was still trying to marshal his furious thoughts when he reached the marketplace. He paused for a moment to catch his breath and watch the women packing up their wares for the day. He had committed himself to so much, and yet got nowhere. And what in the world was he going to do now?

First, he thought, he must write to the Bishop of Oporto. That had been no idle threat; he well remembered with what affection Caterina had spoken of him on their happy voyage out. And then, he must look a little into the affairs of the firm of Gomez, Sanchez and Brown. Something Joe Camo had said had made him wonder whether they, like the Wares, might not have been hard hit by the years of war. It seemed all too likely when once he started really thinking about it. But this brought him to another problem. Was he going to declare his interest to Camo? And should he not consult Caterina first? He wished more than ever now that he had not let that door shut

239

behind him, but it was too late for that kind of afterthought. Anyway, the answer was obvious. The more widely news of their engagement was spread, the greater the protection for Caterina.

'Craddock.' Was it the second time his name had been spoken? He looked up and saw Major Dickson, his arms full of bundles.

'Dickson! What in the world are you doing here?'

'Buying fruit at a price I can afford. I enjoy this market. It's a pity the prices they charge our troops are so much higher. But what's the news with you, Craddock? Are you on your way to dine at the Factory?' They had fallen into step side by side as they crossed the emptying marketplace.

'Maybe. I hadn't thought.' Here was a chance to tell his tale, and perhaps to learn something too. He knew Dickson for a man very much at the centre of things. 'I've just come from the Gomez house,' he went on. 'Congratulate me, Dickson, I am the happiest of men. Miss Gomez has said she will be my wife.' There, it was out, and he was glad.

'Goodness gracious.' Dickson suddenly sounded very Scots. 'I do congratulate you, Craddock. But—' a pause, 'with her father's consent?'

'No, there's the rub. I've just been shown the door and told not to come back.'

'Drastic,' said Dickson. 'And odd, surely. I

thought the word in town was that he fetched her over just so as to get himself a biddable son-in-law. Excuse me—'

'No need to apologise. Lord knows I have made such a public fool of myself, here in Oporto, I must seem like anyone's tool. But evidently not one Gomez wants—'

'So something has happened to change his views. I wonder what.'

They had left the marketplace now and plunged into the tangle of lanes that led down to the English Factory and the quay. 'Has it struck you, Craddock, that we are so busy fighting our own war that we tend to forget just how hard things are here in Oporto? Those market women are close to starvation, many of them. It's hard not to buy from all of them, and the prices are absurd. It can hardly be worth their walking in from their hovels in the country round, but they do it just the same. And their men just as desperate. I don't altogether like the feel of things here. And if things are so bad at the grassroots, who knows what is going on higher up? Maybe Gomez doesn't feel his affairs can stand up to the inquisitive eye of a prospective son-in-law.'

'And proposes to shuffle his daughter off to the silent sisters before she starts asking awkward questions!' exclaimed Jeremy. 'That's what he plans, you know, the day after the Wares' party.'

'Monstrous,' said Dickson. 'We can't let

that happen. What do you plan to do?'

'I thought I'd write to the Bishop of Oporto.' It sounded absurdly inadequate as he said it. 'He's her godfather, I believe.'

'He's also a very busy man down in Lisbon. Several days' ride away, and no guarantee of an immediate answer. Oh, a useful threat, I grant you, but for more immediate protection, I suggest you make sure to introduce the young lady, as your fiancée, to the guest of honour at the party next Tuesday. I know we are not supposed to mention the name but you and I both know he's always had an uncle's eye for a pretty girl, and he's great on the Anglo-Portuguese alliance. Entirely between ourselves, it is partly because of something I said to him, last time I was upriver, about the state of things here in Oporto that he is making this "surprise" visit. Your problem might come quite apropos to his thinking. Would you be appalled to find yourself married to the girl out of hand, with an honour guard of British dragoons?'

'No, but she would.' He regretted the words the minute they were spoken, but Dickson was laughing.

'You make me quite long to meet the young lady.' He paused at the corner of the Rua Nova dos Inglesas. 'I must get rid of my burden of fruit. Shall I see you at the Factory, Craddock? I'm off upriver in the morning to meet the great man.'

242

'Not today, I think. I feel I rather owe it to my landlady to tell her my news before it reaches her by the Portonian grapevine.'

'You are absolutely right, and how Mrs Ware would hate to hear you call her your landlady. So, the news is public?'

'As public as possible. The engagement, that is. No need to speak of old Gomez's reaction. The more I think about it, the more I hope he will sleep on it and settle for me as a lesser evil.'

'Ah,' said Dickson, 'But less than what?'

Left alone, Jeremy looked at his watch. Joe Camo observed the Portuguese habit of siesta and should be just back in his office. There was comfortable time to call on him before the Wares' English dinner hour. And if anyone could throw light on the Gomez business it would be Joe Camo.

He was glad to find Camo alone, reading vintage reports in his sumptuous, mahogany-furnished office.

'Of course I have a moment for you. I'm glad enough to leave this depressing reading.' He put down the last report. 'It is going to be a bad winter, here in Porto. But what can I do for you, Craddock? Don't tell me those Emersons have changed their minds again?'

'No, it's not that. Something quite else.' How very awkwardly it came in the context of the Emersons. 'The case is, Camo, that I am the happiest of men. Miss Gomez has said she will be my wife.'

'Caterina Gomez? Well, I'll be—' He broke off, held out his hand. 'I do congratulate you, Craddock, with all my heart. I've not had the pleasure of meeting her, but a delightful young lady, by all reports, and full of character.'

'She's going to need all of it. Her father has turned me down, forbidden me the house.'

'Has he so? On what grounds, may I ask?'

'My wretched health.'

'But you don't believe that is the real reason?'

'No, I don't think I do. That *éminence grise* of his, Father Pedro, was with him throughout the interview. I did wonder—'

'As well you might. A pity the old man did not send for his daughter sooner. He's the only active partner in the firm, did you know? And not active enough, by what I hear. Don't think it's a fortune you are marrying, Craddock.'

'It's a woman!' Absurd to be angry. 'And she needs protection, Camo. Her father means to send her to the Little Sisters of Saint Seraphina.'

'The silent order? You can't mean it.'

'I'm afraid so. The day after the Wares' party. You know how things go on here better than most, Camo. Could he do it?'

'Her father, and she not of age? Oh yes, he could do it all right, and it would be the devil's own job to get her out again. What are you going to do, Craddock?'

'I wish to God I knew. First of all, I mean to

write to the Bishop of Oporto, who is her godfather. Is there a ship sailing for Lisbon, Camo?'

'No, and if there were, it would take too long to get an answer back, still less by courier, granted the state of the roads. But you write your letter, Craddock, and I will see it goes off by the swiftest route.'

'Thank you. I knew I could count on you.'

'Your best friend, and the young lady's, is going to be public opinion. It's a pity the Portuguese gentry have chosen to ignore Miss Gomez, they would be her strongest allies at this point.'

'Major Dickson suggests I make a point of introducing her as my fiancée to the guest of honour at the Wares' party, enlisting his support.'

'And a very good idea. I will leave you in peace to write your letter, Craddock, while I make arrangements for its delivery.'

* * *

'He refuses his consent.' After the brief, stormy interview with her father, Caterina had told her furious tale.

'Refuses? But it was he—'

'Precisely. He says he didn't know Mr Craddock was such a sick man. Unfit to help him in the business. He claims. Beyond that, he refused to discuss it. Just said we should be packing our things.'

'For the silent sisters?'

'Yes, but we're not going.'

'Of course not. But—have you any money, Cat?'

'Not a *scudo*. I spent it all on drawing materials, and not much good has come of that. I had hoped that maybe after the party I'd sell some of my pictures. No chance of that now. Thank goodness you were able to write to your mother and tell her how hopeful things look for little Lewis.'

'Yes.' Harriet managed a laugh. 'He'll be living off the fat of the land, bless him, once my mother knows there is a rich great-grandmother in the background. Do you know, Cat, the more I think about it, the more I think you had best tell the old lady about this threat of your father's. She's bound to hear about it anyway, and it will come best from you.'

'You are absolutely right,' said Caterina. 'I'll write a quick note and have Tonio get it across the canyon before night. With a bit of luck there will be one from her soon, telling me what she means to do about Luiz. And what the lawyers say. I should think it would take some fixing to turn my Lewis from a bastard into the Fonsa heir.'

'And what will they make of you?'

'I wish to goodness I knew. If only there had been more time to talk. She's formidable, that old lady. I did wonder if she might not want me out of the picture...'

'Have him all to herself? You couldn't allow that.'

'Of course not. Time to cross that bridge when we come to it.' Oh, goodness, with all this going on, I've done nothing about warning Jeremy Craddock. I hardly like to write to him, even if we are supposed to be engaged. And my father has forbidden him the house, did I tell you that?'

'No,' said Harriet. 'How absolutely Gothic. Do you think he is in his right mind, Cat?'

'I think he has talked to no one but Father Pedro for so long that he has quite forgotten what the real world is like.'

'But surely, at the office—'

'They are all his inferiors there, terrified of him—'

'It can't be good for the business,' said practical Harriet. 'In fact, Mr Ware did say something, the other day, that made me wonder a little. Oh, Cat, you do know, don't you, that if he should ever ... that if I ... oh, I don't even dare think of it, but there would always be a home for you.'

'Dear Harryo.' They kissed each other silently.

'But he won't,' said Harriet. 'His mother won't let him. And I'm not sure that I should, even if he were still to want me when I'd told him.'

247

'Don't think about it, love. It makes me superstitious. And, besides, I must write my dreary tale to the old lady. Do you realise that in less than a week's time, the day after the party, we may be condemned to the silent sisters.'

'Yes,' said Harriet soberly. 'I do indeed.'

CHAPTER FOURTEEN

Jeremy Craddock dropped what he did not know was his bombshell at the Wares' dinner table that evening. He had been glad to find Mrs Ware and her son dining alone, and seized an early chance to ask them to join him in a toast: 'To my fiancée,' he said. 'Miss Gomez has made me the happiest of men.'

'Miss Gomez?' Wine spilled from Mrs Ware's glass. 'I don't believe it!'

'Mother—' Frank shot a warning glance at the liveried servants waiting at table. 'I do congratulate you, Craddock.' He raised his glass and drank. 'A delightful girl. It will make our party on Tuesday more of a celebration than ever.' Another quick look for his mother, who was sitting rigid between them, scarlet spots clashing with the rouge on her normally pale cheeks. 'You will be settling with us here in Oporto then?'

'I'm not so sure of that. Her father dislikes

the match, I am sorry to say. He has actually forbidden me the house. I was hoping for your good offices, Ware, to keep me in touch with my fiancée.' He was furious with himself for having failed to recognise Mrs Ware's plans for her son and Caterina. What a blind fool he had been.

'Nonsense.' Mrs Ware found her voice. 'Of course Gomez dislikes the match. You'll have no part in this, Frank.'

'I am sorry to disagree with you, mother.' He looked from her to Jeremy. 'But what in the world has got into old Gomez?'

'He talks of sending the two girls to the Little Sisters of St Seraphina.'

'What?'

'On Wednesday.'

'But he has no right—'

'Certainly none as regards Miss Brown, but Joe Camo says a Portuguese father could do this to his daughter if he wished.'

'Barbarous,' said Frank.

'Well, they are,' said his mother, who seemed to have recovered herself. They none of them noticed that one of the footmen had slipped quietly from the room.

*　　*　　*

The servant who took Caterina's second note to Madame Fonsa brought back only her answer to the first one. The old lady had already retired to her room when he got there, he explained, and nobody dared disturb her until next day. The note he brought was short and to the point, written in the old lady's own spidery hand: 'Thank you. Keep away from him.'

'As if I would do anything else,' Caterina told Harriet. 'It's Jeremy I'm worried about now. I do hope she gets up early and does something at once.'

'Poor woman,' said Harriet. 'Her own grandson. She must have so hoped you would prove him innocent. I'm afraid you must face it, Cat, it's bound to take a bit of time for her to make up her mind. And then she will have to prove to the authorities that she's not the mad old thing people have thought her. I have the horridest feeling that Luiz is going to hear about your "engagement" and do something drastic to Jeremy Craddock long before his grandmother does anything about him. I do think you ought to warn Mr Craddock, Cat.'

'But how?'

'Well, you can't tonight, that's for sure.' She put down her sewing. 'It's been a long day. I think bed, don't you?'

'Yes.' But Caterina sat up for hours in her bedroom, trying and failing to write a warning note to Jeremy about Luiz. It was impossible, she decided at last. Her story was not one to be told in writing. She must see him somehow.

It was pouring with rain again in the

morning and there was no word from across the canyon. 'I doubt if anyone would cross in this,' said Caterina gloomily as she and Harriet finished an anxious breakfast.

'And no one will call either,' said Harriet. 'Oh how I wish we were in England, love, and all well.'

'I wish we had never come!'

'Oh, no.' Harriet turned to the door, where Tonio had appeared.

'The Senhor Ware has called, *minha senhora*. He apologises for the early hour and asks to see you urgently. Alone.'

'Me?' Harriet sat as if paralysed for a moment, looking at Caterina. 'Cat—' She paused, tried again. 'If he should—if it were . . . I'd have to tell him—'

'I think it's time for some telling,' said Caterina. 'Off you go, love, don't keep the urgent gentleman waiting. And don't let him go without seeing me.'

'Of course not.' Here at least was a reliable messenger.

Harriet was trembling when she joined Frank Ware in the library, where he had been shown by a servant surprised and interested by the early visit.

'Miss Brown—' He came forward as the servant closed the door silently behind her. 'Harriet! Craddock told us his good news last night. It's the best I ever heard. Or it would be if it were not for this lunacy of old Gomez's. Is it

251

really true that he means to pack the two of you off to the silent sisters next week?'

'On Wednesday.' Her hand was still in his.

'We can't let it happen,' he said. 'Craddock is doing his best to stop it, but it will take time.'

'And there is no time.'

'Exactly. I'm glad you see it. Harriet!' The way he used her name said it all. 'I had meant to wait until I had a future to offer you, but I can't now. You must give me the right to protect you both, you and your friend. Let's not pretend with each other, my love, there's no time for that. We love each other, you and I, we know it. Say you'll marry me, Harriet?' He was beginning to pull her to him, happily sure of her answer.

'No! Not yet.' She held back, meeting his eyes, with tears in hers. 'It's not your future that's the problem, Frank Ware, it is my past.'

'I don't care a straw for your past. And anyway I know about it, love. My mother had enquiries made, I am ashamed to tell you. She told me just the other day. I know all about your mother, and your birth, and the home for foundling children. It doesn't matter, I tell you. It's you I want to marry, not your mother. And, besides, one must respect her for making her own way in the world. Just what I mean to do myself.'

She stood there, for a long moment, meeting his eyes, thinking about it, horribly tempted. Then: 'I am more grateful than I can say. It

252

only makes me love you more, makes it harder, but I have to tell you. There is more.'

'More?'

'And worse.'

'Worse?' Did he blench?

'Much worse.' She went steadily on. 'My mother had ambitions for me. Things were going well with her then. She sent me to a boarding school for the daughters of gentlemen. I made friends with an upper-crust girl there, was asked to stay with them. Mother thought it was wonderful, such a chance for me. Sent me off rejoicing. A girl without friends, without protection, without a name of her own. Little Miss Brown.' She paused, took a deep breath. 'I wasn't seduced, Frank, I was raped, quite casually, because it was a wet afternoon. Not a member of the family, just a hanger-on. I didn't dare tell anyone. How could I? But I went home pregnant.'

'Harriet!' At some point he had sat her down on a little sofa, sat himself close, and put a protective arm around her. Now it tightened. 'And the baby?'

'Stillborn. I cried myself sick.' Her eyes were far away as she remembered how hungry little Lewis had eased her misery. 'I still dream of her.'

'Her? A little girl? Like you ... Harriet, we'll have more—' He stopped, searching for words. 'Harriet, you can—It didn't?—'

'Oh yes. It was just bad luck, they said. Only

253

they thought it good luck of course.'

'You poor child. How old were you, Harriet, and then we'll say no more about it?'

'Thirteen,' she told him, and let him pull her, at last, into the haven of his arms.

* * *

Counting out sovereigns for the Emersons, Jeremy Craddock realised that the payment was going to leave him uncomfortably short of funds, just when he looked like needing them most. The information they provided had better be good, he told himself, as he dressed quickly for his ten o'clock appointment. He had decided overnight that there was no chance of catching Frank Ware alone before he left for the office, and wild horses would not make him breakfast alone with Mrs Ware today. He would get himself a cup of coffee on his way to the Emersons' house, though it would probably be very nasty.

It was pouring with rain again, dripping through his umbrella, and he found himself envying the Portuguese peasants the curious straw thatches in which they braved the weather. The bag of sovereigns was heavy; his feet were wet; he found no café; he was in a very bad temper when he reached the Emersons' apartment, sharp at ten.

They were sitting comfortably over a breakfast of coffee and rolls and he saw with a mixture of irritation and pleasure that a cup had been laid for him.

'You'll join us, Mr Craddock?' Rachel reached out for the coffee pot. Her pale hair was neatly braided round her head this morning and it made her look years older. With no sun outside, the little room was dark and gloomy, a million miles from the sea cave where she had enthralled him.

'Thank you.' He put his bag of sovereigns down with a little click on the breakfast table, close to his hand.

'Sugar? Milk? Pass Mr Craddock the rolls, my dear,' she turned a wife's glance on her husband. 'I was sure you could not face breakfast with your outraged hostess, Mr Craddock.' She smiled at him and he hated her. 'We are to congratulate you, I believe. Quick work, Mr Craddock.'

Now he hated her entirely: 'You know already?'

'I imagine all Oporto knows by now. And that you are forbidden the house. Had you considered that you might find yourself left with the girl and not the fortune?'

'If there is a fortune,' said Ralph Emerson.

'That is not what I came to discuss.' Anger grated in Jeremy's voice. 'You have some information for me, I trust.' It irked him to find himself hungrily eating her bread.

'Indeed we have. And you, I am glad to see, have the needful for us. You won't believe how the duns come down when they hear you are booked to leave. It's a lady you need to investigate, Mr Craddock, Madame Feuillide, a dressmaker. She makes for your fiancée, I believe, as for everyone else of note here in Oporto. Never for me. I couldn't afford her prices. But of course being so expensive is what makes the ladies adore her. Clever of her, when you think she has been in French pay ever since she came here, almost twenty years ago. Oh, a clever lady, Madame Feuillide, with a spy in every household and an ear at every door. It is not just poverty that makes us wait upon ourselves, it's common sense. What the servants don't know, they can't report back. I have no doubt she is wondering this morning what use she should make of your surprise engagement.'

'So she has been your paymaster?' He immensely disliked this harping on his engagement.

'Not directly. We are not supposed to know about her, but I am no fool either, and it was not too difficult to follow the chain and find her at the end of it. She does not—I hope she does not —know that we know. If she does, all the more reason for our being on the next boat home. So—' reaching out for it, 'we get our money, Mr Craddock?'

'Not yet.' She had convinced him, but his hand closed over the bag of sovereigns just the same. 'As I remember it, Mrs Emerson, you said that Oporto leaked like a sieve. The understanding was that you would tell me about all the leaks.'

'A servant in every house. I told you. And us, of course. I don't wish to brag, Mr Craddock, but it is remarkable what I have been able to pick up from my patients. And my clever Ralph as he walked about the quays. Are you going to make a point of introducing your fiancée to Lord Wellington when he comes next week? I would, if I were you. He has an eye for the girls, they say. I'm really sad not to be able to stay and meet him.' She laughed, and he wondered how he could ever have thought her laugh delightful. 'Don't look so anxious, Mr Craddock, there's no one to hear but us three. The secret of the "very important guest" is safe with us.' Once again she stretched out a hopeful hand for the gold.

But his was still firm on the bag. 'I am absolutely certain that you meant more leaks than one,' he persisted. 'I'm armed, by the way, don't think of violence.'

'Violence is not our line,' she told him. 'That's been our strength—and our weakness—all along. As to these "leaks" you are so insistent about, I suppose what I had in mind when I made that rash remark was Madame Feuillide's connection with the household across the valley from your new fiancée's house. Ask her about the Sanchez family, Mr Craddock. I had meant to look into

257

it, but there's been no time, with all this endless packing and arguing about bills. And another thing, while you sit there looking so obstinate, dear Jeremy, be honest with yourself and admit that I have done you a great deal of good, though not perhaps just what you expected. But, of course, you never did suffer from the falling sickness, did you?'

'You knew all the time?'

'Of course I knew. I may be a spy, but that does not mean I am not a healer too. You owe me that money.'

'Perhaps I do.' He handed it over and left, still fuming.

'Congratulations,' said Ralph Emerson when Jeremy had been seen safely off the premises. 'You didn't tell him. Why not I wonder?'

'Sheer devilry, I think. He should not have engaged himself so soon.' It had stopped raining, which was something. Jeremy turned down towards the quay. His next call must be on Frank Ware in the blessed privacy of his office. He would persuade him to call at the Gomez house that very day and arrange for Caterina to meet him as soon as possible. There was so much he had to say to her. He must warn her about Madame Feuillide the dressmaker and ask her about the Sanchez household. She would know where they could inconspicuously meet. The cathedral, perhaps?

But when he got to Frank Ware's office it

was to learn that he had not come in that morning. 'He sent word that he would not be in until late afternoon, *senhor*.'

'Might he be across at Villa Nova de Gaia?' Jeremy was shocked by the look of dust and inactivity about the Ware offices, a sharp contrast to the atmosphere at Webb, Campbell, Gray and Camo. Things must be bad with the Wares. No wonder Mrs Ware had hoped for a marriage between her son and Caterina Gomez.

'I do not think so, *senhor*,' the man told him. 'There is not much need.' He pocketed Jeremy's tip and smiled a sly smile. 'We think perhaps he is making a morning call.'

Fool that he was not to have thought of this. Frank's mother might still be hoping for a match between her son and Caterina Gomez, but he had seen Frank and Harriet together often enough to know why Caterina had turned not to Frank but to himself for help. The news of old Gomez's threat would have sent Frank hotfoot up to the house this morning. He left the depressing office and walked rapidly uphill. With a bit of luck he might catch Frank emerging from the Gomez house and persuade him to go back in and give his message. Reaching the house without meeting him, he took one indecisive turn up and down the lane outside, then thought this ridiculous and pulled sharply at the bell.

Old Tonio opened the door, and gave him no

chance to speak. 'This door is closed to you, *senhor*.' He spoke unnecessarily loud. 'Do not give me the pain of having to turn you away.' As he spoke, he slipped Jeremy a small, tightly folded note.

'I only wished to ask if Mr Ware were here.' Jeremy took the hint and spoke clearly for the presumably listening ear.

'He left some time ago, *senhor*.'

'Then I will trouble you no further, but give my kindest regards to the *senhoras*, if you are allowed to.'

'Which I am not.' The door closed noisily in his face.

He went down to the corner of the lane, well out of sight of the closed door, before he opened the note. 'This afternoon. In the cathedral. The silver altar. C.'

What a double-dyed fool he would have been if he had not come, he thought, as he started back across the market-place. Caterina had not been able to name a time for their meeting. He would simply have to spend the afternoon in the cathedral waiting for her. He stopped and bought some fruit to pass for lunch from a gaunt market woman and remembered what Dickson had said about how starved and wretched they were. 'And this for you, mother.' He impulsively handed her an extra coin and got vehemently blessed for it. Just how bad were things in Oporto, he wondered, and was ashamed that it had taken

Dickson to alert him to the real state of affairs. He should have reported on it long since. Pitiful to have let himself waste so much time dreaming ridiculous dreams of Rachel Emerson. He would order his thoughts while he waited in the cathedral and write a full report tonight to send by Monday's boat to Plymouth. At least Caterina's plight had settled his own plans for him. Even if it were to cost him his job, he could not leave without either taking the two girls with him or seeing their affairs settled some other way. But Frank Ware's visit that morning might well have changed everything.

He stated to climb the busy stinking lanes that led up to the cathedral. He was comfortably sure that Harriet would accept Frank if he proposed. But what then? He paused to look up at the squat twin towers of the cathedral, looming against the sky. A gloomy building. He looked at his watch. It was technically afternoon by now, but he knew the habits of the Gomez household well enough to know that there was no way Caterina would be able to come out for another hour or so. The sun was out, drying puddles on the cathedral steps, and he found a dryish spot to sit and eat his fruit and wonder how much he would tell Caterina when she came. He could hardly ask her about the dressmaker and the Sanchez family without some explanation. How very much he disliked the idea of telling her he had used her and Harriet Brown as cover for his spying.

And what a selfish wretch he was to be thinking of this now. The first thing was to protect the two girls from the threat of the silent sisters. Gomez's refusal to accept him as prospective son-in-law had been a setback, but he rather hoped Frank Ware would step into the breach. He had probably already done so. Until last night he had discounted Frank, thinking him clay in his mother's hands, but that had changed now. The worm had turned. Caterina would bring the news that she and Harriet had arranged to go to the Wares' for sanctuary. That would let him quite off the hook. His pretence engagement would no longer be needed as protection for Caterina, and the best thing he could do for her would be to take Monday's boat for Plymouth and leave her to break off the false engagement at her leisure, on whatever pretext she pleased.

How very strange. He did not want to go. He thought about it a little and decided that he could not leave before the party, however well that might suit Caterina. He badly wanted to meet Wellington, and besides there were altogether too many overtones about that party. He could not possibly imagine missing it.

The great bell of the cathedral chimed the hour and he got rather stiffly to his feet. Time to go inside and find a quiet corner in which to wait for Caterina. He knew the Portuguese people's easy relations with their church well enough to be sure that there would be such a place where he could sit unnoticed and seem to pray, and go on trying to collect his ragged thoughts.

Music and the smell of incense greeted him as he pushed open the heavy cathedral door. It was Friday, of course. He should have expected a service. It was just as well that Catherina had named the side chapel where the silver altar had been protected from the marauding French by its coat of concealing paint. There were fewer people there and he was able to find himself a secluded seat not too far from the entrance.

It was a long wait. The service was almost over when Caterina slipped quietly into the pew beside him, and knelt at once to pray, ignoring his quick movement of recognition. Impatient thoughts seethed in his head as she prayed. In a little while the service would be over and their talk more likely to be overheard.

Her first words astonished him. 'I am afraid I have put you at risk,' she pushed back her black veil a little so that the words were channelled directly to him only.

'At risk?' He leaned his head close to hers. 'What can you mean? Surely your father would not—'

'No, no, he thinks the matter settled. He has spoken; that is all there is to it. He means us to

263

go to the silent sisters on Wednesday, Harriet and I, just the same. I've risked your life for nothing. I am so sorry.'

'Risked my life?' What madness was this?

'Listen, please. I have to tell you. I should never have involved you.'

'But I am glad to be involved! I am just sorry it has proved so little help. And there are things I have to tell you too. How long—'

'As long as we need. We're not the first, and we won't be the last to use the church for the wrong purpose. But I think we had best talk in Portuguese.' Changing to that language. 'To be less noticeable. Frank Ware came this morning,' she told him. 'Harriet has accepted him, I'm glad to say, but it solves nothing for me. He vows he will take us to his mother on Wednesday, but Father Pedro says I will not be let go. And I am afraid my father could do it.'

'Yes,' he said soberly. 'I talked to Joe Camo—I hope you don't mind—and he said he thought your father's word would be paramount. He urged that I present you to Lord Wellington at the party on Tuesday. He thinks your best protection lies there.'

'But I am afraid something may have happened to you before that.'

'To me? What in the world do you mean?'

'You must have heard the stories about me.' She plunged right into it. 'Well, they are true. There was a man; my father found us together. I was sent to England. He is here in Porto; he

264

thinks he owns me, body and soul. He will have heard, by now, about our "engagement". He will kill you, I think, or arrange to have you killed. I never thought; I was desperate; I am so ashamed. He is a revolutionary, you see, a tool of the French, and in league with violent men. Anything could happen.'

'Who is he?' he asked. And then, because he must: 'But Caterina, *does* he own you, body and soul?'

'No! Thank God. But it took me too long to realise it. I won't make excuses; too late for that. I have none. I have risked your life for nothing. Please, for my sake, for my peace of mind, take the next Plymouth boat. I'd never forgive myself if anything happened to you.'

'And leave you to the silent sisters? Never. But who is he, Caterina?'

She bent a little closer and he got a familiar, heart-stirring hint of the perfume she always wore. 'Luiz de Fonsa y Sanchez,' she whispered so low that he could only just catch it. 'He is in hiding, out at Madame Feuillide's. He left with the French in 1809, can't show his face in town. He believed their tales of an independent kingdom of Lusitania, hopes to use them for his own ends. But I think they are using him. He's planning revolution, here in Porto, wanted me to spy for him. I'm afraid I did answer some of his questions; it makes me so ashamed. I was a fool, beglamoured. And then I realised how he had changed, poor Luiz.

Or how I had. But the thing is, don't you see, he thinks I'm his property, his thing to do with as he likes. When he hears of our "engagement" he will be out of his mind with rage, might risk everything for revenge on you. That's why you must take that Plymouth boat. And be desperately careful in the mean time.'

'Impossible,' he said. 'I can't leave now. But you are right about Madame Feuillide; that's what I came to warn you about, that she is in French pay. And has some kind of connection with the house across the canyon from you. Of course,' he remembered, 'the Sanchez house.'

'Yes. Luiz's family home. He can't go there himself, but he told me he has a spy there.' No need, and no time, to tell him about the old lady. 'He's dangerous, Mr Craddock, do please believe that.' She leaned close again. 'You remember that attack on Father Pedro? I think Luiz was responsible for that.'

'Why?'

'He wanted him out of the way. He had his own plans for me, you see. Still has. He is going to be terribly angry. He never could bear to be crossed. He talked, half in earnest, of coming disguised to the Wares' party on Tuesday. To keep an eye on me, he said. Did you know that Madame Feuillide plans to stay with them for the party? To be available for us young ladies, she said.'

'But you don't believe it?'

'No. Something is planned for that party.

266

I'm sure of it. I wish I knew how she had persuaded Mrs Ware to have her there.'

'It surprises you?'

'Yes, it does a little. I'm not quite sure why. Something about the way they speak of each other. Call it woman's instinct, if you like, but don't laugh at it.' She pulled her veil close around her face. 'I have been away as long as I dare. Do, please, for my sake, be very careful. I'd never forgive myself. Luiz is—' she paused, thought about it, 'dangerous. You'll speak to Wellington the minute he gets here?'

'Just as soon as I can. I've not been much help so far, but, Caterina, I promise you can count on me. Trust me for that. Whatever happens.'

'Thank you, I do.' She rose, genuflected to the altar, and left him.

CHAPTER FIFTEEN

The cathedral was quiet now, the service over, and the dim light getting dimmer. Jeremy sat where he was for a while, trying to make sense of it all. Why was it so hard to think clearly, dispassionately? He knew, really. It was because of Caterina and this unknown Luiz. It was not the threat of danger that sent the blood racing furiously through his veins; it was their relationship. They had been lovers, she and this young Portuguese traitor. It put her beyond the pale; an outcast from society.

And who was he to think so? He who had dangled after Rachel Emerson, let her lead him by the nose so ignominiously. He could suddenly not bear to sit still a moment longer, but rose to his feet and hurried out of the cathedral into the gathering dusk. And yet he must be quiet, must think it all out. He should have stayed in the cathedral, the only peaceful place now that the Ware house was so full of activity. Something twitched in his mind about the Ware house. The party? What had Caterina said about the party? She seemed to think Luiz's plans revolved around it. That he might not act till then. No, that was not it. Niggling at the back of his mind were all the postponements. It had been the recurrent theme of his early days with the Wares. Mrs Ware announcing that the wine had not come, the party must be put off again, the floors were not ready ... And then, suddenly, it had been fixed for next Tuesday.

And all the time, part of his mind had been on Wellington, trying to decide how to approach him, how much to tell him. He had never met either of the two powerful Wellesley brothers, and very much wished now that he knew more about them. It was absurd that he had been given no contact here in Oporto, and because of his own ambiguous position he had no useful friend in the British establishment here. The best thing he could do was to go straight to the top, to talk to Wellington himself, and not just about Caterina. But how?

And that was another thing, restless at the back of his mind. Had the news of the 'very important guest' come before or after the moment when Mrs Ware finally fixed the date for her party? He rather thought he had heard it after, but then Mrs Ware might easily have had earlier information. He knew her for the spider at the heart of the British colony's web of gossip. It had certainly all come very much at the same time: the party and the very important guest and the hope that he would find his way from the dinner at the English Factory to the festivities down the road. Well, of course, tuft-hunting Mrs Ware would want this hero for her party. Nothing odd about that.

Hardly noticing what he was doing he had climbed to the height above the cathedral that Wellington's troops had stormed two years before so as to retake Oporto. He stopped by the ruined seminary to look at the sunset blazing out to sea. Was he actually beginning to think again? He felt his mind clear, as if after an illness. What had they done to him, Rachel Emerson's subtle hands? What kind of hypnotic trickery had she practised on him? Never mind that. She would be gone tomorrow: it was over. And this was not the moment to be brooding about the past. The sense of urgency was strong upon him. It was time he started to behave like a sensible man.

*   *   *

The house doors swung open as Caterina's sedan chair stopped in the courtyard, and Tonio hurried out to greet her. 'Thank the good God you are back at last, *minha senhora.* Your father has been asking for you; he has a caller; it's the old lady from across the valley, would you believe it, the Senhora Fonsa herself. She came in her carriage; they could not believe their eyes in the stable yard. Her servants carried her in, as if she were a queen. She made Senhor Gomez send Father Pedro away, said she must talk to him alone. They've been at it half an hour. And now he wants you.'

'What did you tell him?'

'What you said. That you had gone to the cathedral to pray for guidance. He said you were to join them the very minute you got back.'

'Then I had best do so. Thank you, Tonio.'

She found the old lady enthroned in her father's own great chair, with Carlotta in attendance beside her, smelling salts in hand. Gomez, deprived of his normal seat, was pacing up and down the room, livid with rage. 'There you are at last, Caterina. What in the world possessed you to go jaunting off to the cathedral without a word to anyone?'

270

'Harriet and the servants knew where I was, father.' She went forward to kiss the old lady on her wrinkled cheek. 'Dear madam, it was good of you to come.'

'Of course I came! And I am enjoying my visit, too, whatever you say.' This to Carlotta, who looked racked with anxiety. 'I shall sleep tonight for a change. And if coming out should chance to kill me, as you seem to expect, Carlotta, well you could call that a good sleep too. But I don't mean it to. I have too much to do; this is the beginning of a whole new life for me. I am come to invite you and your friend, whatever her name is, to live with me,' she told Caterina. 'The whole town is shocked at this talk of the silent sisters, and so I have told your father. If I had been consulted three years ago, you would have married my grandson. Now you are to be my grand-daughter. I have been telling your fool of a father how things stand in my family. The Fonsa money has always been mine, to do with as I please. I meant it for Luiz, but when he disgraced himself and us by joining the French two years ago I had to think again. He'll never touch a *scudo* of mine, and neither shall that hopeless father of his. So, child, here is my offer. Pack up your traps, come across the valley to brighten an old lady's house, and, if we suit, you shall be my heir.'

'I'm overwhelmed.' It was true. How gravely she had misjudged old Madame Fonsa, and how she admired the speed with which she had

271

grasped and taken advantage of the new situation.

'One stipulation, mind you.' The old lady's dark-rimmed eyes held Caterina's. 'This idiotic engagement your father speaks of, to some invalid of an Englishman; that must be broken off before I receive you. I'll have no hanger-on.'

Odd that it should grate on her nerves to hear Jeremy Craddock so summarily dismissed. But, 'That's not a problem,' she said coolly. 'Mr Craddock only proposed to me out of the kindness of his heart, because he knew how intolerably I was placed. He will be glad enough to be released. But Miss Brown has a hanger-on,' she smiled at the old lady now. 'Harriet has engaged herself to young Mr Ware, just this morning, and I doubt he will give her up so easily.'

'Oh, I don't mind Mr Ware,' said the old lady graciously. 'That's settled then. You will dispose of this Mr Craddock.'

She turned a sharp glance on Senhor Gomez who had looked increasingly foolish as he listened helplessly to the arrangements being made. 'I take it you will admit the poor young fellow to your house so that your daughter can put paid to his pretensions?' She left no time for Gomez to answer, but turned back to Caterina. 'I shall need to make a few changes in my household before you arrive. You will deal with young Craddock while I do that, and then, on Wednesday, with this ridiculous party safe over, come to me, you and Miss Brown, instead of to the silent sisters. You can hardly object to that.' The dark eyes flashed back to Gomez. 'She will not need a *scudo* from you; it can all go to Father Pedro's friars, if that is really what you wish. And the name of Gomez gone for good.' Her claw of a hand reached out to clutch Caterina's. 'I mean to ask you to change your name to Fonsa when I rewrite my will. You won't mind that?'

'No.' Caterina met her father's angry eyes squarely. 'I won't mind that at all, dear madam.'

*   *   *

'If I had only known she was so clever.' Caterina was telling Harriet about the interview. 'It takes care of everything, don't you see? Presently we will bring over little Lewis, child of a secret marriage, I suppose. England is a long way off. And he will be a Fonsa like me.'

'And the old lady will then leave everything to him,' warned Harriet.

'I am sure you are right, but why should I mind that? Lewis will never let his mother starve. Oh, Harriet, how soon do you think we will be able to get him here?'

'With that formidable old lady behind you? Pretty soon, I would think. I must say I quite long to meet her.' She paused. 'Now all you have to do is dispose of poor Jeremy Craddock. And the sooner and the more publicly the better, don't you think? To remove the threat from Luiz? I take it your father made no objection?'

'My father knew he had not a leg to stand on. I have to say, Harriet, that it was a great pleasure to see him so completely at a stand. That was a masterstroke of Madame Fonsa's about wanting me to change my name. It went deep. I almost felt sorry for him.'

'Not quite, I hope.'

'Oh, no, not quite. Harriet, sometimes I think of what it must have been like for my poor mother ... Will you be as glad to get out of this house as I shall?'

'Yes, I am afraid so. But, Cat, should you not be summoning Mr Craddock? I do think the sooner you let him off the hook the better.'

'You are absolutely right. I'll send at once, though it's too late for him to come today. I do hope Madame Fonsa is none the worse for being out in the evening air. I could see that Carlotta, her maid, was worried to death about her.'

'I wonder what it will be like living there?'

'Better than here, I am sure.'

'How sad that is.' Jeremy had dined at the English Factory and did not get Caterina's note until very late indeed. Whatever it was that made her want to see him so urgently, and with her father's permission too, would have to wait until morning. He had meant to be down at the quay to watch the Emersons safe on board the *Washington*, was glad to have a reason for avoiding this. He was sure they meant to go. In fact, Rachel Emerson's obvious eagerness to be gone before the party was yet another cause for anxiety. She had explained it by talk of the threat of war between England and America, but this seemed an unlikely enough story in retrospect. He had mentioned the possibility of war, casually, over dinner at the Factory the night before and it had been greeted with gales of dismissive laughter by the military men of the party.

He was thinking about this as he crossed the marketplace. Had Rachel Emerson gone on deceiving him to the end? It seemed all too likely. He stopped. A hand was tugging at his coat. He turned back, surprised, and recognised the haggard old woman from whom he had bought fruit the day before. She was selling little tight bouquets of flowers today. 'Buy one for your pretty lady, *senhor*?'

Well, why not? It was his first visit to his 'fiancée' after all, thought it was disconcerting that the old woman seemed to know this. 'Thank you, mother.' He took the flowers and handed her a lavish handful of small coins.

'God bless you, *senhor*.' She smiled gap-toothed at him. 'It is dry today, the sun is

275

shining, but there will be a storm on Tuesday, St Bruxa's Eve. Best stay home that day, you and the pretty lady together.'

'What do you mean?' But she had turned her back on him to cajole another possible customer.

He arrived at the Gomez house very thoughtful, but for the moment Caterina's news drove everything else from his head. 'You mean to go and live there?' He could not believe his ears. 'And what in the world will your Luiz think of that?'

'Not my Luiz,' she said. 'And Madame Fonsa and I could hardly discuss him in front of my father. I mean to call on her today, ostensibly to tell her that I have done her bidding and you and I are no longer engaged. That will give us a chance to talk. But I haven't thanked you properly.' She held out an impulsive hand. 'I am more grateful to you than I can say.'

He took and held it, resisting a strong urge to kiss it. 'Are you sure you will be happy there? It seems a rash enough move to me. Should you not rather let me take you back to your English grandmother?'

Now she wished she had told him about little Lewis. But this was not the moment for that revelation. 'Old Lady Trellgarten is poor as a church mouse,' she told him. 'I would only be a burden on her. And I *like* Madame Fonsa. I can be happy with her, I think.'

276

'And her grandson?' He had just realised that the curious feeling that plagued him was jealousy. How ridiculous.

'Poor Luiz,' she said, making it worse. 'God knows what is going to happen to him. You must tell everyone at once that I have broken off our engagement because of my father's objections. I won't breathe easy until I am sure that Luiz knows. Lord, I will be glad when that party of Mrs Ware's is safely over.'

'We are going to cut a couple of fairly ludicrous figures at it, I am afraid, you and I.'

'Yes, aren't we,' she said cheerfully. 'If that is the worst of it! Are those for me?'

'Of course. Stupid of me.' He had dropped the flowers on a garden table when she broke her news to him. 'They were for my fiancée,' he said wryly. 'Take them as a dear friend, Caterina. But they come with a warning.' He described his two encounters with the old woman. 'What should I think about that?'

'It confirms all my instincts,' she said. 'Something is going to happen at that party.'

'I think so too. All the British colony will be gathered under one roof.'

'And Lord Wellington,' she reminded him.

'Yes, and that's a funny thing. All those postponements. Can you remember whether the news of Wellington's visit came before Mrs Ware finally fixed the date for that party?'

'No.' She thought about it. 'But it was very much at the same time. But you cannot suspect

277

Mrs Ware?'

'She's a very silly woman. And, by the sound of her, Madame Feuillide a very clever one. You don't think that perhaps some mixture of blandishment with a touch of blackmail...?'

'Oh dear, yes I do. Did you know that Madame Feuillide plans to spend the night of the party at Mrs Ware's house? That surprised me when she told me, but of course it would make sense if she has some kind of hold over her. And I am afraid we are none of us heroines to our dressmakers. I can easily imagine some silly secret of poor Mrs Ware's that she would rather die than have exposed to public scorn.'

'Or let someone else die?'

'I don't think she has much imagination,' said Caterina. 'What are we going to do? Should we not go to the authorities?'

'Which? Portuguese or English? I wish your bishop was here. We could trust him. Or Colonel Trant, but the acting governor is an entirely unknown quantity. For all I know he might be implicated in a move against the unpopular British, if that is really what is afoot. And the last thing we want to do is exacerbate the feeling against us. Just imagine how delighted the French would be to see the Portuguese and the English at each other's throats.'

'That's it, of course,' she said. 'That's what Madame Feuillide is planning. She is using Luiz just as she is Mrs Ware.'

'And we have to stop her without seeming to. Could you make Luiz understand that, do you think?'

'Not a chance. He thinks women are to be played with, not listened to. But there must be someone you know who would believe you.'

'I feel such a fool.' He came out with it at last. 'It is more than time I told you. I am here on false pretences, have been all along. I'm not here for my health; there's nothing wrong with that, it was merely a cover. I was sent as a spy, to find out who was leaking information to the French. I used you, as a cover Caterina, you and Harriet. Forgive me?'

'You were very useful to us on the way out.' She smiled at him. 'I confess I had wondered a little about your health, but it was no business of mine. And you found your spy, I take it, in Rachel Emerson. Poor Mr Craddock.'

'And her husband,' he said savagely. And looked at his watch. 'They will be on board ship by now, thank God, and good riddance. And my report goes to England on Monday's ship.'

'To England?'

'Yes, that's the devil of it. I was given no contact here, told I was entirely on my own and would be disowned if I should get into any kind of trouble.'

'How very stupid of your employers. It does leave us rather at a stand, does it not?'

He could have kissed her for that 'us'. 'I

279

think it has to be Wellington himself,' he said. 'I hope to God he gets here in good time before the party. And that I can find some means of getting to talk to him at once. I've been racking my brains about that. I had counted on Major Dickson to put me in touch, but he has gone upriver to meet the general.'

'I'm sure Frank Ware could help you about that,' she said. 'Did you know that he and Harriet are engaged? That is one good thing that has come out of my father's threats.'

'I wonder what Mrs Ware will think about that.'

'So do I, but I cannot say that I care.'

CHAPTER SIXTEEN

Harriet, too, had written a note the night before, and while Caterina entertained Jeremy on the sunlit terrace, she was closeted with Frank in the library. 'So you see,' she said at last, 'our problems are all to be solved by this good fairy of a Madame Fonsa. She has rolled up Senhor Gomez horse, foot and guns and we are spared the Little Sisters of St Seraphina. So, if you please, Mr Ware, we will pretend yesterday's events did not happen. I shall never forget your kindness in my hour of need, but it is over, and that must be an end to our engagement. You have had time to think about it; you must know that I am right. Please, dear Frank, make it easy for me, and let this be goodbye.'

'Never.' He had hold of both her hands. 'You are going to marry a poor man, Harriet my darling, but you are going to marry me, and soon. I told my mother last night. She was not pleased, there's no use pretending; we both knew she would not be. I have to tell you, my dearest love, that I do not think it will be possible for us to start our married life here in Oporto. My mother would make life impossible for you. So I am going to sell out to John Croft, who made me an offer for what remains of my unlucky business some time ago. He was good enough to say he would find me a place in his firm, but I think London would suit us much better, do not you? Away from Oporto's busy tongues?'

'But, Frank—'

'No buts, my own. You are my own; you let me see it yesterday, and it is too late now to pretend second thoughts. You have changed my life, Harriet. I am my own man at last, no longer just my mother's son. But it will be easier to make the change away from here. John Croft and Major Dickson both promise me help in finding work in London; it is merely to wait until something is settled there, and then we will be married, you and I, and say goodbye to Oporto and its thousand eyes and ears. But it is good to know that you will be safe with Madame Fonsa in the meanwhile. She is one of Oporto's great ladies.'

'Your mother will stay here?' She had to ask it.

'Yes. Croft promises her an annuity from the firm, God bless him. She will be able to keep the house, so long as she is prepared to go on taking lodgers after Craddock leaves. I wonder where he and Miss Gomez plan to live?'

It was not her place to tell him that Caterina was out in the garden with Jeremy that very moment, breaking off their engagement. 'He is here now,' she said, hearing voices from the terrace.

'An early caller like me, and I hope as happy as I am. May I have the chance to say so?' And before she could stop him, if indeed she wanted to, he had opened the door into the hall just as Caterina and Jeremy entered it from the garden. 'Miss Gomez, Craddock,' he moved forward impulsively. 'It is good to have the chance to tell you both how very happy I am for you. And for myself—' turning back to include Harriet.

'Dear Mr Ware,' Caterina smiled at him with great affection as Jeremy Craddock stood silent at her side. 'We do thank you, but I am afraid we do not deserve your good wishes. Mr Craddock only offered for me out of the goodness of his heart, to save me from the silent sisters. Now that threat is lifted, thanks to Madame Fonsa, I have released him from

282

the engagement. We would be most grateful if you would spare us the pain of making a public announcement to that effect. Perhaps, if you were to tell your mother, Mr Ware—?' She smiled, to take the sting out of it.

'She would certainly tell the world. But I am so sorry—' What could he say?

'Don't be sorry, it has made us the best of friends.' She took a quick decision. 'But we want to talk to you. Would you come into the garden with us? Both of you.'

Safely out on the terrace, she turned to Jeremy. 'Will you explain?'

Jeremy thought fast. 'We are a little anxious, Miss Gomez and I, about your party,' he told Frank. 'I had a warning about it from an old market woman this very morning.'

'A warning—what on earth did she say?'

'Something about expecting a storm on Tuesday, and staying safe at home, my pretty lady and I.' With a smile for Caterina. 'She said it was some day or other—St Bruxa's Eve. I never heard of a saint called that.'

'Not a saint,' Caterina exclaimed. 'A devil. You didn't tell me that!'

'It quite slipped my mind.'

'And nobody warned your mother.' Turning to Frank. 'How could I have forgotten the date? St Bruxa is the patron devil of the witches, here in Portugal. They call them *bruxas*,' she explained. 'Next Tuesday is her night—like your Halloween, only it is much

283

worse—a night of wicked licence. No sensible person stirs abroad if they can help it. Someone should have told your mother, Frank.'

'But who would?' It was almost a groan. 'The British don't know, and the Portuguese must have seen it as a chance to make fools of us, or worse. But what's to do? Impossible to change the date now. With Wellington coming—Oh!'

'Just so,' said Jeremy. 'Think what a disaster if he should be caught up in one of the outbreaks of mob violence we know the Portonians to be capable of. Could you have a quiet word with the authorities, Ware? It will come better from you than from me.'

'Indeed I will. And I'll speak to John Croft too. He's a good friend of Wellington's. The great man may well be staying with him; he often does when he is in town. We must hope he tears himself away from his fox-hunting upriver in good time, and gets here to advice us. He is the master strategist, after all, but even I can see that the moment of danger will be when the men leave the Factory after dinner and walk down to our house. What a disaster if they should encounter a mob of witches and warlocks.'

'*Bruxas* and *lobishomes* and *feiticeiras*,' Caterina told him. 'And none the less dangerous for having such outlandish names. Kill a man on Bruxa's Eve, and leave marks on his throat, and all Porto will believe that he has been killed by the *lobishomes*—you call them werewolves.'

'There will have to be patrols,' said Jeremy. 'Ware, do you think that your friend Croft would arrange for me to meet Lord Wellington? Without asking too many questions?'

'I'm sure he would, if I asked him to. Without asking too many questions?' With a friendly smile for Jeremy.

'Precisely. And I do thank you. Oh—and Ware, let's not alarm your mother with these fears of ours?'

'I should rather think not,' said Frank Ware.

*   *   *

'Just the same, I wish you would hear something from Luiz,' said Harriet. It was Sunday morning and the two girls had just come back from Mass at the Franciscans'.

'Or even from Madame Feuillide. I quite agree with you. They must have heard about my "engagement" by now. I don't know quite what I was afraid of, but I confess I do find this silence ominous.'

'I'd noticed you were keeping quite close to the house,' said Harriet. 'And very wise too. I rather wish it would start raining again.'

'I told Jeremy Craddock to keep out of dark alleys. I just hope he took me seriously. But I must say, it is a relief that Madame Fonsa has

285

found Luiz's informant in her house and got rid of him.'

'Do you think he has one in this house too?'

'I do hope not.' With a quick glance at the door. 'Madame Fonsa is sure that nothing will happen until the day of the party, and I think I agree with her. She is clever, that old lady. I wish you could have seen the letter she wrote to your mother, but she sent it straight off to catch the Plymouth packet. She had had her lawyer there and arranged about funds in Bath and everything. Just think, if your mother can find someone to bring him, Lewis could be here in two weeks or so. It all seems too good to be true. Oh Harryo, I would be so happy if I wasn't so frightened.'

'I know,' said Harriet. 'I feel just the same.'

'I wish Lord Wellington would get here.'

'Even if it does mean travelling on Sunday? So do I.'

* * *

Jeremy Craddock got his report safe on board the Plymouth packet on Monday afternoon and had returned to the discomforts of the Ware house when Croft's summons to meet Wellington came. He was glad to get out of the house again. Mrs Ware had not spoken to her son except on matters of business since he had told her of his engagement. She went about her preparations for the party red-eyed and simmering, a volcano ready to erupt. Jeremy just hoped that the inevitable explosion would not happen until after the party, and promised himself that he would find other lodgings as soon as it was over, if, indeed, he did not take the next boat for England, as of course he should. Why did he not want to go? He could not remember ever being in such a state of confusion about his own plans. What in the world was the matter with him?

His summons had been to John Croft's house rather than his office and he spent the short walk down the Rua Nova dos Inglesas trying to order his thoughts: the great man was notoriously impatient of muddled thinking.

The Croft house made him realise the pretentiousness of Mrs Ware's. Here, glowing mahogany and silver, and the family story painted by Gainsborough and Romney, spoke of years of solid, prosperous living. The main Croft vineyard, he knew, was forty miles or so upriver at Cima Douro, and Croft himself was a known expert in the business.

He had not met him before, and liked him on sight. This was a man to be reckoned with. 'I am surprised that you have not got a crowd outside the house,' he said, when the first greetings were over, and Croft had explained that Wellington was still busy with the reports he had found waiting for him. 'I thought Wellington was adored in Oporto.' Had he perhaps hoped that an enthusiastic reception for the liberator of Oporto might put paid to any plans the French might have for next day?

'It was Wellington's own wish,' explained Croft, gesturing his guest to a seat. 'He very much dislikes being mobbed, however enthusiastically. He came downriver in one of the wine barges Dickson commandeered for his military supplies, and waited for dusk to slip ashore with the crew at Villa Nova de Gaia. The first I knew of his arrival was when he banged on my door an hour ago.'

'He's wasted no time.'

'He never does. Ah.' A servant had entered the room. 'He'll see you now.'

Wellington was in the big dining-room, with papers spread all over the mahogany table. He looked up at Jeremy without moving, the cold blue eyes sharp under frowning brows. 'You were most urgent to see me, Mr Craddock. Sit down. Explain.'

'I was sent here as a spy.' Jeremy wasted no words. 'To find the source of the leak in Oporto.'

'Nobody told me. But that's no surprise. And you found it, Mr Craddock?'

'I found several.' He plunged into his story, aware that this was a remarkable listener. The few questions Wellington interjected helped to clear up points about which he was still doubtful himself.

'So you think this Miss Emerson told you the whole tale in the end?' The cold eyes held his.

'I thought so at the time, sir. Now, in retrospect, I am not so sure. She seemed—' He paused. 'Too pleased with herself.'

'Ah. No need to look so cast down. I am sure you were right to let them go. Trouble with the Americans is something we could do without just now. The place is bound to be riddled with spies. Impossible for you to flush out the lot. And this young fool Luiz de Fonsa y Sanchez is tilting at some windmill of his own. Kingdom of Lusitania! Mind you,' thoughtfully, 'they fight well, that Loyal Lusitanian Legion. I'd liefer have them with me than against. And your thinking is that their demonstration will play into the hands of the French and leave me with Oporto to take all over again.'

'Worse than that.' It warmed Jeremy to be consulted like this. 'I am sure they mean to kill you, sir. That's their first priority. I am more and more certain that the date of the party was changed so that it would coincide with your coming. St Bruxa's Eve was just a happy coincidence for them.'

'Flattering,' said Wellington. 'Well, I don't mean to be killed. Thank you, Craddock. You have done well. Tell your employers back in England that I said so. For what that is worth! And ask Croft to come to me, would you?'

The interview was over. Jeremy felt as if he had been put through a very efficient mangle. He gave Croft the message and emerged into the dark street. Where now? Too late to call on Caterina, though he longed to do so. How strange that the fact of telling his story to that acute listener had made him realise that his feelings for Rachel Emerson had never been more than an illusion. He had loved Caterina almost from the very first, certainly from those happy days at Falmouth. It was from his own feelings, as much as from her sharp eyes, that he had hidden on the crossing. Too successfully. I wonder if she has ever done a caricature of me, he thought, and turned reluctantly at last towards the misery of the Ware household.

*   *   *

'I told him everything and he told me nothing.' Jeremy summed up the interview for Caterina early next morning. He had been relieved to be admitted without question by old Tonio. 'But he said I was right to let the Emersons go,' he told her. 'I had been worrying about that.'

'Yes, I can imagine.' How beautiful she was, in her plain morning dress, listening so intently.

'Caterina!' But this was not the moment. 'I'll tell you one thing, I'm not worrying any more, now I have met Wellington. It will be all right tonight. I'm sure of that.'

'He must be quite a man.'

'He is! But I'm ashamed. With all this going

on, I have not thought enough about you. How are you proposing to get to the party tonight, you and Miss Brown?'

'Why, in our sedan chairs, of course. Very early, long before the witches and warlocks are out. When she invited us Mrs Ware told us to come early, before the others guests. I expect she regrets it now, but never mind. Is she very angry about Frank and Harriet?'

'I am afraid she is. She goes about looking ready to burst. I am glad you are to be there early; perhaps you may be able to calm her a little. But you must let me come and escort you.'

'An Englishman! You're not thinking, Mr Craddock. I am a Portuguese *fidalgo*. They are my people. It's you British who are at risk tonight.'

'But what about Luiz? What's this?' He was annoyed at the interruption.

'A note from Madame Fonsa.' She read it quickly. 'Good gracious, what a woman! She has invited herself to Mrs Ware's party. Proposes to go in her carriage and will take us with her. Now that *will* mean an early start. It is twice as far to the Wares' house by carriage. Does that make you feel better?'

'Yes, I must say it does. What an intrepid old lady. I wonder how Mrs Ware will take it?'

'Perhaps you should go back and explain to her, just in case she does not know, that Madame Fonsa is one of the greatest ladies in

Portonian society and is doing her an immense, an unprecedented honour.'

'Miss Gomez—'

'So formal!' The dark eyes mocked him. 'You called me Caterina just now.'

What had he meant to say? Instead: 'Did you ever draw my caricature?'

'Oh, dear me, yes. But hardly a caricature. I can't tell you what a hero of romance I made you look. Goodness, what a long time ago that happy journey seems.'

'Yes, a lifetime—' But he had thought of something else. 'And, Luiz, have you drawn him?'

'Why, yes.' She was blushing, and he was suddenly, furiously angry.

He controlled it: 'May I see? Just in case—It would be useful to be able to recognise him.'

'Of course it would.' She reached into a portfolio and riffled through the drawings it contained. 'Here you are, and here. That's not a bad likeness.'

'He's devilish handsome.' Jeremy fought down a tide of rage. 'How well you draw.' He was in control again.

'Thank you.' Dryly.

'Caterina—' But this time he was interrupted by Harriet, who bounced into the room, brimful of news. 'There's a proclamation being made about the streets,' she told them. 'Tonio heard it on his way back from market. The British Parliament has voted

£100,000 for the relief of Portuguese suffering during the war, and Wellington is here to arrange its distribution. Mr Croft is going to handle it, apparently. I suppose Wellington told you about that when you saw him last night, Mr Craddock?'

'Not a word.' Jeremy was ashamed to be irked by this. 'He keeps his own council, and one must respect him for it. Oh, I knew it was under discussion before I left England, but I thought it was meant mainly for the peasants who lost everything when the Lines of Torres Vedras were built. If Croft is handling it, he will know who was worst hit by the fighting here. It's splendid news! It's hard to see how anyone could whip up anti-British feeling in Oporto tonight.'

'Money's not everything,' said Caterina.

'No, but when you remember that it was Wellington himself who liberated Oporto from the French you have to see that it is a powerful combination.'

'So long as you are not pro-French. Goodness, Mr Ware, we did not hope to see you this morning!'

'Forgive me for bursting in on you, but I've no time to lose today. My mother sent me to ask if you had heard anything from Madame Feuillide. She was supposed to come first thing this morning to help with the final arrangements, but there has been no sign of her, and no message.'

'Well that is a piece of good news,' said Jeremy. 'Wellington has lost no time. I imagine she has been arrested as a suspected French sympathiser. I do wonder if anyone else was arrested with her.'

'So do I,' said Caterina. 'But, Mr Ware, don't tell your mother until after her party. And now, if you gentlemen will excuse us, Harriet and I must think about making ourselves beautiful for it.'

CHAPTER SEVENTEEN

It was strange to put on the evening gowns Madame Feuillide had made while knowing she was under arrest. 'I hope they aren't too hard on her,' said Harriet as they gathered their wraps around them and made their way through the house to the stable yard.

'She'll talk her way out of it,' said Caterina. 'I just wish we knew—'

'I know.' No need to speak Luiz's name. Harriet caught her friend's hand and pressed it. 'Poor Cat, I am *sorry*!' Luiz was her one-time lover, the father of her child, and the best she could hope for him was that he was safe away to a discredited life in France.

'I hope they have got him,' said Caterina. 'Oh, look, she is using the old Fonsa coach.' The huge lumbering vehicle had just pulled into the yard. 'With the Fonsa arms on it, do you see?'

'I am afraid I don't understand,' said Harriet.

'No, love, why should you? She wants to be seen as Fonsa today, not Sanchez in her son-in-law's carriage, bearing his arms.'

'And her grandson's. I see. Oh, poor Madame Fonsa.'

'Nothing poor about her,' said Caterina. 'You wait till you meet her.'

Carlotta was sitting beside the old lady in the dank-smelling carriage, and surrendered her place reluctantly to the two girls. 'Take good care of my lady,' she told Caterina. 'And I'll be there before you, *senhora*.'

'Carlotta is to pick up what news she can on the way,' explained Madame Fonsa as she received Caterina's kiss and looked Harriet briskly up and down. Then she smiled at her. 'You have been a good friend to my Caterina, I know. I am sorry to hear we are to lose you to marriage so soon, Miss Brown.' The carriage doors closed on them. 'We will go on speaking English, I think, just to be on the safe side.' The carriage wheels groaned as it moved off, and she leaned forward to speak close to the two girls sitting opposite her. 'I heard from my man. They got Madame Feuillide, but Luiz escaped. It's hard to know whether to be glad or sorry.'

'It depends what he does,' said Caterina

bleakly.

'What do you expect?'

'Something terrible, madame.' They did not talk much after that.

It had been a dark day, with scurrying rain storms, and the light was beginning to go when the carriage drew up outside the Wares' house in the Rua Nova dos Inglesas. Frank was there at once to help them alight, with Carlotta anxious by his side, and his mother in all her finery hovering in the doorway.

'I am more than honoured,' she dropped her deepest curtsey for Madame Fonsa, gave Caterina a brief, wintry smile, and managed not to see Harriet at all. 'I am so glad you brought your maid, madame. Madame Feuillide has failed me; I cannot imagine why. I was counting on her—'

'My Carlotta will do anything in her power to help your guests,' said the old lady, and moved indoors on a tide of obsequious thanks.

It was a curious party. Since dinner at the Factory did not take place until the English hour of six, and most of the senior male members of the English community were at it, Mrs Ware was left to entertain the old men, the wives, the dowagers and the young, until their lords and masters chose to tear themselves away from the vintage port and walk down, with the guest of honour, to grace her establishment. Until then, the rest of the party must mark time as best they might. There were lavish refreshments, and music, of course, and a little half-hearted dancing. Young ladies sang and one young lady played the harp, rather badly, Caterina thought. But she had preoccupations of her own. News of her swiftly broken engagement was obviously out. She was aware all the time of censorious glances, whispers behind fans, a drawing away of elderly skirts. She ignored it, busy trying to see the faces of the menservants. She knew that Mrs Ware had hired extra help for the occasion, and could not forget what Luiz had said about masquerading as one of the flunkeys. But it was a most difficult task. Wax candles had been lit in sconces throughout the house by now, and it was full of shadows and dark places. And the footmen all looked alike, resplendent in powdered wigs and high-collared livery that did not necessarily fit. She thought that instinct would tell her if Luiz were near, but could not be sure of it. Oddly, she did not feel very much afraid. She knew Luiz well enough to be sure that vengeance on her would take second place to whatever else he had planned for tonight. He was a frighteningly single-minded man, and the more she thought about it, as she chattered and smiled and curtseyed, the more convinced she was that he was here somewhere. Or out in the street, waiting for Wellington? He would never have run for safety. Not Luiz.

Jeremy Craddock brought her a glass of

lemonade and she told him this, *sotto voce*. He had stayed away from the Factory dinner, partly as guest of the house, partly to watch out for Luiz. 'He must know we will be looking for him here,' he whispered back. 'Most likely he will be in the street. That is why we are going up to meet Lord Wellington.'

'You're going—?'

'Yes, Frank and I. And there are soldiers in the streets. No need for anxiety there. I expect tomorrow we shall be laughing at ourselves for all this worry.'

'I do hope so, but I don't quite believe it. I know Luiz, you see. He won't have run for it.'

Could she possibly love him still? Jeremy felt a sudden blaze of anger and pity. 'Caterina, I am sorry. I hadn't thought—'

'Don't think,' she said. 'There's no time for that.' And was suddenly engulfed in a bevy of English girls who had been getting up their courage to approach her, the notorious heroine of the occasion. After being aware all evening of being the focus of unkind gossip, it was pleasant to find herself included in this chattering, cheerful group of young people, and she was sorry when a maidservant managed to catch her attention and tell her that Madame Fonsa was asking for her. 'She is not well, *minha senhora*.'

She made swift apologies and turned to follow the messenger. 'This way?' she asked, surprised, when the girl turned towards the

298

stairs.

'Yes, *senhora*,' she said hurriedly. 'She fainted, and we took her up to the mistress's room.'

'Fainted? Have you sent for the doctor?'

'Of course. But she has been asking for you.'

*   *   *

Jeremy and Frank reached the English Factory just as a cheerful, talkative group emerged from it, Lord Wellington's spare figure unmistakable in their midst. There was a crowd in the street, but it was a friendly one and burst into a ragged cheer when the liberator of Oporto appeared. 'All's well so far,' Jeremy said to Frank as they started back down the crowded street.

'Yes, not a werewolf in sight. Have we been starting at shadows, do you think?'

'I do hope so,' said Jeremy soberly.

Mrs Ware was at the door again to greet the guest of honour in his plain, impeccable evening dress, and babbled of the honour he was doing her poor house as she led him indoors. The musicians struck up 'See the Conquering Hero', and there was a good deal of cheerful confusion as she led him between bowing and curtseying rows of guests to the inner room where Madame Fonsa sat enthroned. Frank, as man of the house, followed close behind, but Jeremy was looking

299

for Caterina.

As the music drew to a rather ragged close, he saw Harriet. 'Where is Caterina?' They asked each other the question almost simultaneously.

'I've been looking for her all over,' Harriet went on. 'She's not in any of the obvious places. She was talking to Miss Sandeman and her friends over there,' she pointed. 'And then when I next looked for her, she was gone. I don't like it, Mr Craddock.'

'No more do I. Oh, it's probably nothing—we shall feel fools in a minute, but I will have a word with the young ladies, just the same.'

'Do. And I will keep looking.'

Miss Sandeman and her friends were too excited by Wellington's arrival to be very helpful, but Jeremy's persistent questions finally elicited a response from one of them: 'A maid came and called her away,' she said. 'I don't understand Portuguese, of course, but I caught the name Fonsa. That's the old lady she came with, isn't it?'

'Thank you.' He left them to their giggles and made his way through the crowd to the main salon where Wellington was standing by Madame Fonsa's chair, laughing his sharp bark of a laugh at something she had just said. Impossible to intrude on this exchange, specially as he had not yet been presented to the old lady, but he was glad to see Frank in attendance, and was making his way towards him, when Madame Fonsa said impatiently: 'But where is Miss Gomez? I sent for her ten minutes ago. I wish to present my protégée to you, milord.'

'Delighted,' said the great man.

Harriet spoke before Jeremy could. 'I have been looking everywhere for her, madame. And so has Mr Craddock.'

'You sent for her?' Jeremy stepped forward. 'Jeremy Craddock ma'am, at your service.'

'Of course I sent for her.' The old face was suddenly haggard. 'What have you done with the child among you? Oh, tell those musicians to stop it!'

'Yes, do, please, Frank.' Mrs Ware stepped forward. 'A servant has just given me this, madame. It seems to be addressed to you.'

The hand that took the note trembled. 'Kidnapped!' She read aloud, her voice wavering only slightly: ' "We have Miss Gomez. Do we kill her? Or will the great Wellington exchange himself for her? We will come for his answer in fifteen minutes." '

*   *   *

'You are mad.' She faced him in the dimly lit attic, breathing heavily from the ruthless manhandling that had got her there. Her dress was torn, her hands were tied behind her back, but she had not been hurt. 'You are entirely out

301

of your mind, Luiz. What do you think to gain by this lunacy?'

'Wellington's death. Or yours. I don't much care which. We'll keep our bargain, either way. He won't come, of course. Even if he should wish to, they won't let him. So—he will be disgraced, and you, my sweet love, will be dead. Pity there won't be time for the painful death you deserve, but I have my escape to make after all.'

'You'll never get out of here!'

'Oh, yes, I will, my dearest life. Do you remember when the Wares used to deign to invite us to play, as children? I came up here, once, in one of our games of hide-and-seek and found a secret door through to the next house. I expect some long-dead Ware had a mistress there, don't you? So, kill you, kill Wellington, whichever, and I am safe away before the pack can come after me.'

'But Luiz, why kill Wellington? He's a friend of Portugal!'

'A fine friend! They care only for their own interests, those British. They let us shed our blood, and destroy our houses, and starve, while he hunts his foxhounds across our ruined fields.'

'You don't know what he is here for, do you? I suppose you have been up here all day.'

'Since dawn. Naturally.'

'There's been an announcement made about the streets. The English Parliament has voted

302

£100,000 for the relief of Portuguese suffering. Wellington is here to arrange for its distribution. That's your enemy, Luiz!'

'I don't believe it! You are making it up. I won't listen.'

'Believe me, or be sorry later. You have let the French tell you a pack of lies. Madame Feuillide has been arrested, by the way. I expect you don't know that either, since you have been shut up here all day. She is a known French spy, has been ever since she came here twenty years ago. What does she care for you and your "Friends of Democracy"? She has been using you, Luiz, for French ends.'

'I don't believe it,' he said again.

'You had better. Think, Luiz.' Urgently. 'Either way, the French gain everything, and you lose everything. I am sure you are right in one thing. Wellington won't be allowed to make the quixotic gesture of exchanging his life for mine. But he's got enemies in England will be glad to see him disgraced, and Portugal will lose a good friend. And you will kill me, Luiz, and go through that secret door of yours, but it won't be your friends waiting for you, it will be the French. You will have served their turn, they'll have no more need of you. They'll give you up to justice, and you know what that means. A stinking prison and a savage death.'

'I don't believe you.' But she thought he was beginning to. And then: 'It's too late.'

'It's never too late. Let me go, Luiz, let me go

down those stairs. Come with me, see me safe through your "friends" on the way, and I promise I will talk you out of this. Your grandmother will help me.'

'My grandmother?'

'She is here. You didn't know that either? Luiz, how little you know. Think about that and stop trusting them.'

'Why should I trust you?'

'I'll tell you why. There is something else, Luiz, something you have a right to know. Kill me, and you kill the mother of your son.'

* * *

The argument had gone on, round and round, back and forth, hopeless. 'We can't let you go,' Croft told Wellington once again.

'I can't not go,' Wellington answered.

Croft was looking at his watch. 'The fifteen minutes are nearly up,' he said. 'When we know what their terms are, we may think of something.'

'No dodging,' said Wellington. 'No fudging. The case is clear.' He bent down to Madame Fonsa. 'Don't fret, ma'am. You will have her back in no time.'

'Here it is.' All eyes turned to Mrs Ware, who had stood a little back from the group of desperately arguing men. 'The second note. For you this time.' She handed it to Wellington.

304

There was a deadly hush as he opened and read it aloud. 'She is in the attic. Come up the stairs alone. Follow the light. When we see you, we let her go. If we do not see you before the next quarter strikes, we will kill her.' And as he read it, the clock in the main hall struck the first quarter of the hour.

A babble of comment broke out, silenced at once by Wellington. 'No time for that. Yes, what is it, Craddock?'

Jeremy came forward to confront Mrs Ware. 'Where did you get that note, ma'am?'

'Why—a servant gave it to me, as before.'

'No. I have been watching you all the time. She is in it too.' He turned to Wellington. 'I did not realise how deep till now. Surely you can use that, sir. I'm sorry, Ware.' He felt Frank Ware rigid beside him.

Frank was looking at his mother with horror. 'It can't be true—' He paused. 'But it is. No use protesting, mother. Too late for that. Your only hope now is to help us save Miss Gomez.'

They were all aware of the desperate minutes ticking away. 'I can't,' she said. 'There's nothing I can do. And if there were anything, I wouldn't!' Her voice rose. 'Vengeance is mine, saith the Lord. For all the slights, for all the whispers, all the condescensions ... I don't much care which of them it is; both if I'm lucky, and him too, your precious grandson, Madame High and Mighty Fonsa. Honouring

305

my house with your presence, after all these years! My poor house!' The horrible parody of her own once fawning voice rose into hideous, screaming hysteria.

'Take her away,' said Wellington. 'Lock her up. It solves nothing, and time is passing. You had better show me the way to your attics, Ware.'

'You must be armed,' said Croft, and they all knew that Wellington had won his point.

'Yes. If you would be so good, Ware? Time's passing. Make haste.'

'In my study. This way. You trust me, sir?'

'Of course. And if the rest of you gentlemen would be so good as to keep out of the way. Comfort the ladies, perhaps? How many floors?' To Frank.

'Three flights and then the attic stairs.'

'Right. You, Ware, and you, and you,' picking out Croft and Jeremy. 'Come with me to the last stair. It's narrow, I take it.'

'Yes.' Handing over the weapons. 'But—'

'No time for buts.' They were in the hall and a quick glance at the grandfather clock showed its hands nearing the next quarter. 'Quiet now.'

If there had been members of the gang on the upper floors, they must have taken flight at the sound of Mrs Ware's hysterical screaming. All was silence and darkness except for the glimmer of light at the head of the attic stair.

'Right.' Wellington had his pistol in his hand now. 'Put out your candles. Wait here for her.'

In the sudden darkness, the light at the top of the stairs seemed to grow brighter. There was a sound of movement on the upper landing. 'Stop there.' Caterina's voice. 'It's all over. We are coming down. Stand back, please, and wait for us. Do you understand? All's well.'

There was a short, stunned silence, then: 'Agreed,' said Wellington. 'We are waiting for you.' They moved a little back in the narrow hall and watched silently as the flickering light grew to reveal Caterina, candle in hand, coming slowly down the stairs. Her dress was torn off one shoulder, her hair hung shaggily round her face; the shadowy figure behind her must be Luiz.

'Thank you for coming, sir.' She looked gravely up at Wellington, quite unconscious of her own dishevelled state. 'This is Luiz de Fonsa y Sanchez. He has made a great mistake. He wants to give himself up. Only, to you, please, to the English?'

Wellington thought about it for a long moment. Then, 'Very well, Miss Gomez. I think you have earned that.'

'Thank you. But who was screaming? That's what did it.'

'My mother,' said Frank Ware.

'I was afraid so. Poor Frank, I am sorry.'

'I should be asking you to forgive us.'

'Too much talk,' said Wellington. 'You, Croft, find a guard for the prisoner. Ware, you had best ask your guests to go home. And

307

Craddock, find our young heroine a shawl and take her down to reassure the old lady.'

'Oh!' Caterina looked down for the first time, and blushed scarlet. 'I do apologise.' She did her best to pull the torn muslin together.

'Now that,' said Wellington, 'you do not need to do.'

'But I must know about my son,' Luiz protested as Croft prepared to take him away.

'His name is Lewis,' Caterina said. 'And he is mine.' She turned to Wellington. 'There is a secret way from the attic to the house next door. He meant to escape by it.'

'Thank you,' said Wellington. 'Which side?'

'I don't know.'

'We'll search both.' He strode swiftly away down the stairs.

'Caterina!' For the moment, they were alone together on the shadowy landing, lit only by the candle in her hand. 'You have a son! I shall love him.' What was he saying? He reached out to take the candle from her as her hand began at last to shake, dripping wax on the floor. He put it down on a step of the stair, took her cold hand in his. 'I seem to understand nothing, but this I know: I love you, Caterina Gomez, always have, always will.' He tried to pull her into his arms, but she resisted, her left hand still clutching the torn muslin around her.

'No, Jeremy.' Very quiet, very firm. Thoughts scuttered through her head: Rachel Emerson ... Little Lewis ... Luiz. 'You will see

308

things quite differently in the morning,' she told him gently. 'And be grateful to me. And now, here in good time is Carlotta, and that shawl.'

*   *   *

Downstairs, the rooms had emptied, and Madame Fonsa's carriage was at the door. 'God bless you.' She rose stiffly from her chair to embrace Caterina, held out a hand to Jeremy. 'I do thank you, Mr Craddock.' Her piercing black eyes moved from him to Caterina and back again. 'Come to me in the morning, Mr Craddock, and tell me the whole tale. No more talking tonight. The child has had enough.'

'Yes.' Jeremy kissed the old lady's hand and then, more slowly, Caterina's. 'I am glad she has you, ma'am.'

'She has. Take me to my carriage, young man. Mr Ware will see to the young ladies.' She let him settle her in her corner of the huge, dark vehicle and leaned back with a little sigh. 'In the morning, Mr Craddock, early, and now, good night!' As he bowed and withdrew, she reached out a clawlike hand to touch Caterina's. 'I thank God you are safe,' she said. 'We'll talk when you come to me tomorrow. Now, be quiet, rest, you have earned it. But I do thank you for my grandson's life. And no tears, please.'

'No tears.' Caterina managed something between a smile and a snuffle and was glad to sit in a quiet daze, Harriet's warm arm around her. The morning would be time enough for thought.

But when they reached the Gomez house, Tonio was on the lookout for her. 'I'm glad you are here, *minha senhora*, your father is still up, he wants to see you.'

'My father?' She could not believe her ears.

'Yes, he is in his study, *minha senhora*.'

'I'll wait up,' said Harriet.

'Thank you.' She was glad that Carlotta had insisted on pinning the shawl securely round her shoulders and had tidied her hair for her.

'Father?' She found him sitting staring into the fire, and thought suddenly how old he looked, how forlorn.

'Caterina. You have a son.' It was not a question.

'Yes.' She had known that the fact of little Lewis would not be a secret for long, once Madame Fonsa went to her lawyers, but had not expected it to be out quite so soon as this.

'And you did not tell me.' Again it was not a question.

'No, father.'

'Fool of a girl!' Out of old habit, he took refuge in anger.

'Could you not see that this changes everything. A grandson. An heir! How old is he? Where is he?'

310

'Three. Harriet's mother is looking after him.'

'And Madame Fonsa means to adopt him as her heir.'

'Yes, father.'

'To call him Sanchez?'

'No, Fonsa.'

'Impossible! He must be Gomez. I have sent Father Pedro back to his order with a flea in his ear. He took too much for granted. I hadn't realised ... Caterina—'

'Yes?'

'Must I apologise?'

'I really think you should, father.'

'Then I will. I do. Don't go to Madame Fonsa, Caterina.'

'But I have said I will.'

'Please, Caterina.'

'I'm very tired, father. Something happened at the Wares' party. You'll hear about it in the morning. Let it wait till then, please?'

'But let him be Gomez?'

'Fonsa y Gomez?' She rose to her feet. 'Goodnight, father.'

* * *

Jeremy did not sleep much. Madame Fonsa's words had been a command and he had promised to obey, but he resented it. Why must he pay his first call to that imperious old lady when all his heart was set on an urgent

311

explanation with Caterina? But he had said he would go, and he did.

'You came. I am glad.' The old lady was ready for him.

'I said I would.'

'A man of your word. I have a favour to ask of you, Mr Craddock, some advice to give you, and an offer to make you. I knew your aunt, by the way. I think I loved her a little.'

'My aunt?'

'Caterina's mother. I suppose you never met her, never thought about her much. Your mother's older sister. They were an unlucky pair, those two. Motherless girls who married the first men who asked them. Disastrous. Don't blame only your mother, Mr Craddock. Look at Caterina's father, and think about your own. And now, my favour. Will you go to England for me, and fetch my great-grandson?'

'Ma'am!' He was dumbstruck by the implications of the request.

She smiled at him very kindly. 'Yes. I like you, Mr Craddock. And I rather hope Caterina does too. Marriage to you would certainly solve some problems for us all. Things are not going to be easy here for any of us, but they are going to be worse for Caterina. Luiz won't behave well, and nor will that father of hers. I had hoped to carry things off for her with a high hand, and with your help I may manage it yet. I am going to adopt the boy, of course, bring him up as a Fonsa, my direct heir.

If you get her, Mr Craddock, you get a rich woman.'

'And a son,' he told her. 'And lucky to have both. But it's her I want, ma'am, though I won't play the hypocrite and pretend the money won't come kindly too. I have to confess to you, as more of a guardian than her father, that I am a younger son, and probably out of a job. But I love her.'

'And I like you. Which brings me to my offer. I dislike admitting it, but I am getting old. I need someone to manage my estates for me. Would you consider the job? After fetching my grandson, of course. You are the obvious person to do that, and it will give Caterina time, Mr Craddock, which is what she is going to need. She is a girl of great spirit, but apt to carry things with a high hand, just as I do. Whatever you do, don't push her, that might be fatal.'

'You're right, ma'am, and I'm deeply grateful. For everything. And, yes, I will be proud to fetch your great-grandson from England, and more than honoured to act as your steward.'

'I like a man who can make up his mind. Good, and good luck, Mr Craddock. They should be up and about in the Gomez house by now. Please tell Caterina I expect them this afternoon.'

'Thank you.' He bent to kiss her hand. 'For everything.'

'So what are you going to do?' Harriet asked. The two girls were eating a very late breakfast on the terrace and Caterina had just finished describing last night's scene with her father. 'Stay here, or move over to Madame Fonsa? Either way, he is going to be a rich baby, your Lewis.'

'Yes, bad for him, I think, but there's not much I can do about it.'

'Marry Jeremy Craddock. Give him a father.'

'You think marriage is the answer to everything, don't you, love? I'm not so sure. But, oh Harryo, I am so happy for you and Frank. It's heartless to say it, but if his mother is really mad, the way is clear for you two.'

'Yes,' said Harriet soberly. 'I think it is. But I want you to be happy too, Cat dear.'

'Happy?' said Caterina. 'What is happy, I wonder? But one thing I do know, I will be happy when I have Lewis here. Oh, look, here come our cavaliers. Be a good friend, love, and see your Frank indoors? But first I must comfort him. He'll want to apologise all over again. How is your poor mother, Mr Ware?' As the two men approached across the terrace.

'Mad as can be, thank God. That great man, Wellington, says there is no question of prosecuting her. In fact, he wants the whole thing hushed up. I was just telling

314

Craddock—We met on the doorstep,' he explained. 'Wellington says it would be bad for Anglo-Portuguese relations if the real story came out. He's had your kidnapper smuggled out of town already,' he told Caterina. 'And we are all to say it was just a vulgar snatch for money. There will be talk, of course, but if we stick to our story it will die down soon enough. I have promised to be responsible for my poor mother.' He smiled at Harriet and took her hand. 'I knew I could count on your support, my darling. And I can only beg for your forgiveness, Miss Gomez.' Turning to Caterina.

'You have it. And my deepest sympathy, and best of all, my congratulations. And now, please, take Harriet indoors and plan your wedding, while I talk to Mr Craddock.'

Carrying it with a high hand, thought Jeremy and realised what a wise woman Madame Fonsa was. He must indeed be very careful. But Caterina's first words amazed him.

'I need your advice,' she said.

'My advice? It's yours, of course.'

'My father has heard about Lewis. I should have known he would. He was waiting up for me when I got home last night. He wants the child for his heir too!' She smiled at Jeremy suddenly and his heart turned over. 'I had no idea how clever I was to have a boy,' she told him. 'He's twice an heir now, my little Lewis, but what am I to do for the best? I promised

315

Madame Fonsa I'd go there; now my father is urgent I stay. He has even sent Father Pedro away.'

'Now that is a gesture.' Every instinct urged him to say, 'Marry me', but he remembered Madame Fonsa's words and restrained himself. 'It seems to me that you need to think very carefully about this, Caterina, for the boy's sake as well as your own. It's hard to advise when I know so little about him. How old is he? Where is he?'

'He is three. He lives with Harriet's mother outside Bath. She keeps a home for children like him.'

'And you couldn't go there to say goodbye to him, the day I fetched you away? Oh, Caterina, I am sorry,' he said impulsively, and was amazed to see tears in her eyes.

'Fancy your thinking of that,' she said. 'Yes, it was bad, but at least I was able to send a message from Harriet's house, promising funds for him. I've been so worried about that, but now Madame Fonsa is sending for him. I can't believe I'll be seeing him so soon, but I have to think, you see, which household would be better for him to grow up in. I'm afraid he will be spoiled rotten in either, and I hate spoiled little boys.'

'Better than neglecting them,' he said. 'Too much love never hurt anyone. What you must remember is that you are in a strong position. They both want him; you can name your own terms. Say you won't make a decision until he gets here; that's reasonable enough. Madame Fonsa has asked me to fetch him, by the way.'

'And you will go?' Her face lit up. 'Oh, Jeremy, that is wonderful! I shall feel so safe if I know he is with you. But—' she remembered. 'Your work! Can you just go like that?'

'I shall,' he told her. 'And it doesn't matter anyway. Spying's a shabby business; I've had enough of it. I've hated it from the moment I found myself having to lie to you and Harriet. It put me all at odds with myself, and everything else. I've not seen straight. But I do now. I know what I want. Madame Fonsa has also asked me to be her steward when I get back. It is a great compliment. She says she loved your mother. Did you know that?'

'No, I never did.' Caterina was silent for a moment, taking in the implications of it all.

Jeremy took a deep breath. 'Had you thought, Caterina, that the best thing of all for your son would be some brothers and sisters? We were both lonely children, you and I, we know what it's like. Caterina—' But she was laughing at him.

'Dear Jeremy—' She held out an impulsive hand and he grasped it in his. 'So you are telling me that Madame Fonsa thinks I should marry you to save my poor tarnished name, and you are advising me to do it for little Lewis's sake?'

'Not precisely that.' He had her other hand

now. 'I am saying Caterina, that I have loved you from the first moment that we met, though like an idiot I didn't realise it until it was almost too late. I wasn't ready. I'll tell you all about it some day, I hope. I think I was afraid of you, Caterina, of the depths in you. You have changed me, made a better man of me. Take the man you have made.' He tried to pull her towards him, felt her gently resist. 'And I promise to beat your Lewis when he is bad.'

'You tempt me vastly!' She still held back, but she was laughing now, tears in her eyes. 'But it is too soon. You must give me time. And think more yourself. Just the other day I thought I still loved Luiz. And we have said nothing about Rachel Emerson.' She overrode his attempted protest. 'She changed you a little, too, I think. But we'll say no more about that. Fetch my Lewis for me, get to know him. You may find you dislike him.'

'Your child? Never. But, Caterina, one is not enough.'

'Think a little, Jeremy. I've never really known him, been his mother. I had to leave him with Harriet and go back to the convent. It nearly killed me; what did it do to him? I need time with him, to make friends, to make amends, before I can think of love or marriage. For now, he must come first. Can you bear with me, be my friend, and his, while I get to know my son?'

'More than a friend, Caterina, please?'

'But less than a lover? I won't offer to be a sister to you, but I'll make a bargain with you. Fetch my Lewis, be our friend, give me a year to be his mother, then let us talk again.'

'A whole year?' He groaned.

'Cut off a day then.' Smiling at him. 'Come to me next Bruxa's Eve.'

'You think this is all a warlock's dream? It's not for me, Caterina.' He bent and kissed her lightly, first on one cheek, then on the other. 'But I'll not plague you further. It's an odd rival to have, a three-year-old boy, but I shall love him just the same, you'll see. It's a bargain then, a year less a day, next Bruxa's Eve.'

She smiled at him. 'Yes, Jeremy. A bargain, but not a promise.'